Magic Pickle

BY SCOTT MORSE
WITH COLOR BY JOSE GARIBALDI

AN IMPRINT OF

■SCHOLASTIC

NEW YORK   TORONTO   LONDON   AUCKLAND   SYDNEY   MEXICO CITY   NEW DELHI   HONG KONG   BUENOS AIRES

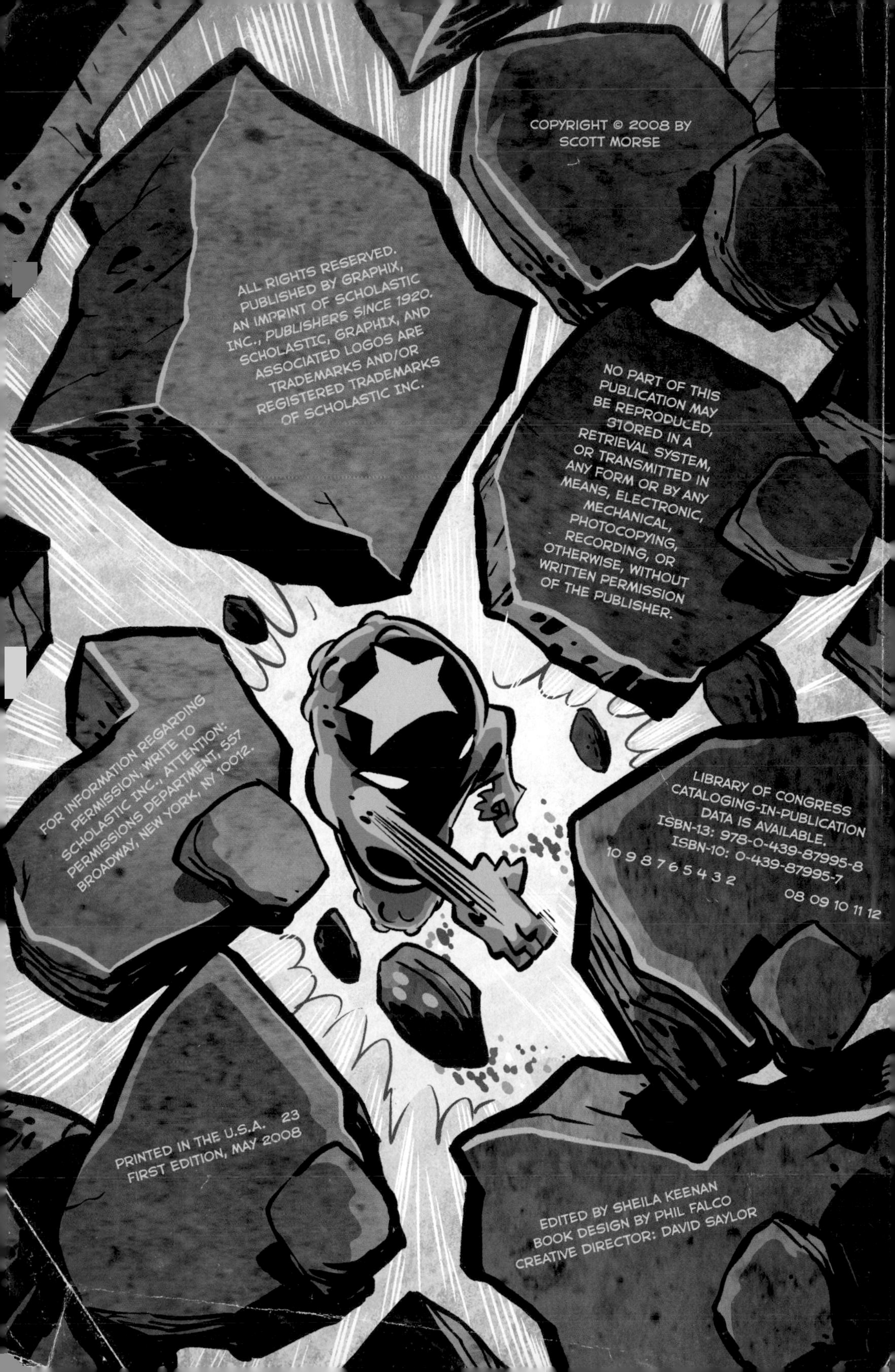

PUBLISHED BY GRAPHIX,
AN IMPRINT OF SCHOLASTIC
INC., *PUBLISHERS SINCE 1920.*
SCHOLASTIC, GRAPHIX, AND
ASSOCIATED LOGOS ARE
TRADEMARKS AND/OR
REGISTERED TRADEMARKS
OF SCHOLASTIC INC.

LIBRARY OF CONGRESS
CATALOGING-IN-PUBLICATION
DATA IS AVAILABLE.
ISBN-13: 978-0-439-87995-8
ISBN-10: 0-439-87995-7
10 9 8 7 6 5 4 3 2 08 09 10 11 12

PRINTED IN THE U.S.A. 23
FIRST EDITION, MAY 2008

EDITED BY SHEILA KEENAN
BOOK DESIGN BY PHIL FALCO
CREATIVE DIRECTOR: DAVID SAYLOR

for
KATIE MORSE
AND
ALL OF HER KIDS...

CHAPTER 1

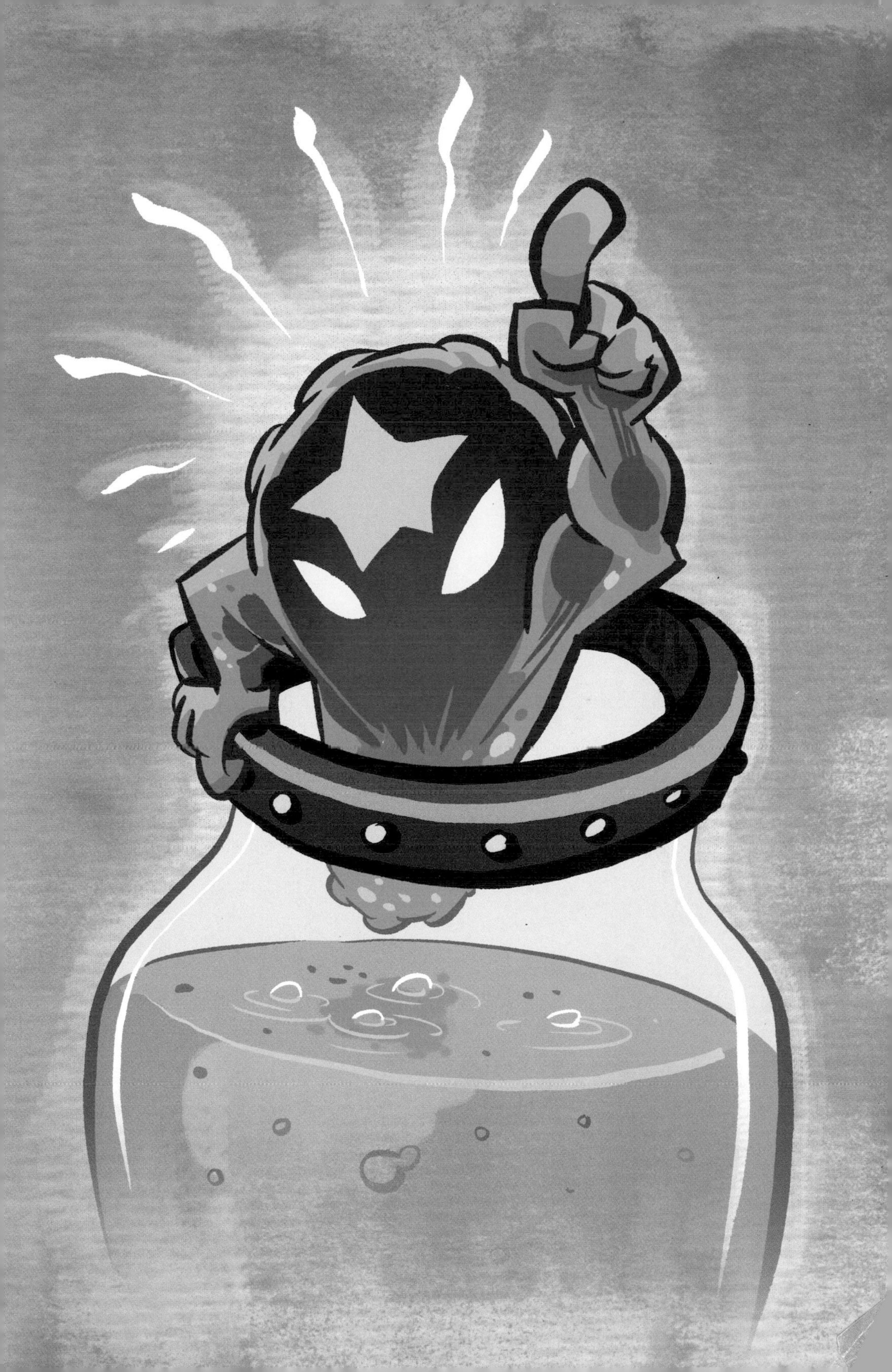

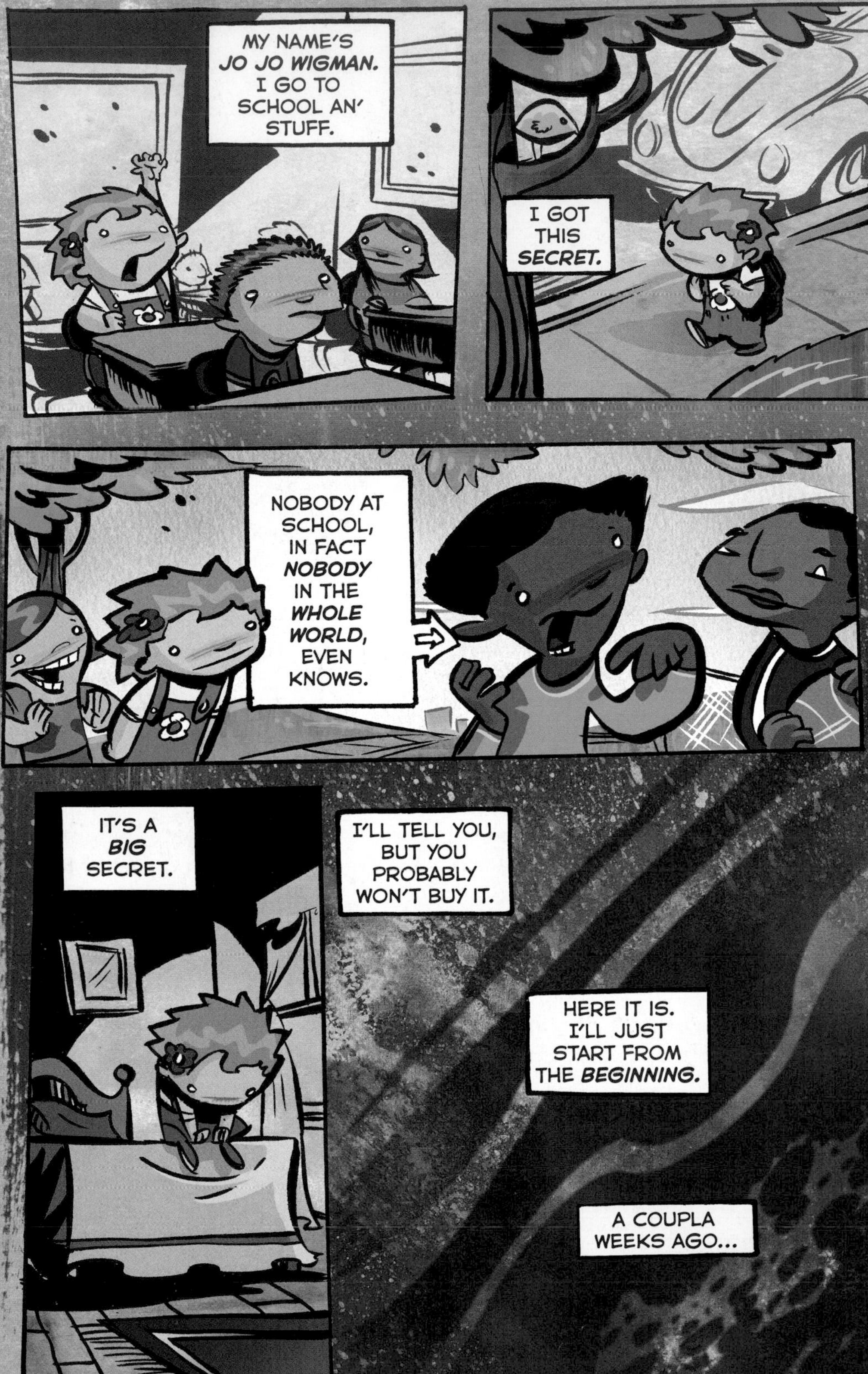

MY NAME'S *JO JO WIGMAN.* I GO TO SCHOOL AN' STUFF.
I GOT THIS *SECRET.*
NOBODY AT SCHOOL, IN FACT *NOBODY* IN THE *WHOLE WORLD,* EVEN KNOWS.
IT'S A *BIG* SECRET.
I'LL TELL YOU, BUT YOU PROBABLY WON'T BUY IT.
HERE IT IS. I'LL JUST START FROM THE *BEGINNING.*
A COUPLA WEEKS AGO...

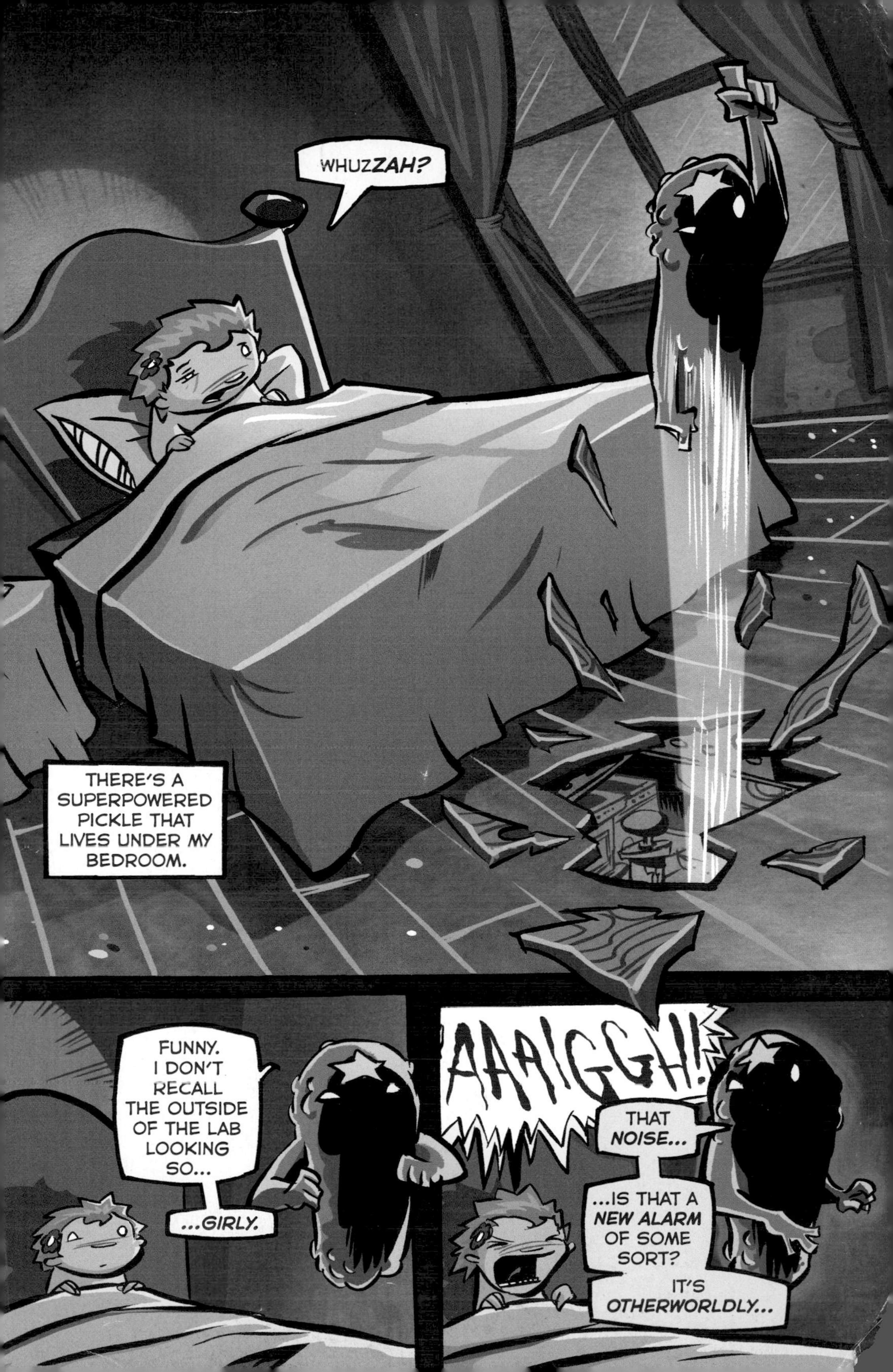
WHUZZAH?
THERE'S A SUPERPOWERED PICKLE THAT LIVES UNDER MY BEDROOM.
FUNNY. I DON'T RECALL THE OUTSIDE OF THE LAB LOOKING SO...
...GIRLY.
AAAIGGH!
THAT NOISE...
...IS THAT A NEW ALARM OF SOME SORT?
IT'S OTHERWORLDLY...

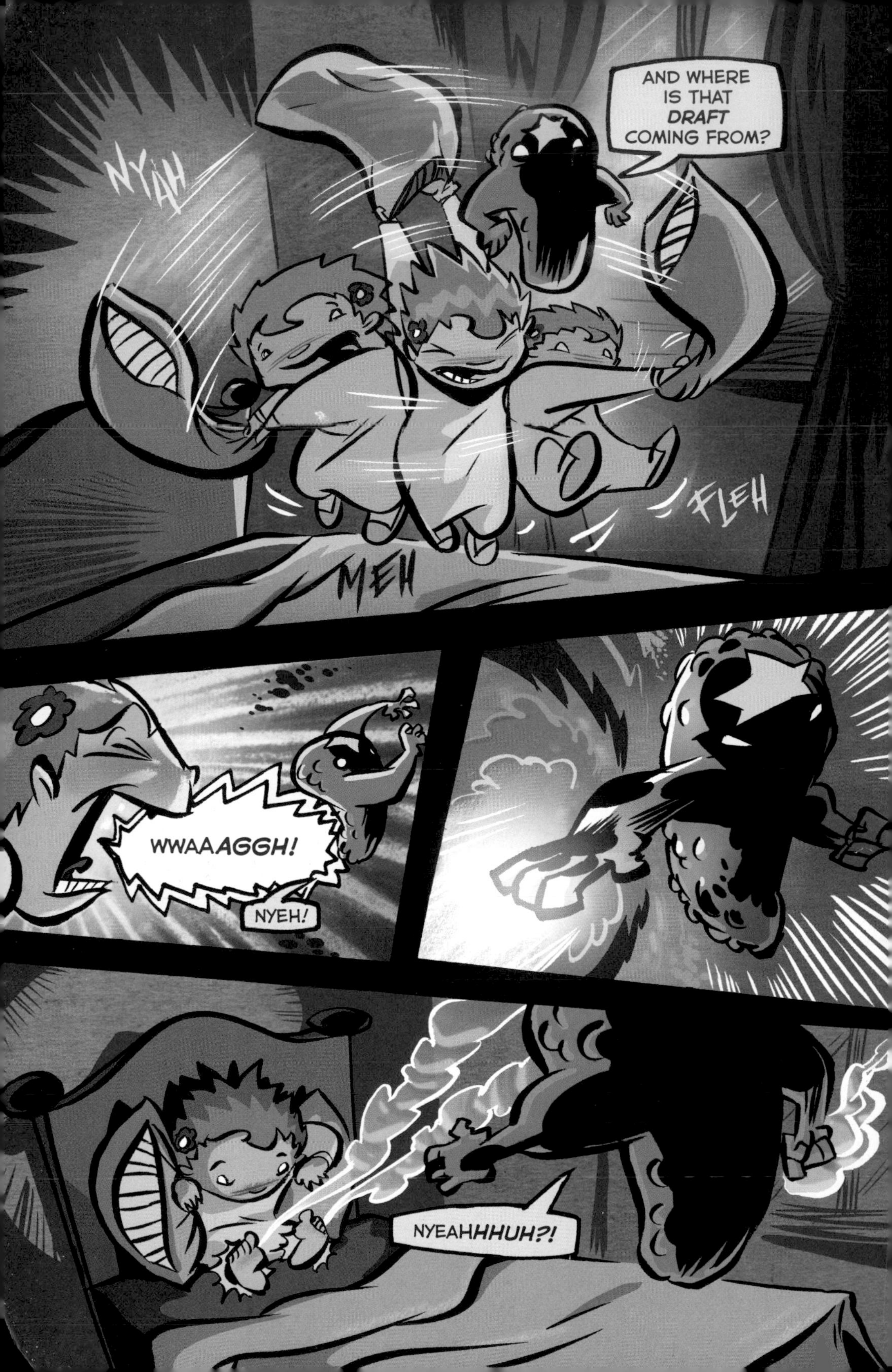
AND WHERE IS THAT DRAFT COMING FROM?
NYAH
FLEH
MEH
WWAAAGGH!
NYEH!
NYEAHHHUH?!

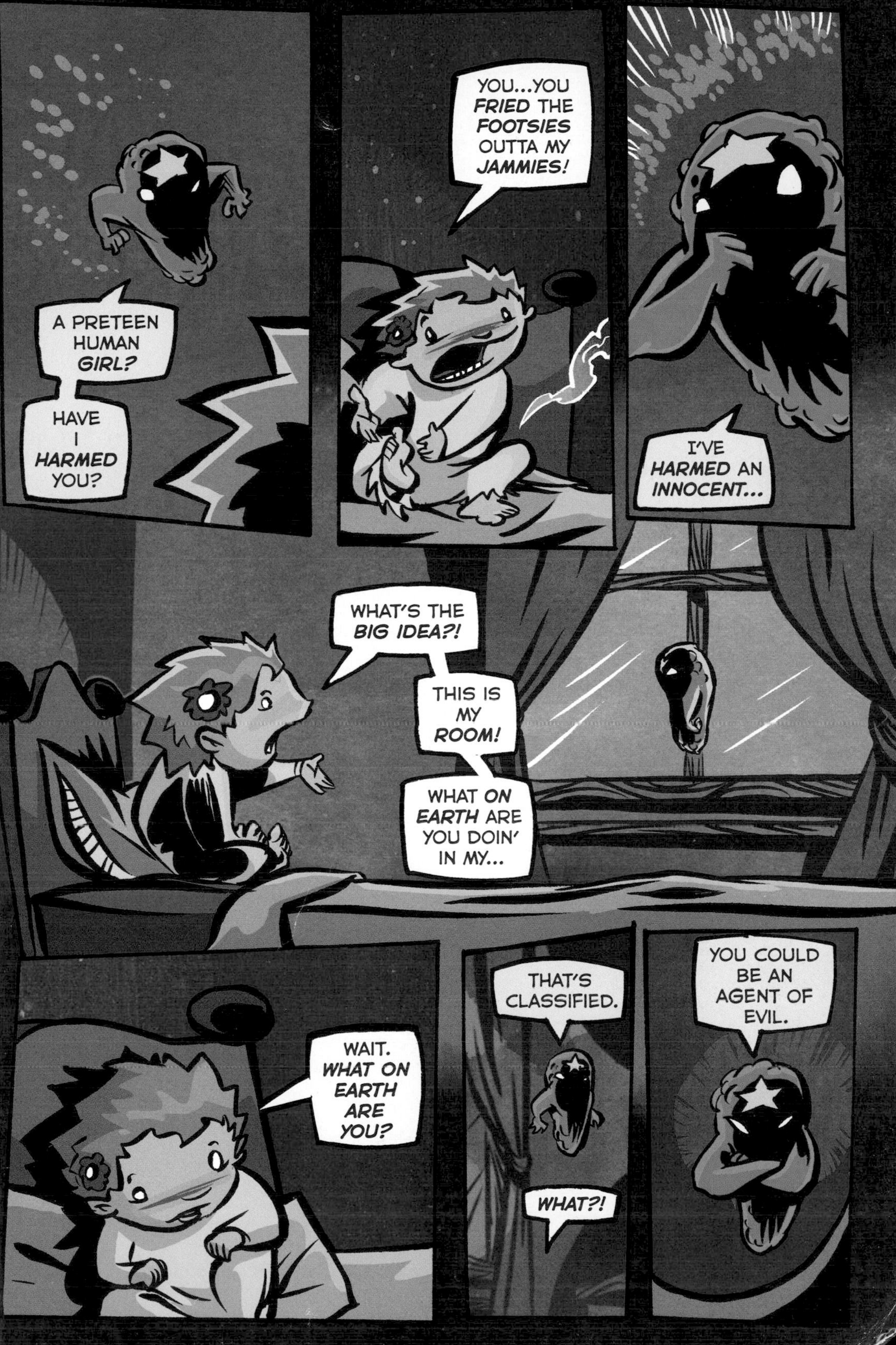
A PRETEEN HUMAN GIRL?
HAVE I HARMED YOU?
YOU...YOU FRIED THE FOOTSIES OUTTA MY JAMMIES!
I'VE HARMED AN INNOCENT...
WHAT'S THE BIG IDEA?!
THIS IS MY ROOM!
WHAT ON EARTH ARE YOU DOIN' IN MY...
WAIT. WHAT ON EARTH ARE YOU?
THAT'S CLASSIFIED.
WHAT?!
YOU COULD BE AN AGENT OF EVIL.

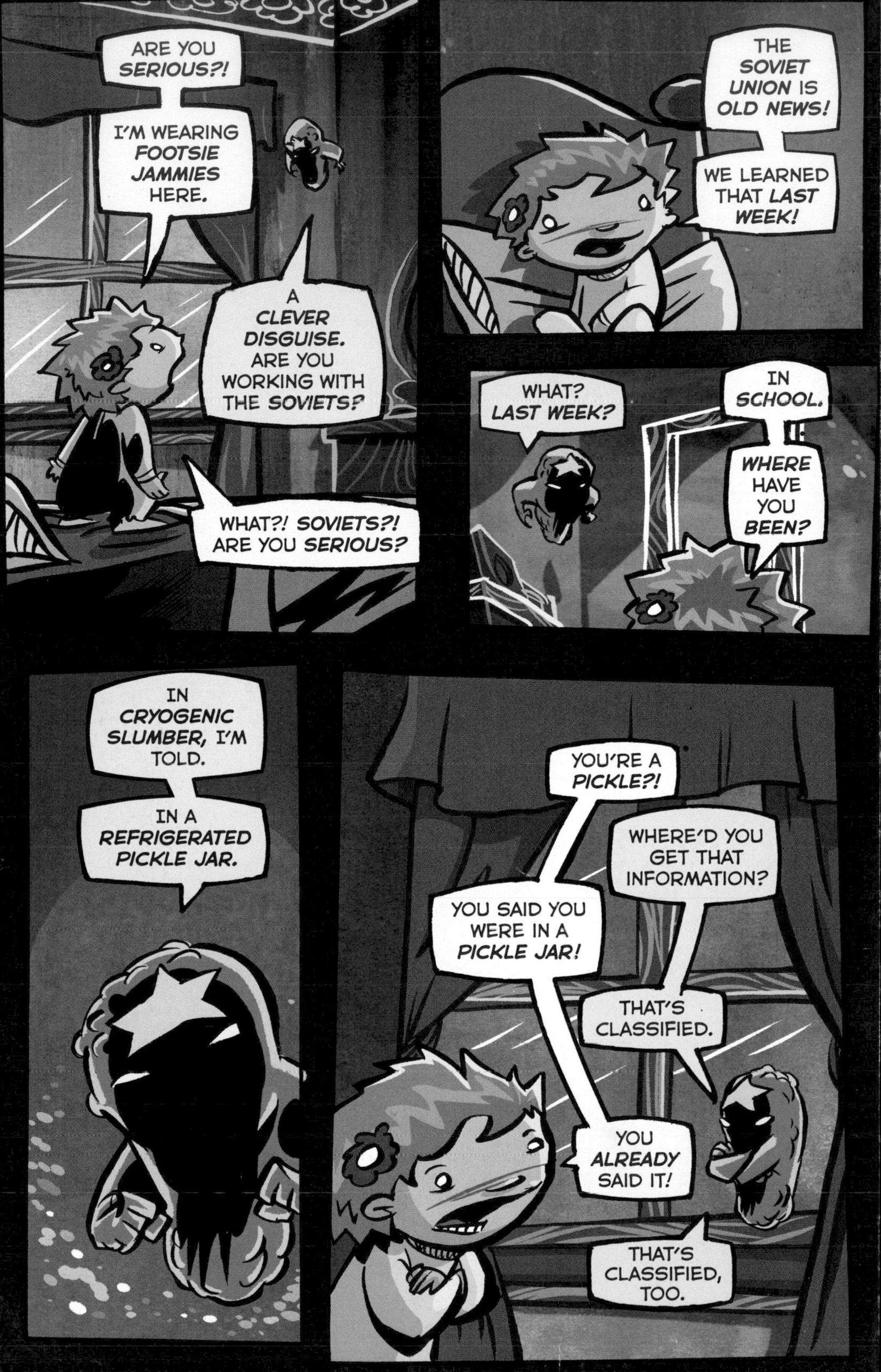
ARE YOU SERIOUS?!
I'M WEARING FOOTSIE JAMMIES HERE.
A CLEVER DISGUISE. ARE YOU WORKING WITH THE SOVIETS?
WHAT?! SOVIETS?! ARE YOU SERIOUS?
THE SOVIET UNION IS OLD NEWS!
WE LEARNED THAT LAST WEEK!
WHAT? LAST WEEK?
IN SCHOOL.
WHERE HAVE YOU BEEN?
IN CRYOGENIC SLUMBER, I'M TOLD.
IN A REFRIGERATED PICKLE JAR.
YOU'RE A PICKLE?!
WHERE'D YOU GET THAT INFORMATION?
YOU SAID YOU WERE IN A PICKLE JAR!
THAT'S CLASSIFIED.
YOU ALREADY SAID IT!
THAT'S CLASSIFIED, TOO.

WAIT A MINUTE... YOU'RE ONE OF THOSE *FRUITS* THAT'S BEEN ALL OVER THE *NEWS*...

...THE ONES WHO *STOLE* ALL THAT MUSEUM STUFF!

WHAT? I'M A VEGETABLE, GIRL. I'M GRADE A PRODUCE.

A *SOLDIER* OF THE *UNITED STATES.*

MY POWERS ARE THE RESULT OF IMPORTANT *SCIENTIFIC ENDEAVOR.* ACCIDENTS HAPPEN, THOUGH, AND HEROES ARE BORN. COUNT YOURSELF LUCKY.

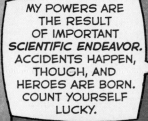

YOU *ARE* ONE OF THOSE *MAGIC FRUITS.*

PICKLE, GIRL.

DON'T TOUCH.

ALRIGHT, A *MAGIC PICKLE.*

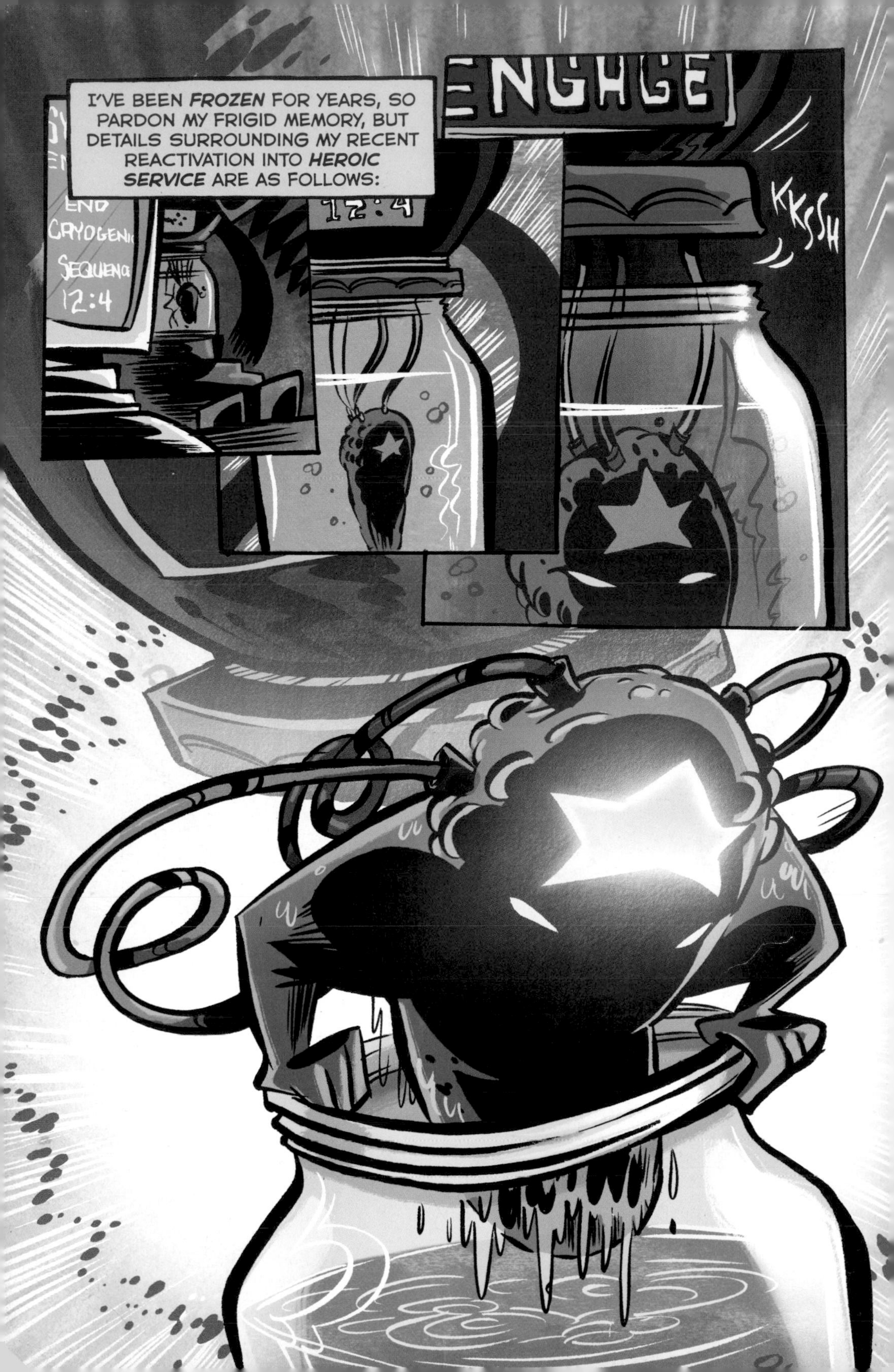

I'VE BEEN *FROZEN* FOR YEARS, SO PARDON MY FRIGID MEMORY, BUT DETAILS SURROUNDING MY RECENT REACTIVATION INTO *HEROIC SERVICE* ARE AS FOLLOWS:
END
CRYOGENI
SEQUENC
12:4
12:4
ENGAGE
KKSSH

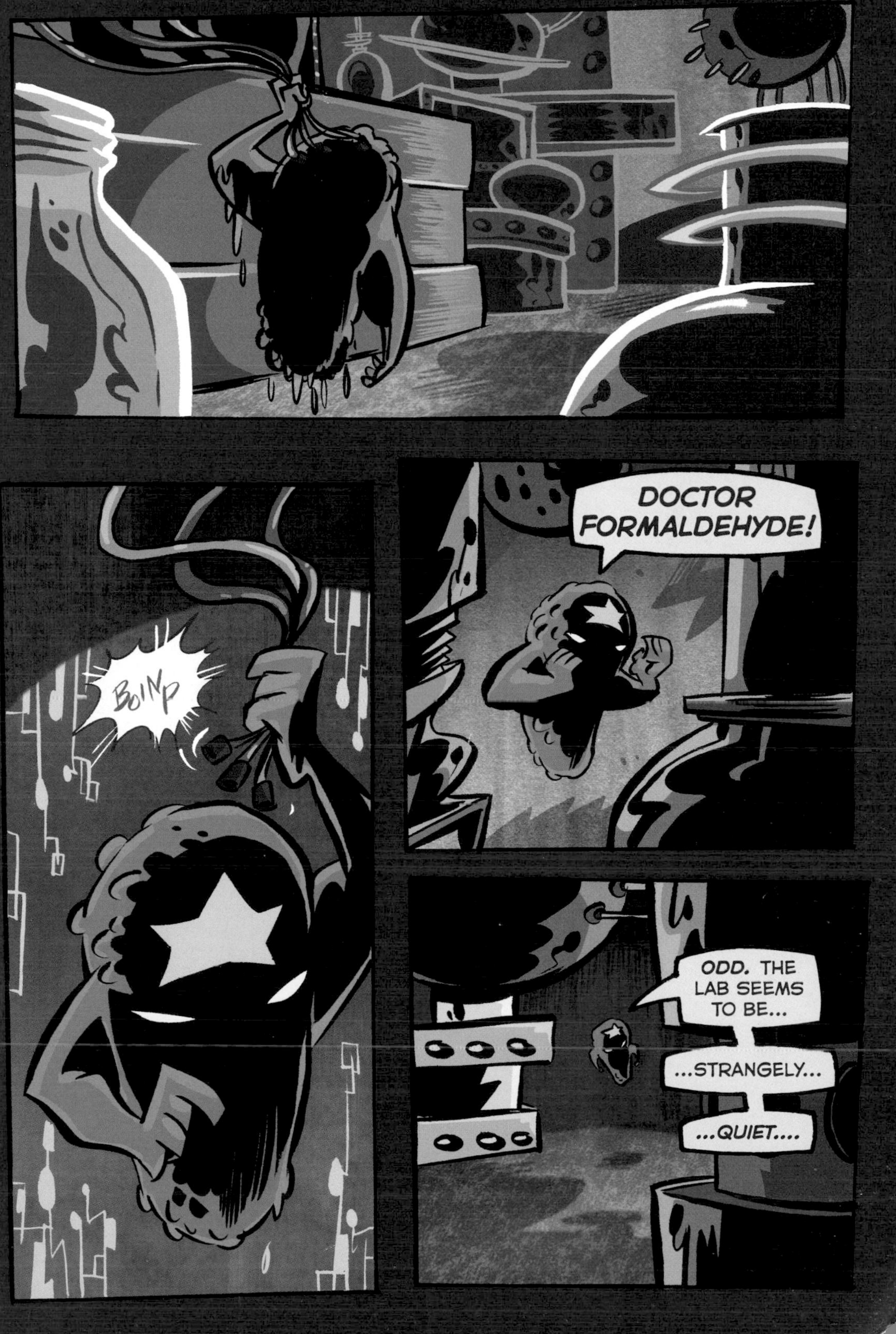
BOINP
DOCTOR FORMALDEHYDE!
ODD. THE LAB SEEMS TO BE...
...STRANGELY...
...QUIET....

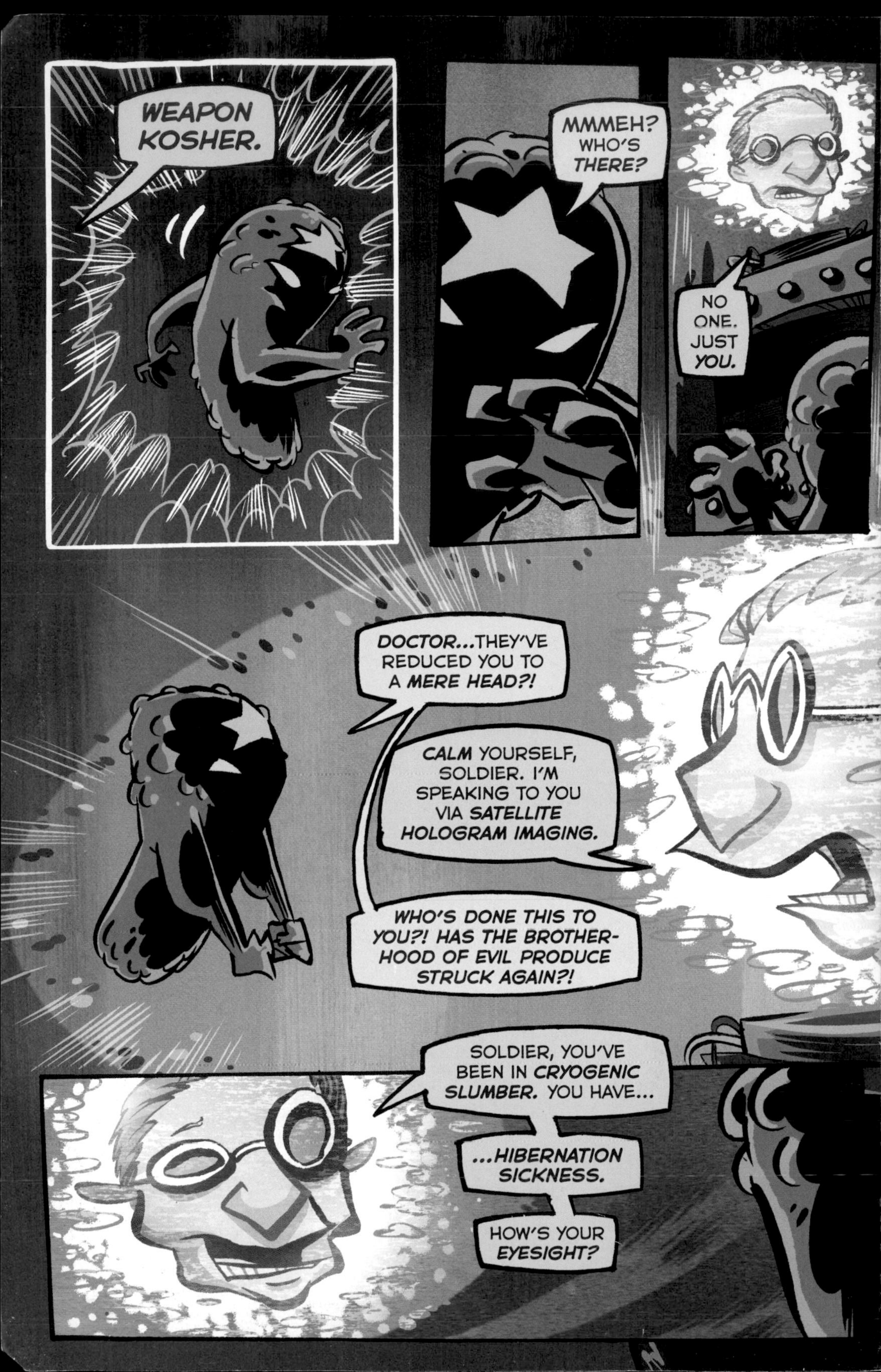
WEAPON KOSHER.
MMMEH? WHO'S THERE?
NO ONE. JUST YOU.
DOCTOR...THEY'VE REDUCED YOU TO A MERE HEAD?!
CALM YOURSELF, SOLDIER. I'M SPEAKING TO YOU VIA SATELLITE HOLOGRAM IMAGING.
WHO'S DONE THIS TO YOU?! HAS THE BROTHERHOOD OF EVIL PRODUCE STRUCK AGAIN?!
SOLDIER, YOU'VE BEEN IN CRYOGENIC SLUMBER. YOU HAVE...
...HIBERNATION SICKNESS.
HOW'S YOUR EYESIGHT?

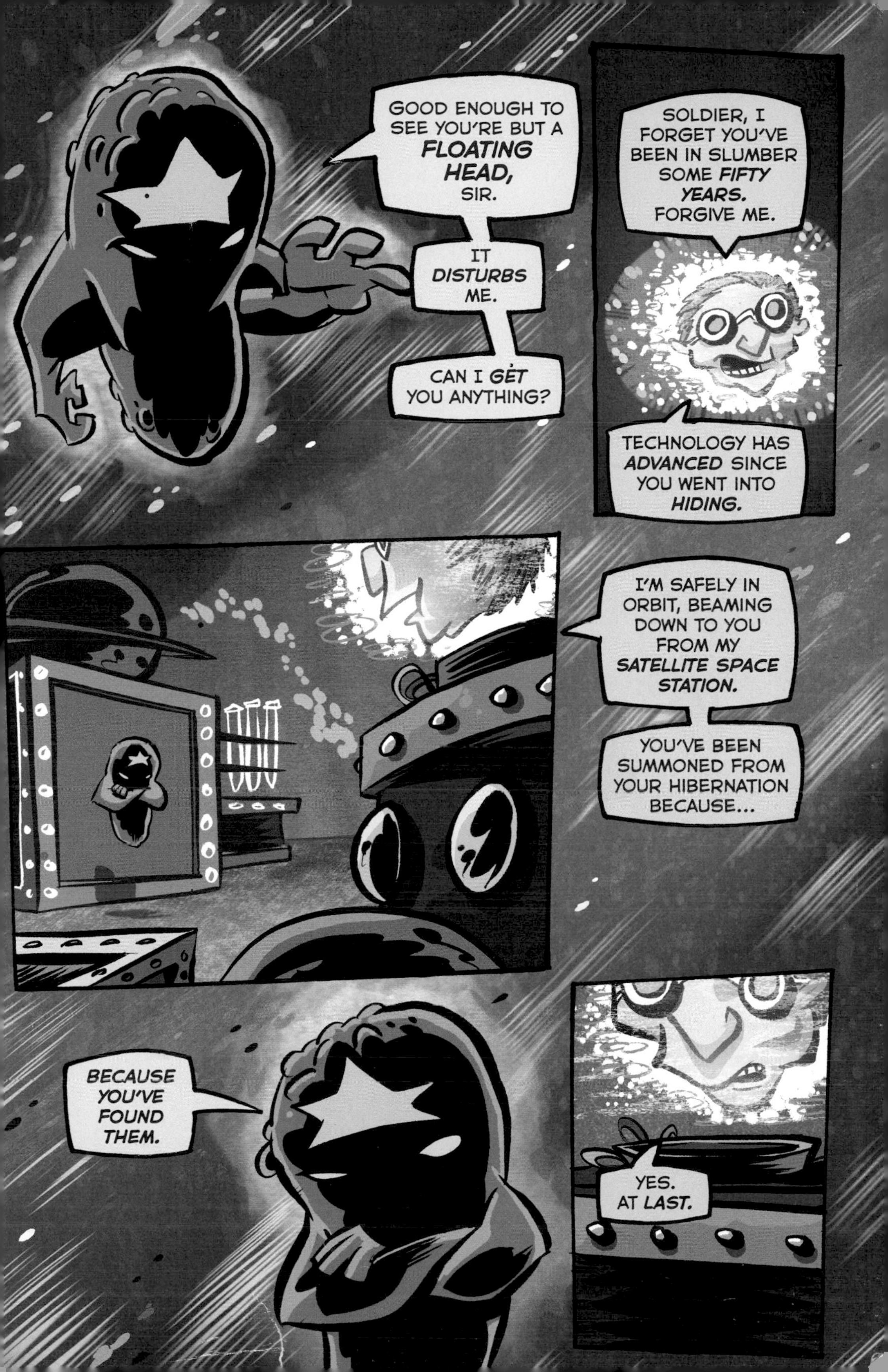
GOOD ENOUGH TO SEE YOU'RE BUT A *FLOATING HEAD,* SIR.
IT *DISTURBS* ME.
CAN I *GET* YOU ANYTHING?
SOLDIER, I FORGET YOU'VE BEEN IN SLUMBER SOME *FIFTY YEARS.* FORGIVE ME.
TECHNOLOGY HAS *ADVANCED* SINCE YOU WENT INTO *HIDING.*
I'M SAFELY IN ORBIT, BEAMING DOWN TO YOU FROM MY *SATELLITE SPACE STATION.*
YOU'VE BEEN SUMMONED FROM YOUR HIBERNATION BECAUSE...
BECAUSE YOU'VE FOUND THEM.
YES. AT *LAST.*

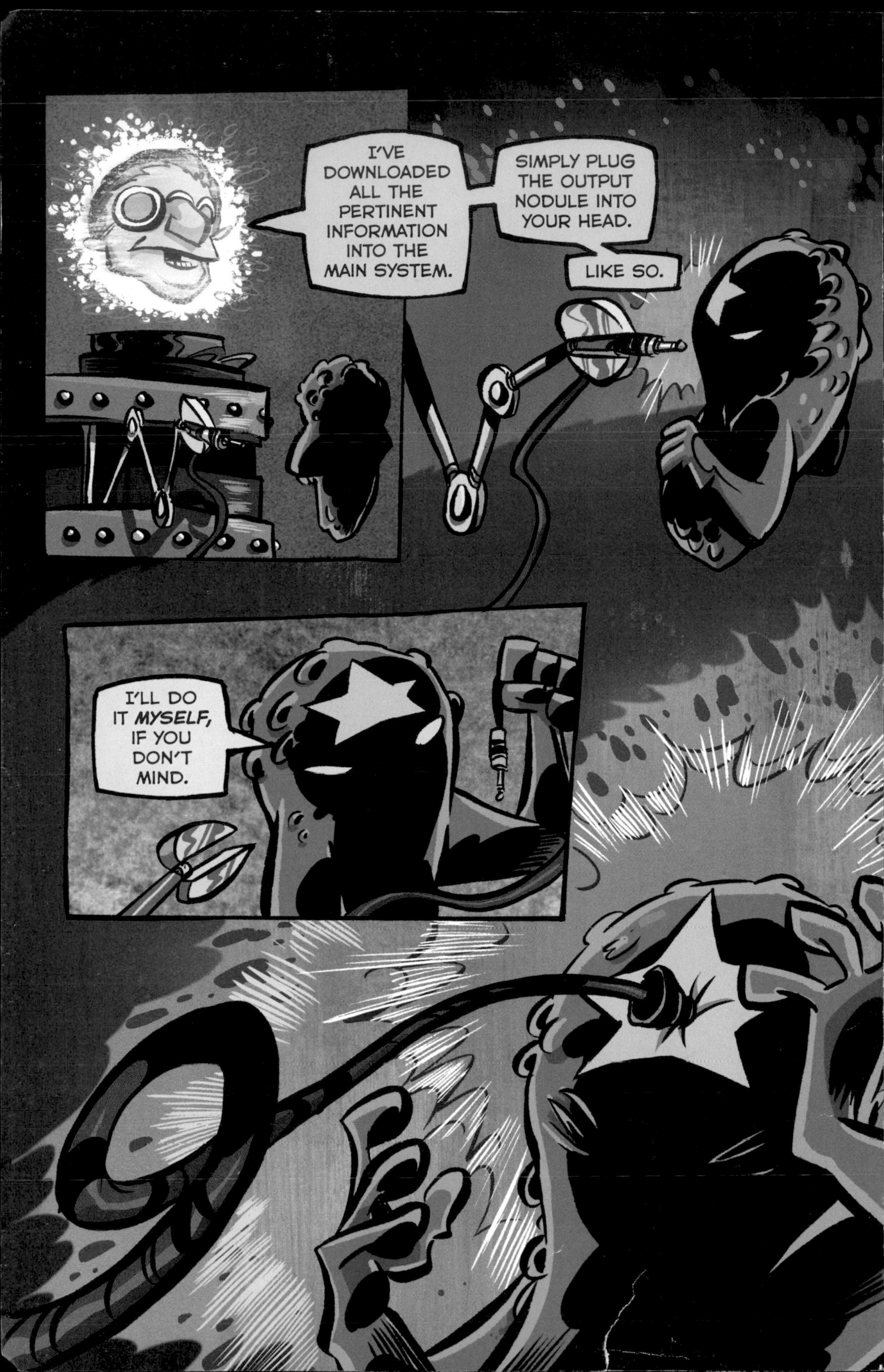
I'VE DOWNLOADED ALL THE PERTINENT INFORMATION INTO THE MAIN SYSTEM.
SIMPLY PLUG THE OUTPUT NODULE INTO YOUR HEAD.
LIKE SO.
I'LL DO IT *MYSELF,* IF YOU DON'T MIND.

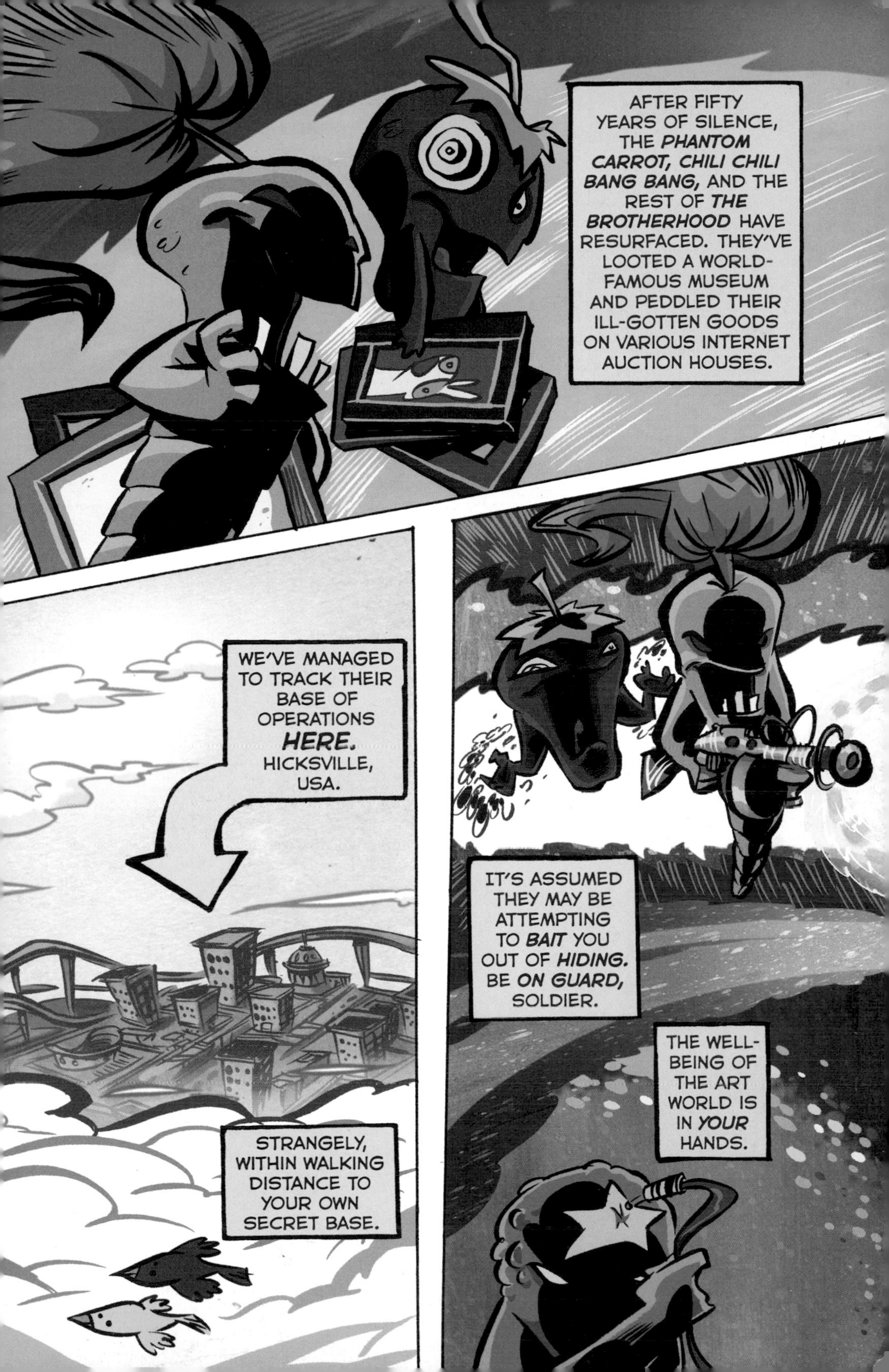
AFTER FIFTY YEARS OF SILENCE, THE PHANTOM CARROT, CHILI CHILI BANG BANG, AND THE REST OF THE BROTHERHOOD HAVE RESURFACED. THEY'VE LOOTED A WORLD-FAMOUS MUSEUM AND PEDDLED THEIR ILL-GOTTEN GOODS ON VARIOUS INTERNET AUCTION HOUSES.
WE'VE MANAGED TO TRACK THEIR BASE OF OPERATIONS HERE. HICKSVILLE, USA.
STRANGELY, WITHIN WALKING DISTANCE TO YOUR OWN SECRET BASE.
IT'S ASSUMED THEY MAY BE ATTEMPTING TO BAIT YOU OUT OF HIDING. BE ON GUARD, SOLDIER.
THE WELL-BEING OF THE ART WORLD IS IN YOUR HANDS.

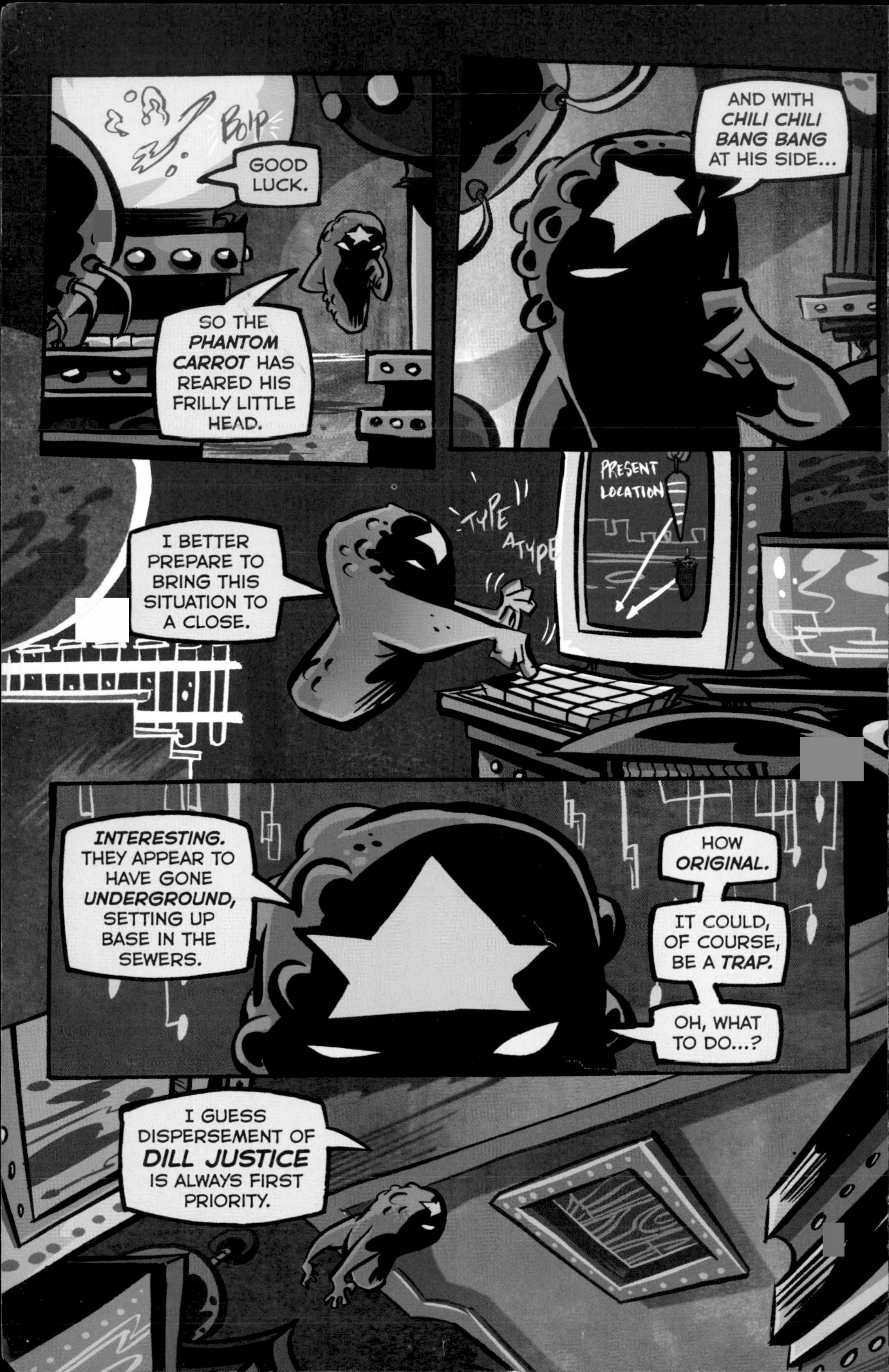
BOIP
GOOD LUCK.
SO THE PHANTOM CARROT HAS REARED HIS FRILLY LITTLE HEAD.
AND WITH CHILI CHILI BANG BANG AT HIS SIDE...
I BETTER PREPARE TO BRING THIS SITUATION TO A CLOSE.
TYPE
A TYPE
PRESENT LOCATION
INTERESTING. THEY APPEAR TO HAVE GONE UNDERGROUND, SETTING UP BASE IN THE SEWERS.
HOW ORIGINAL.
IT COULD, OF COURSE, BE A TRAP.
OH, WHAT TO DO...?
I GUESS DISPERSEMENT OF DILL JUSTICE IS ALWAYS FIRST PRIORITY.

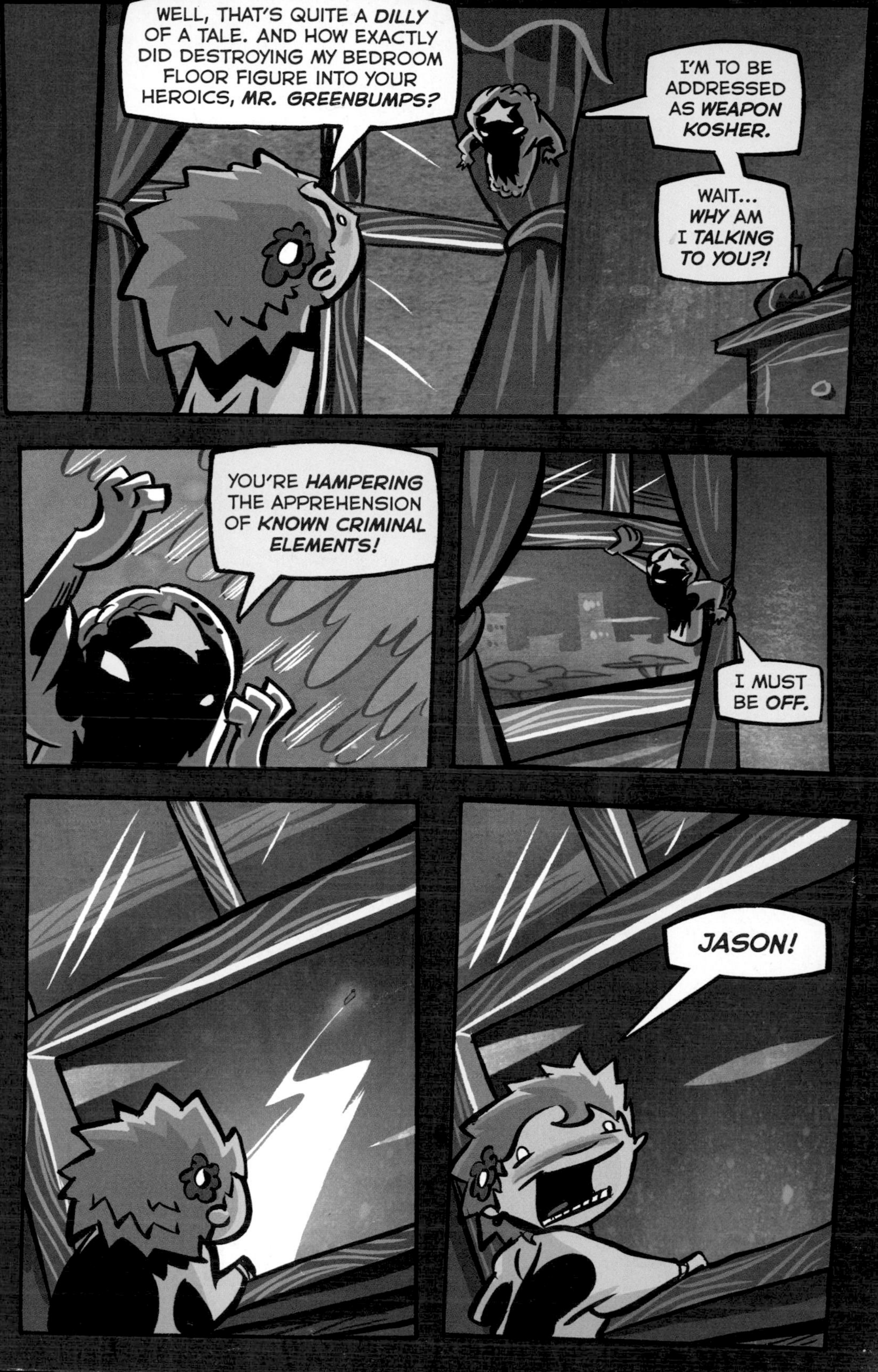
WELL, THAT'S QUITE A DILLY OF A TALE. AND HOW EXACTLY DID DESTROYING MY BEDROOM FLOOR FIGURE INTO YOUR HEROICS, MR. GREENBUMPS?
I'M TO BE ADDRESSED AS WEAPON KOSHER.
WAIT... WHY AM I TALKING TO YOU?!
YOU'RE HAMPERING THE APPREHENSION OF KNOWN CRIMINAL ELEMENTS!
I MUST BE OFF.
JASON!

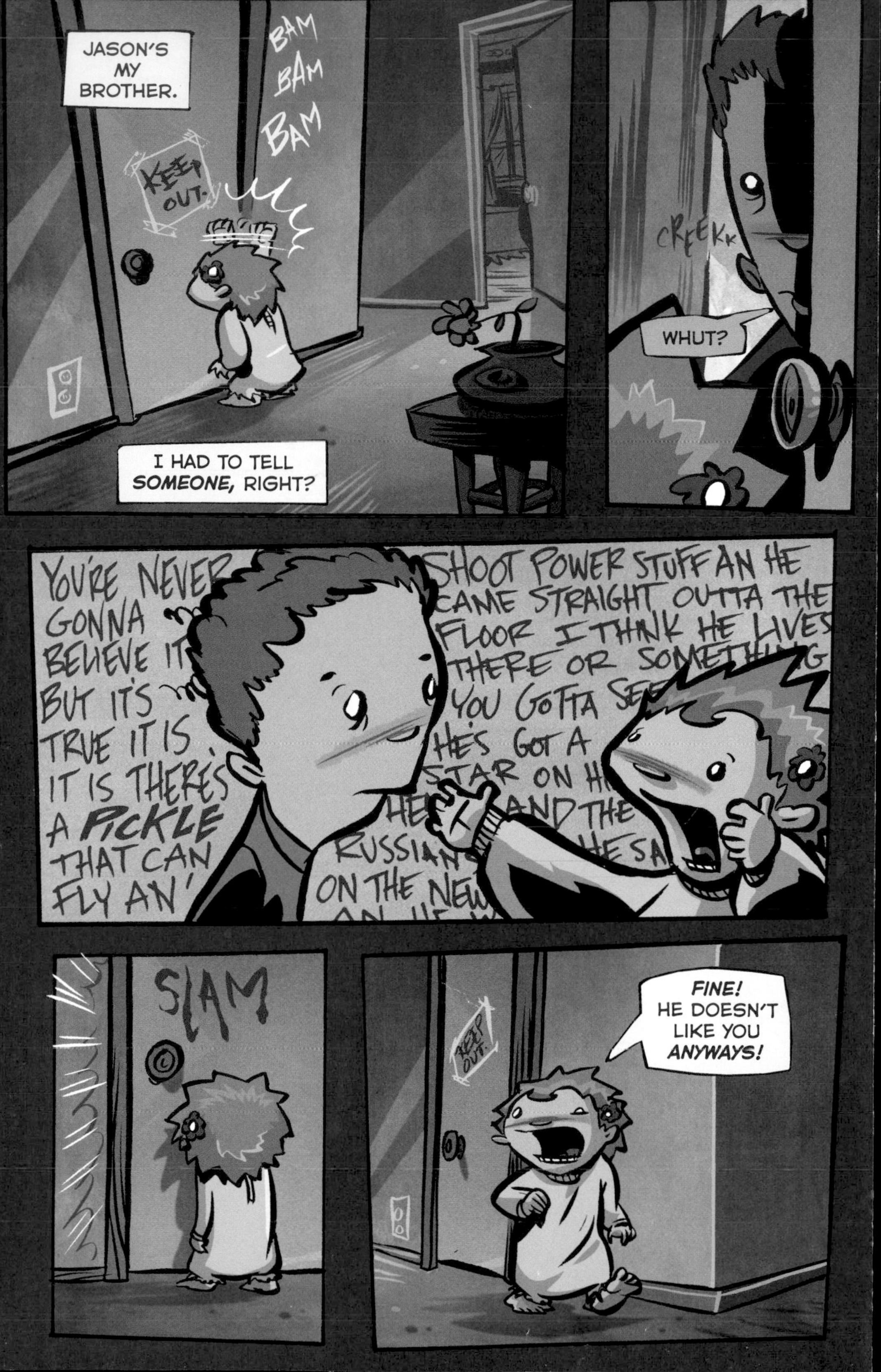
JASON'S MY BROTHER.
BAM BAM BAM
KEEP OUT.
I HAD TO TELL ***SOMEONE,*** RIGHT?
CREEKK
WHUT?
YOU'RE NEVER GONNA BELIEVE IT BUT IT'S TRUE IT IS IT IS THERE'S A ***PICKLE*** THAT CAN FLY AN'
SHOOT POWER STUFF AN HE CAME STRAIGHT OUTTA THE FLOOR I THINK HE LIVES THERE OR
YOU GOTTA
HE'S GOT A
STAR ON
RUSSIAN
ON THE
SLAM
KEEP OUT.
FINE! HE DOESN'T LIKE YOU ***ANYWAYS!***

CHAPTER 2

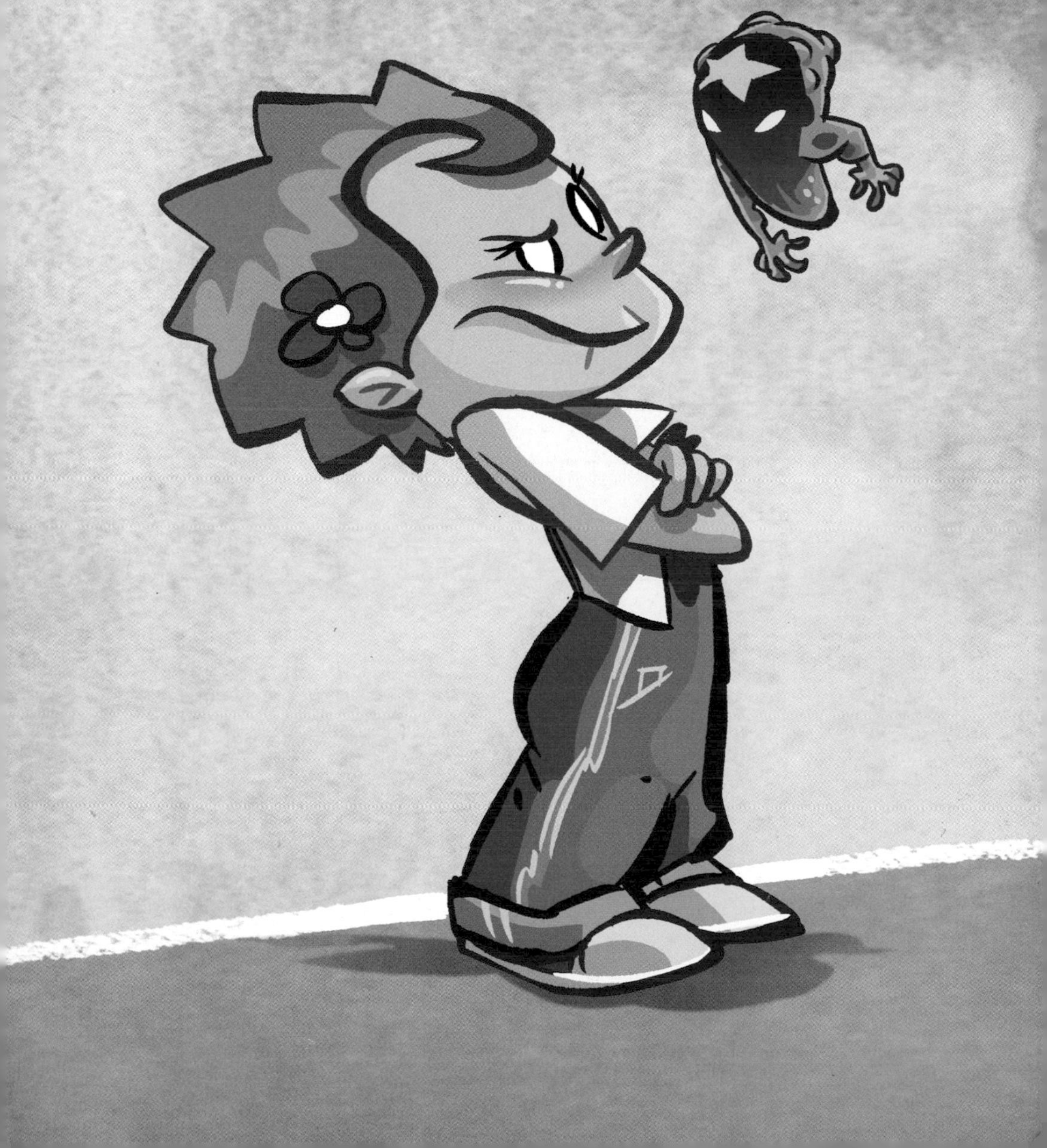

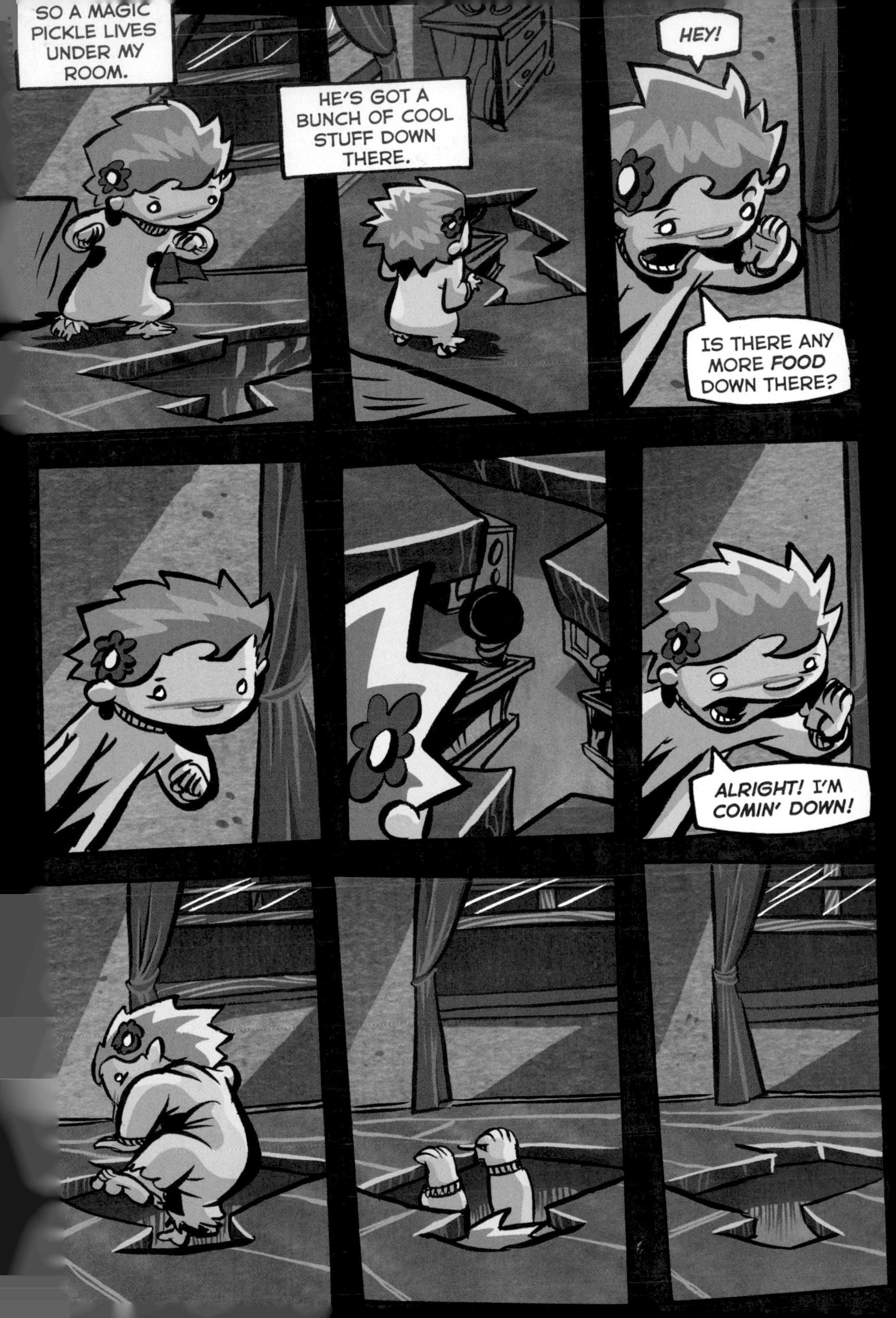
SO A MAGIC PICKLE LIVES UNDER MY ROOM.
HE'S GOT A BUNCH OF COOL STUFF DOWN THERE.
HEY!
IS THERE ANY MORE *FOOD* DOWN THERE?
ALRIGHT! I'M COMIN' DOWN!

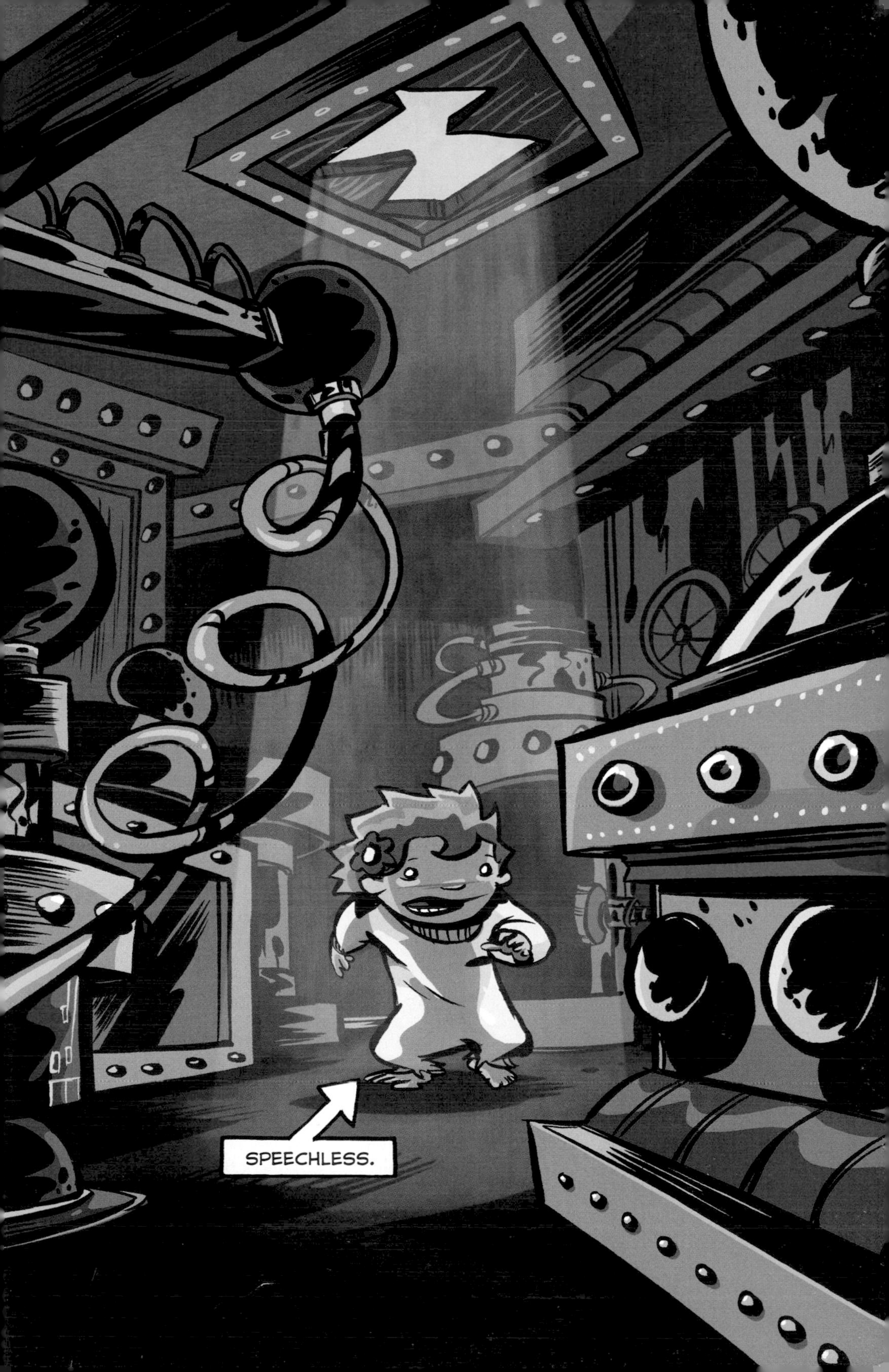
SPEECHLESS.

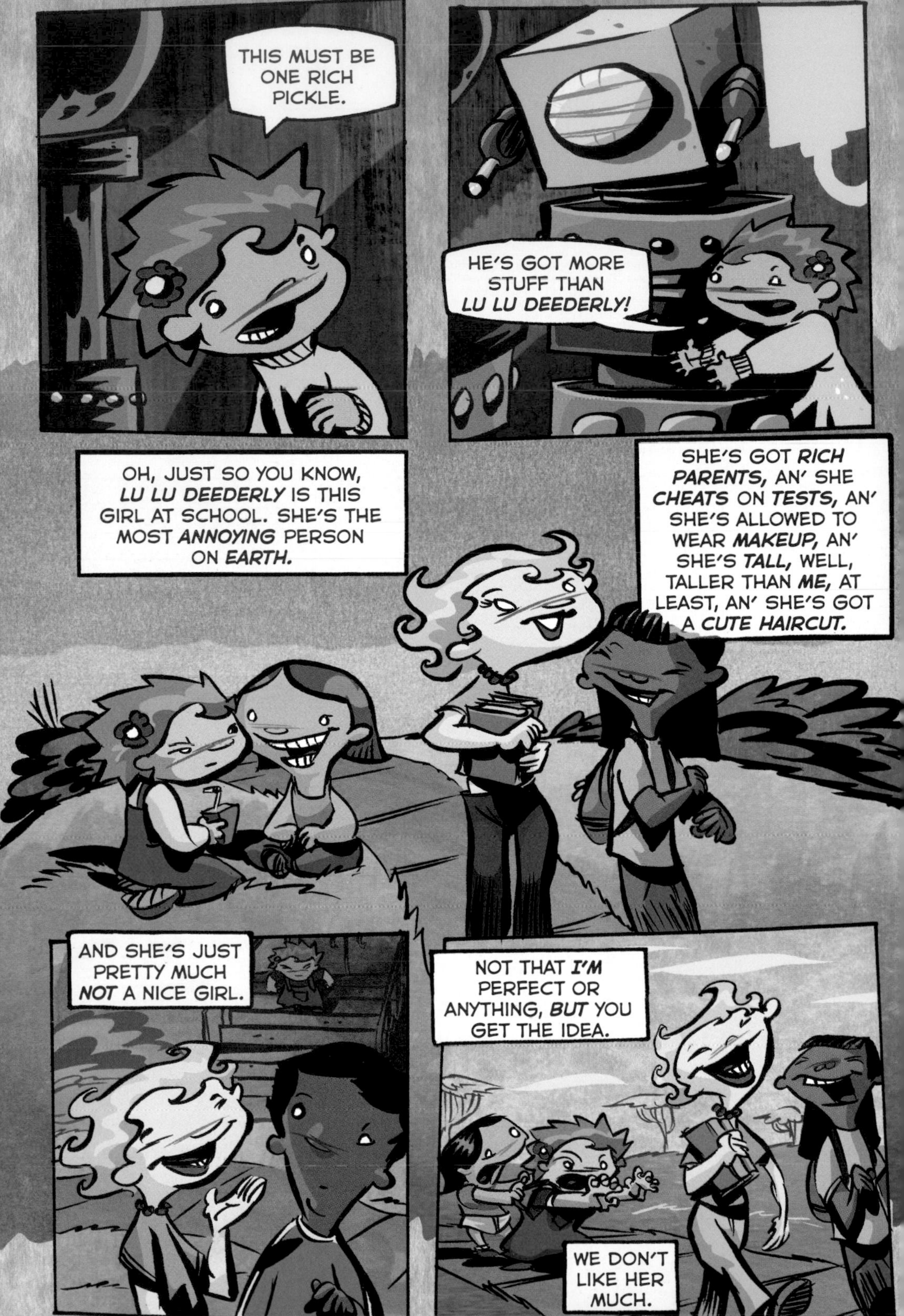
THIS MUST BE ONE RICH PICKLE.
HE'S GOT MORE STUFF THAN *LU LU DEEDERLY!*
OH, JUST SO YOU KNOW, *LU LU DEEDERLY* IS THIS GIRL AT SCHOOL. SHE'S THE MOST *ANNOYING* PERSON ON *EARTH.*
SHE'S GOT *RICH PARENTS,* AN' SHE *CHEATS* ON *TESTS,* AN' SHE'S ALLOWED TO WEAR *MAKEUP,* AN' SHE'S *TALL,* WELL, TALLER THAN *ME,* AT LEAST, AN' SHE'S GOT A *CUTE HAIRCUT.*
AND SHE'S JUST PRETTY MUCH *NOT* A NICE GIRL.
NOT THAT *I'M* PERFECT OR ANYTHING, *BUT* YOU GET THE IDEA.
WE DON'T LIKE HER MUCH.

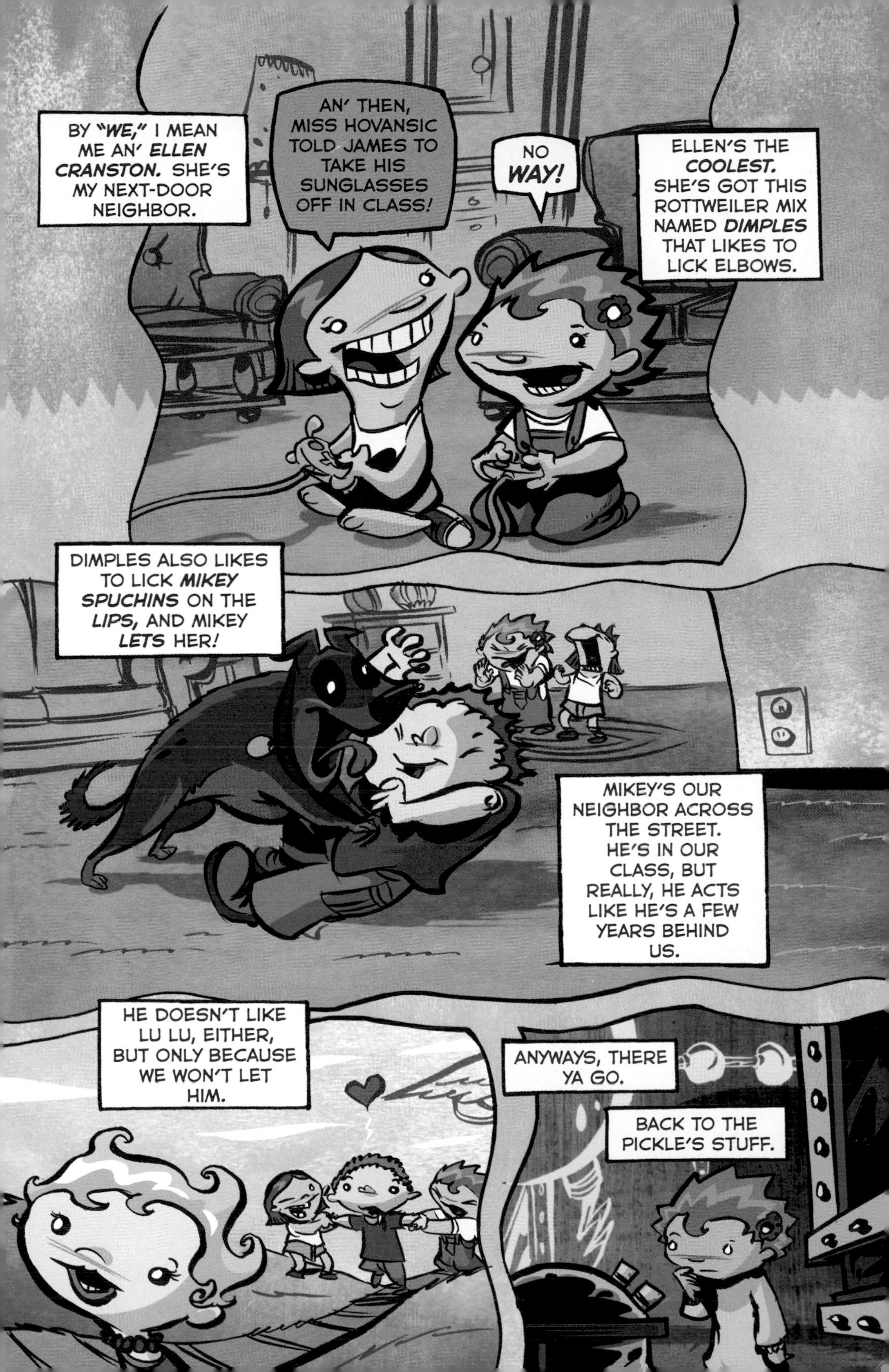
BY "WE," I MEAN ME AN' ELLEN CRANSTON. SHE'S MY NEXT-DOOR NEIGHBOR.
AN' THEN, MISS HOVANSIC TOLD JAMES TO TAKE HIS SUNGLASSES OFF IN CLASS!
NO WAY!
ELLEN'S THE COOLEST. SHE'S GOT THIS ROTTWEILER MIX NAMED DIMPLES THAT LIKES TO LICK ELBOWS.
DIMPLES ALSO LIKES TO LICK MIKEY SPUCHINS ON THE LIPS, AND MIKEY LETS HER!
MIKEY'S OUR NEIGHBOR ACROSS THE STREET. HE'S IN OUR CLASS, BUT REALLY, HE ACTS LIKE HE'S A FEW YEARS BEHIND US.
HE DOESN'T LIKE LU LU, EITHER, BUT ONLY BECAUSE WE WON'T LET HIM.
ANYWAYS, THERE YA GO.
BACK TO THE PICKLE'S STUFF.

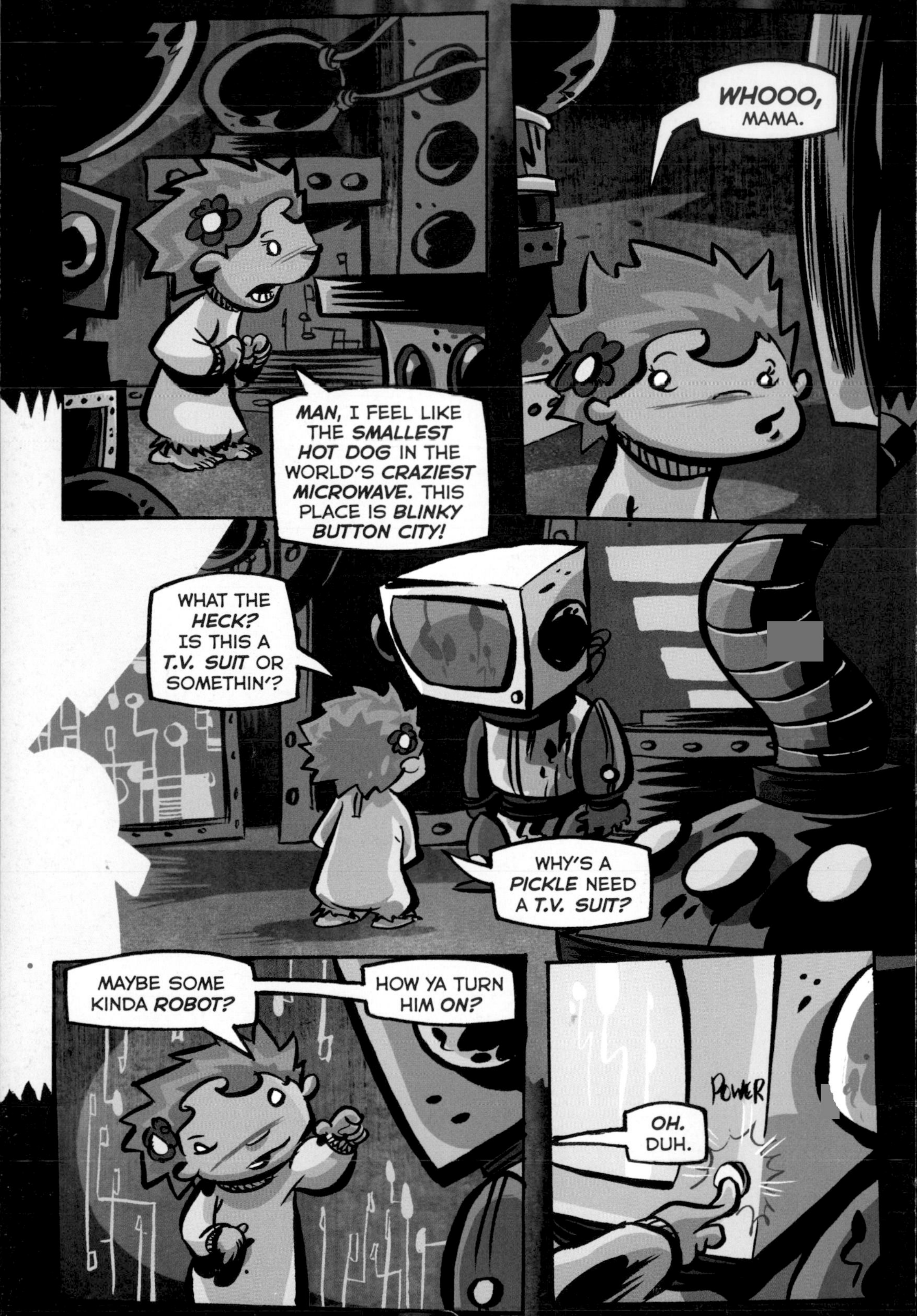
MAN, I FEEL LIKE THE SMALLEST HOT DOG IN THE WORLD'S CRAZIEST MICROWAVE. THIS PLACE IS BLINKY BUTTON CITY!
WHOOO, MAMA.
WHAT THE HECK? IS THIS A T.V. SUIT OR SOMETHIN'?
WHY'S A PICKLE NEED A T.V. SUIT?
MAYBE SOME KINDA ROBOT?
HOW YA TURN HIM ON?
POWER
OH. DUH.

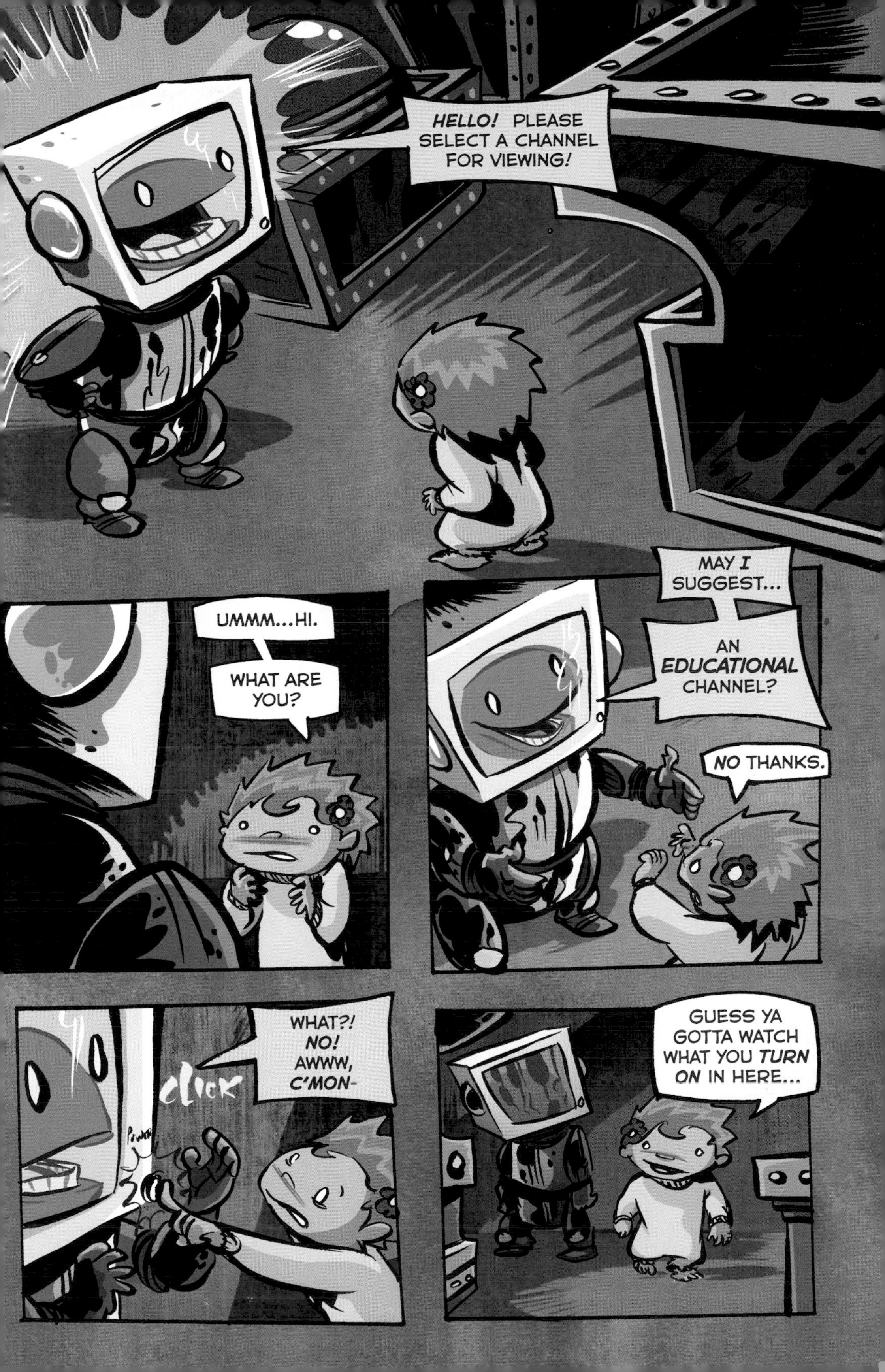

HELLO! PLEASE SELECT A CHANNEL FOR VIEWING!
UMMM...HI.
WHAT ARE YOU?
MAY *I* SUGGEST...
AN *EDUCATIONAL* CHANNEL?
NO THANKS.
CLICK
WHAT?! *NO!* AWWW, *C'MON-*
GUESS YA GOTTA WATCH WHAT YOU *TURN ON* IN HERE...

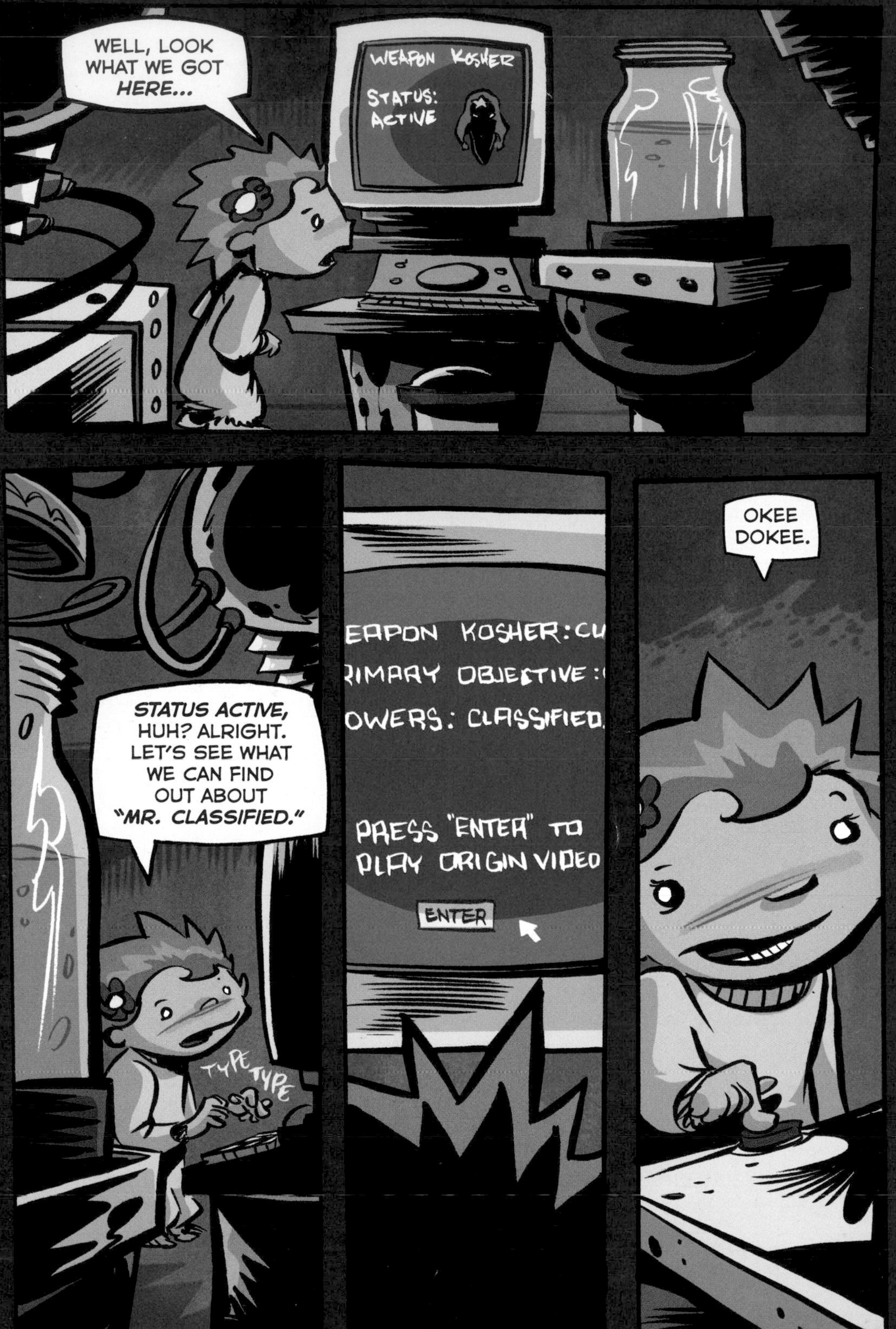
WELL, LOOK WHAT WE GOT *HERE...*
WEAPON KOSHER
STATUS: ACTIVE
STATUS ACTIVE, HUH? ALRIGHT. LET'S SEE WHAT WE CAN FIND OUT ABOUT *"MR. CLASSIFIED."*
TYPE TYPE
EAPON KOSHER:CL
RIMARY OBJECTIVE:
OWERS: CLASSIFIED.
PRESS "ENTER" TO PLAY ORIGIN VIDEO
ENTER
OKEE DOKEE.

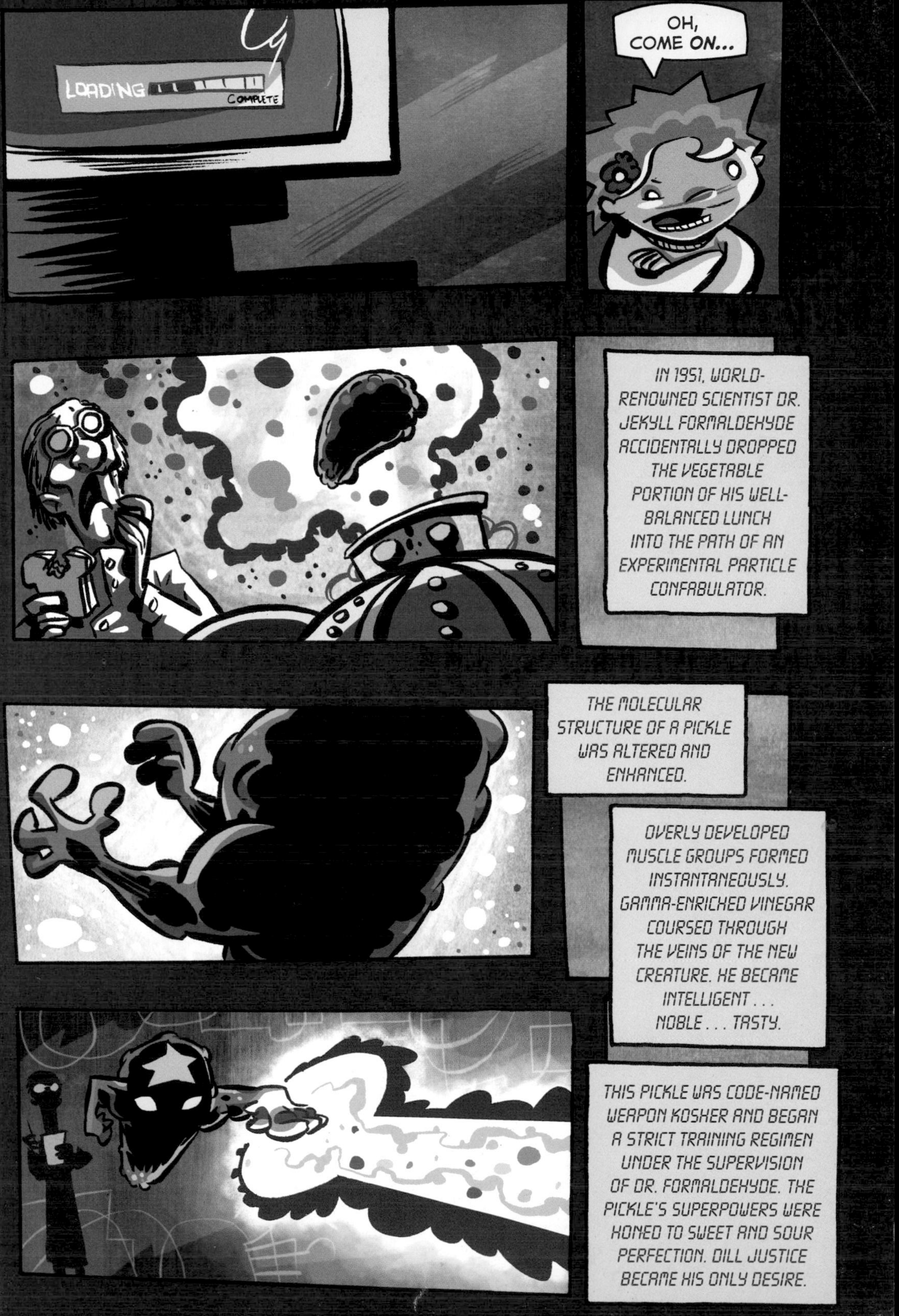
LOADING
COMPLETE
OH, COME ON...
IN 1951, WORLD-RENOWNED SCIENTIST DR. JEKYLL FORMALDEHYDE ACCIDENTALLY DROPPED THE VEGETABLE PORTION OF HIS WELL-BALANCED LUNCH INTO THE PATH OF AN EXPERIMENTAL PARTICLE CONFABULATOR.
THE MOLECULAR STRUCTURE OF A PICKLE WAS ALTERED AND ENHANCED.
OVERLY DEVELOPED MUSCLE GROUPS FORMED INSTANTANEOUSLY. GAMMA-ENRICHED VINEGAR COURSED THROUGH THE VEINS OF THE NEW CREATURE. HE BECAME INTELLIGENT . . . NOBLE . . . TASTY.
THIS PICKLE WAS CODE-NAMED WEAPON KOSHER AND BEGAN A STRICT TRAINING REGIMEN UNDER THE SUPERVISION OF DR. FORMALDEHYDE. THE PICKLE'S SUPERPOWERS WERE HONED TO SWEET AND SOUR PERFECTION. DILL JUSTICE BECAME HIS ONLY DESIRE.

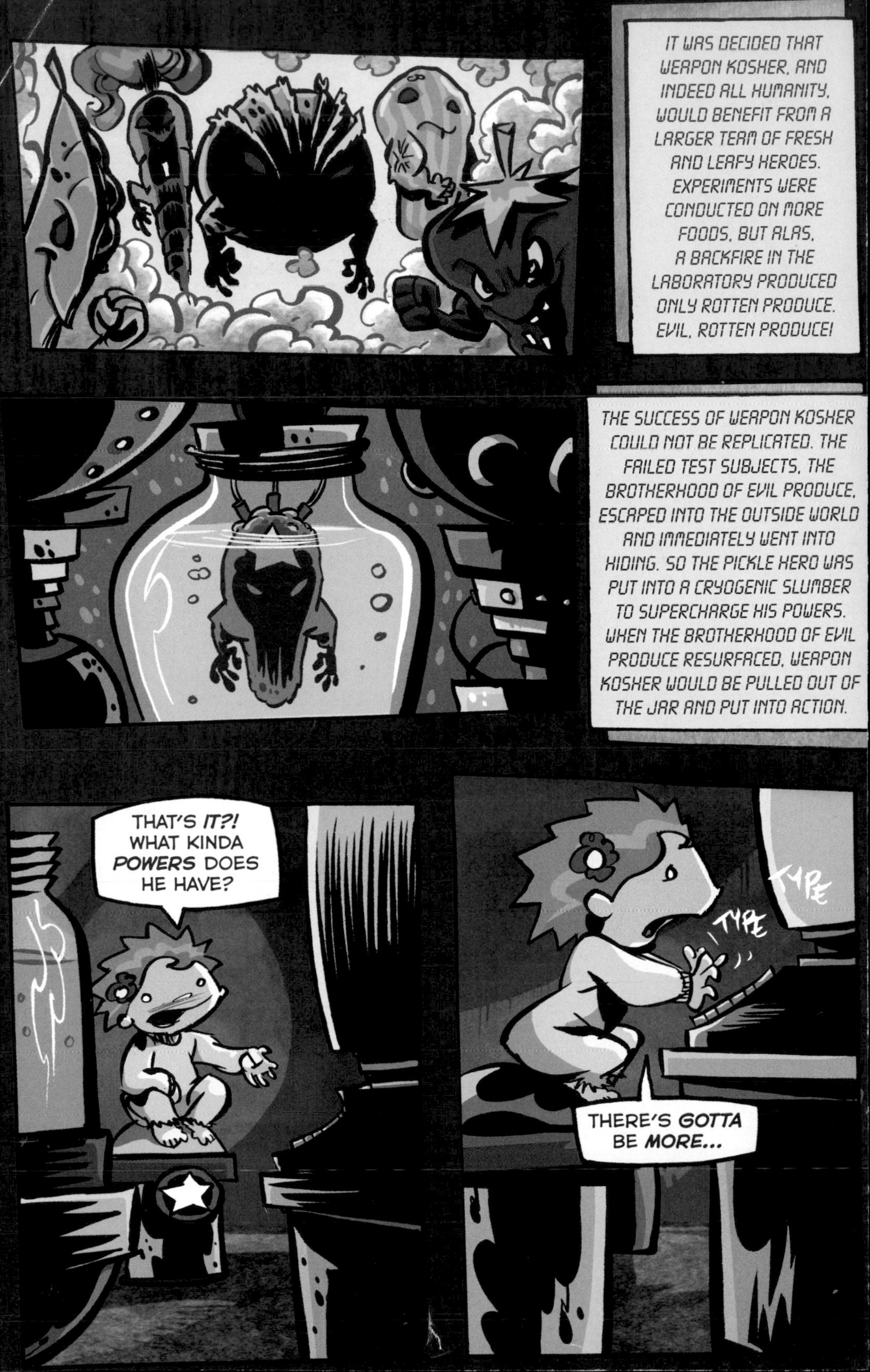
IT WAS DECIDED THAT WEAPON KOSHER, AND INDEED ALL HUMANITY, WOULD BENEFIT FROM A LARGER TEAM OF FRESH AND LEAFY HEROES. EXPERIMENTS WERE CONDUCTED ON MORE FOODS, BUT ALAS, A BACKFIRE IN THE LABORATORY PRODUCED ONLY ROTTEN PRODUCE. EVIL, ROTTEN PRODUCE!
THE SUCCESS OF WEAPON KOSHER COULD NOT BE REPLICATED. THE FAILED TEST SUBJECTS, THE BROTHERHOOD OF EVIL PRODUCE, ESCAPED INTO THE OUTSIDE WORLD AND IMMEDIATELY WENT INTO HIDING. SO THE PICKLE HERO WAS PUT INTO A CRYOGENIC SLUMBER TO SUPERCHARGE HIS POWERS. WHEN THE BROTHERHOOD OF EVIL PRODUCE RESURFACED, WEAPON KOSHER WOULD BE PULLED OUT OF THE JAR AND PUT INTO ACTION.
THAT'S *IT?!* WHAT KINDA *POWERS* DOES HE HAVE?
TYPE
TYPE
THERE'S *GOTTA* BE *MORE...*

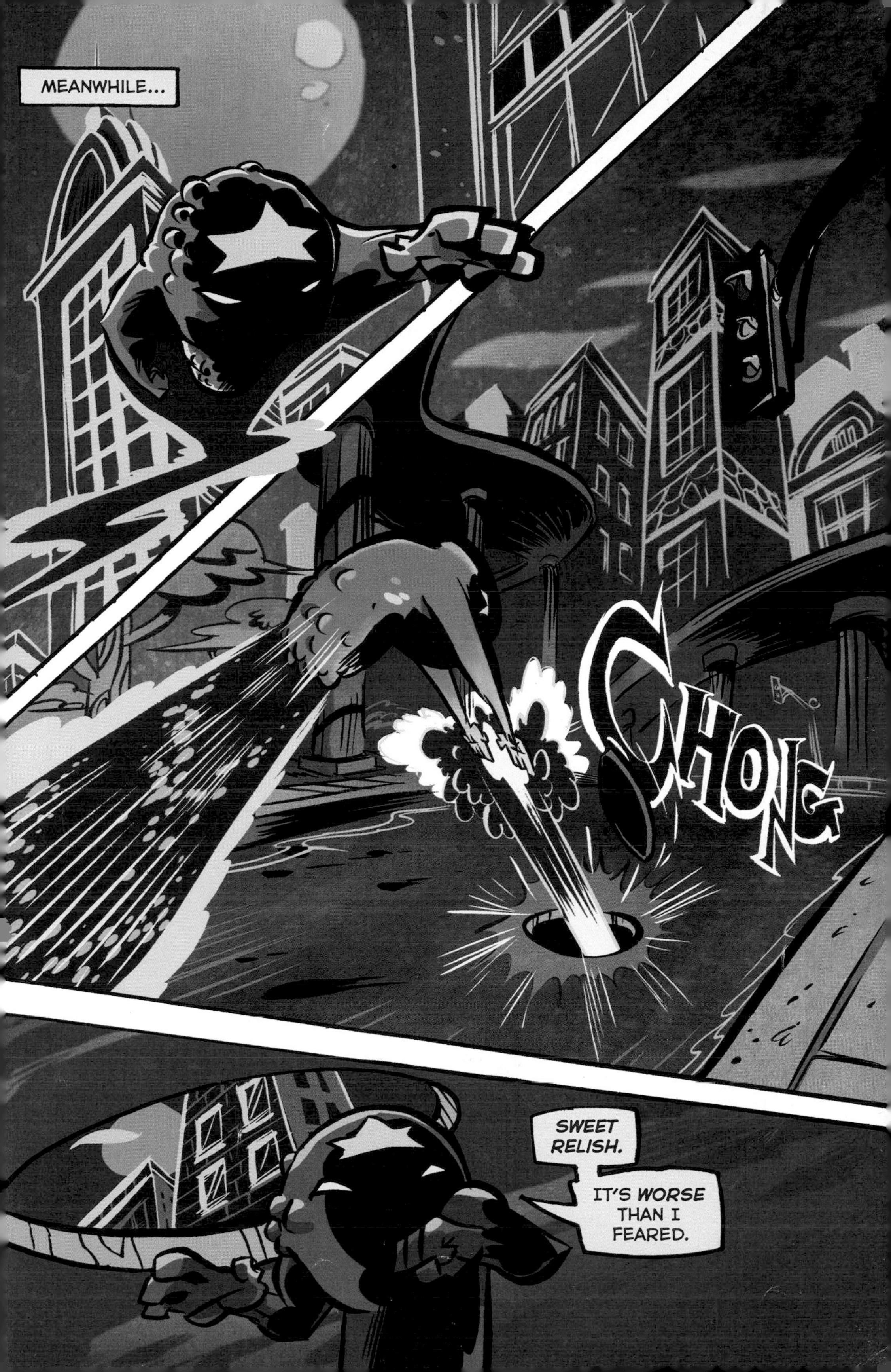
MEANWHILE...
CHONG
SWEET RELISH.
IT'S WORSE THAN I FEARED.

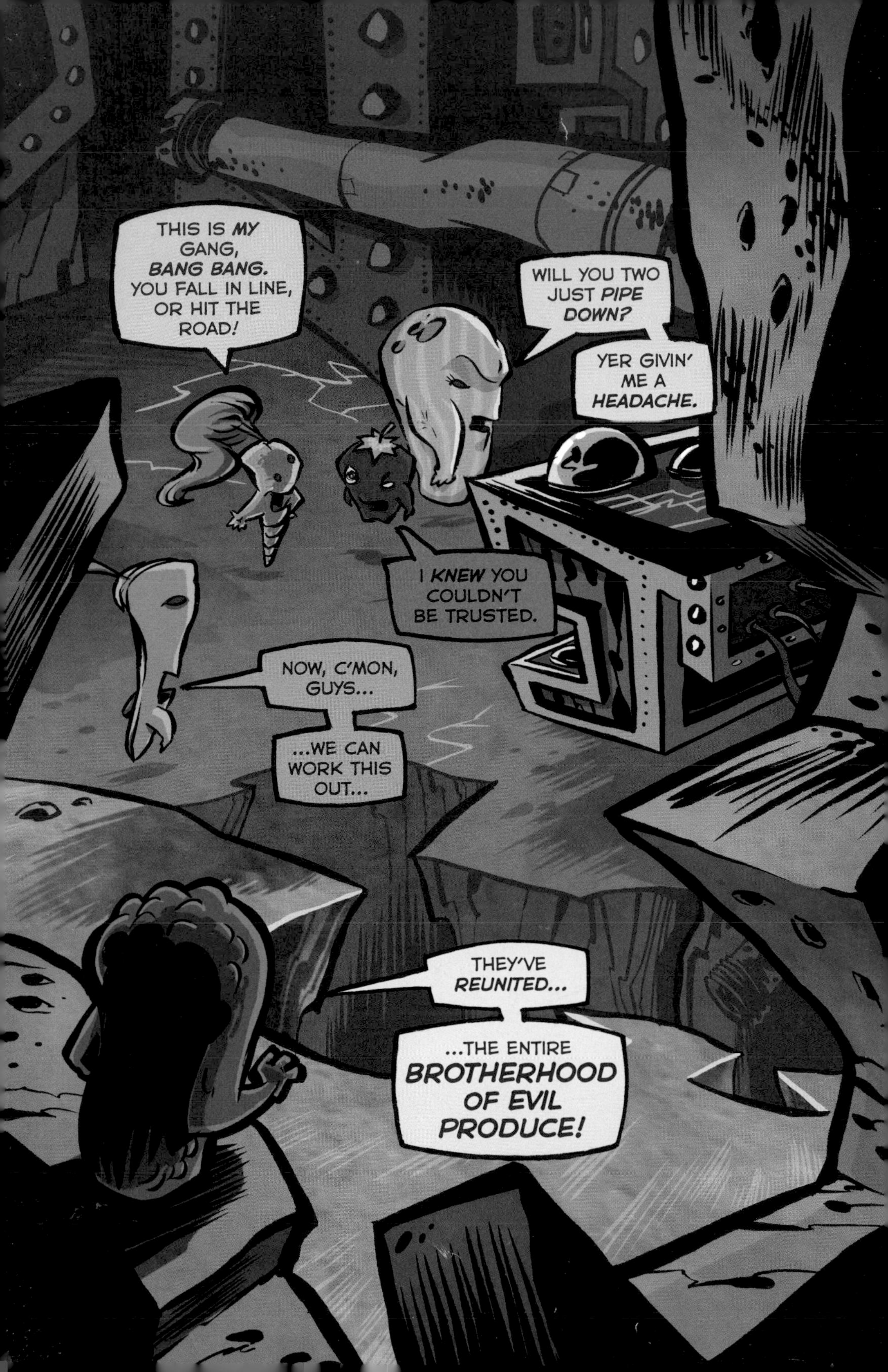
THIS IS *MY* GANG, ***BANG BANG.*** YOU FALL IN LINE, OR HIT THE ROAD!
WILL YOU TWO JUST *PIPE DOWN?*
YER GIVIN' ME A ***HEADACHE.***
I ***KNEW*** YOU COULDN'T BE TRUSTED.
NOW, C'MON, GUYS...
...WE CAN WORK THIS OUT...
THEY'VE ***REUNITED...***
...THE ENTIRE ***BROTHERHOOD OF EVIL PRODUCE!***

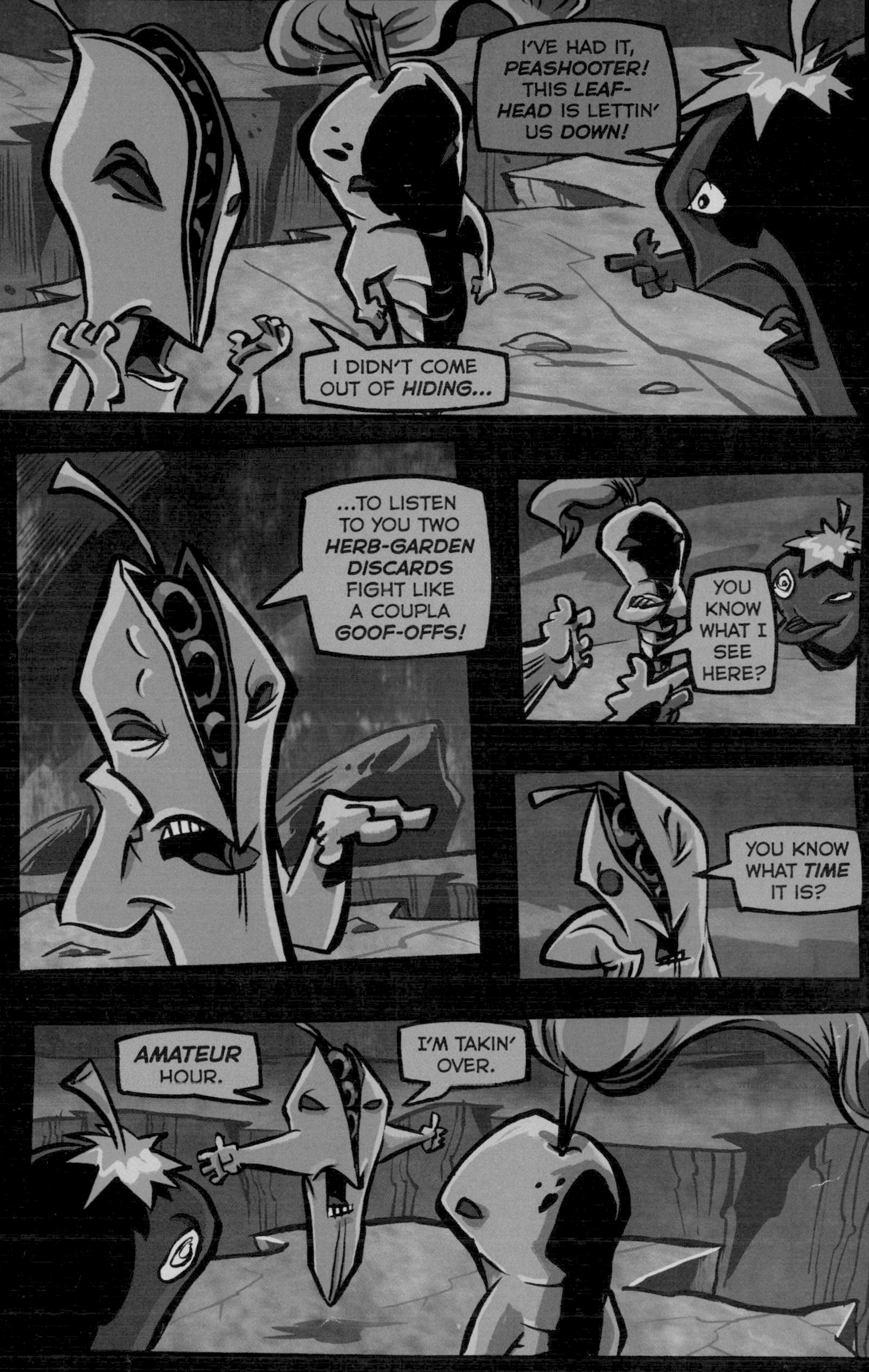
I'VE HAD IT, PEASHOOTER! THIS LEAF-HEAD IS LETTIN' US DOWN!
I DIDN'T COME OUT OF HIDING...
...TO LISTEN TO YOU TWO HERB-GARDEN DISCARDS FIGHT LIKE A COUPLA GOOF-OFFS!
YOU KNOW WHAT I SEE HERE?
YOU KNOW WHAT TIME IT IS?
AMATEUR HOUR.
I'M TAKIN' OVER.

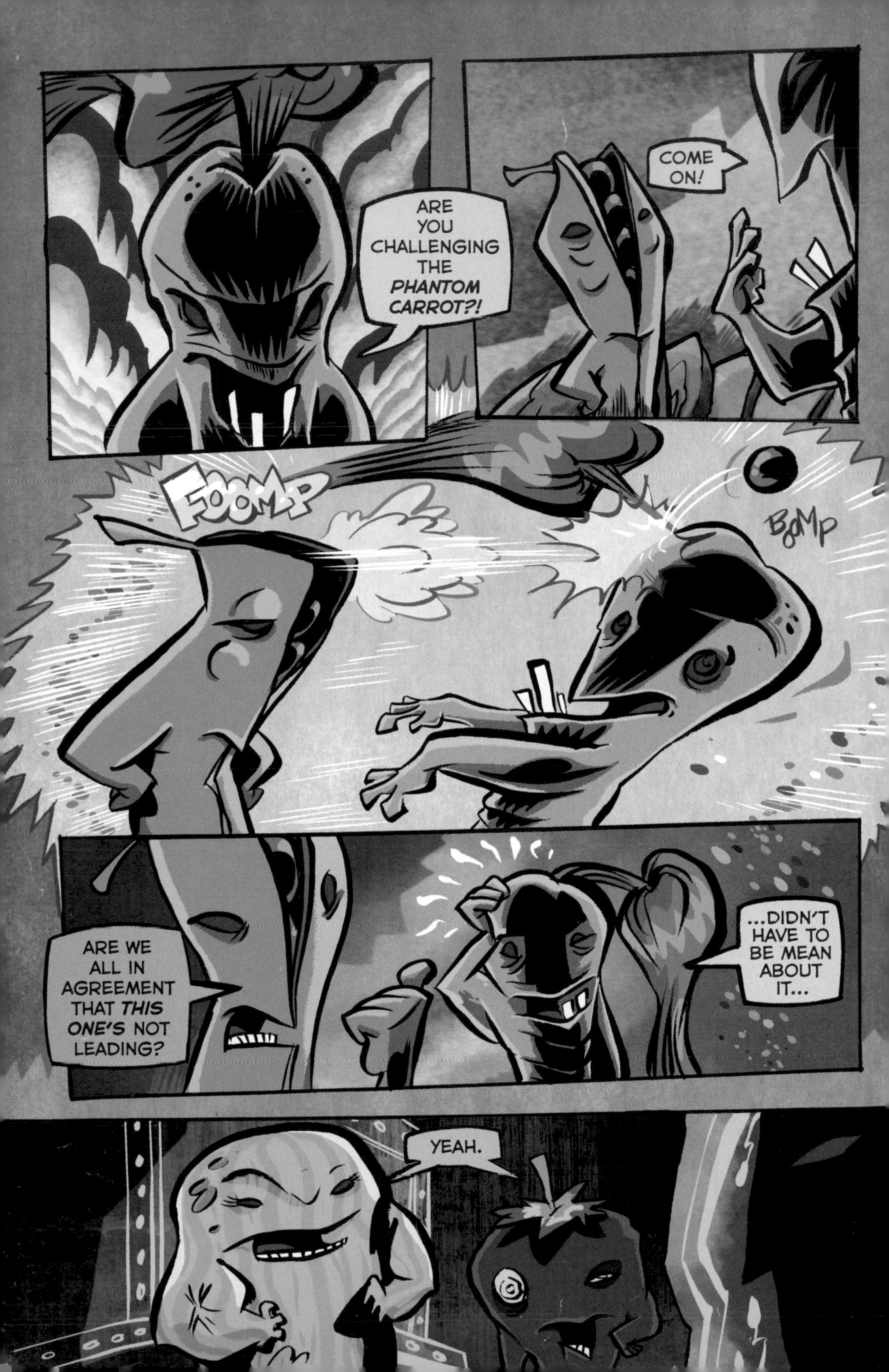
ARE YOU CHALLENGING THE *PHANTOM CARROT?!*
COME ON!
FOOMP
BOMP
ARE WE ALL IN AGREEMENT THAT *THIS ONE'S* NOT LEADING?
...DIDN'T HAVE TO BE MEAN ABOUT IT...
YEAH.

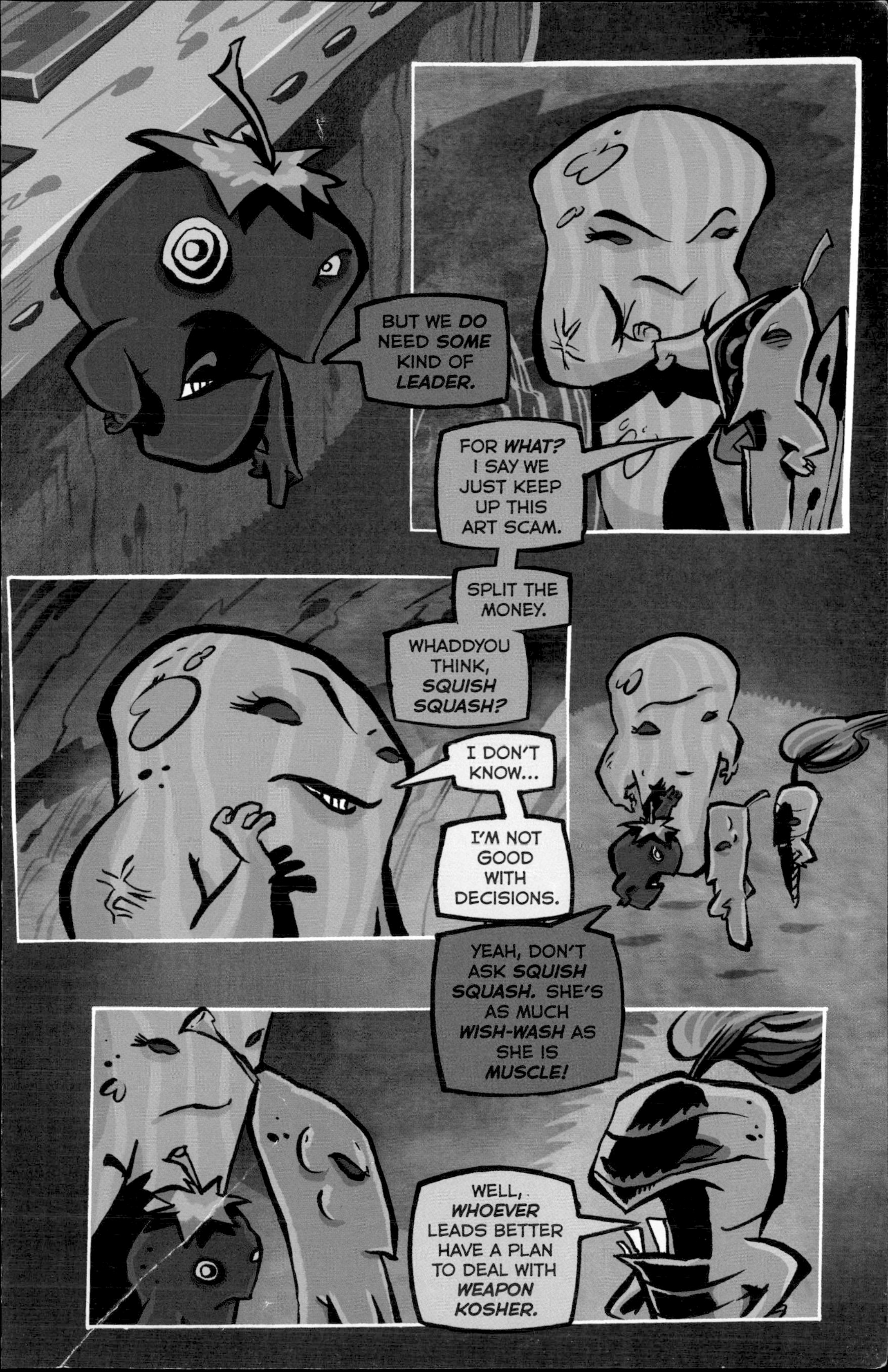
BUT WE DO NEED SOME KIND OF LEADER.
FOR WHAT? I SAY WE JUST KEEP UP THIS ART SCAM.
SPLIT THE MONEY.
WHADDYOU THINK, SQUISH SQUASH?
I DON'T KNOW...
I'M NOT GOOD WITH DECISIONS.
YEAH, DON'T ASK SQUISH SQUASH. SHE'S AS MUCH WISH-WASH AS SHE IS MUSCLE!
WELL, WHOEVER LEADS BETTER HAVE A PLAN TO DEAL WITH WEAPON KOSHER.

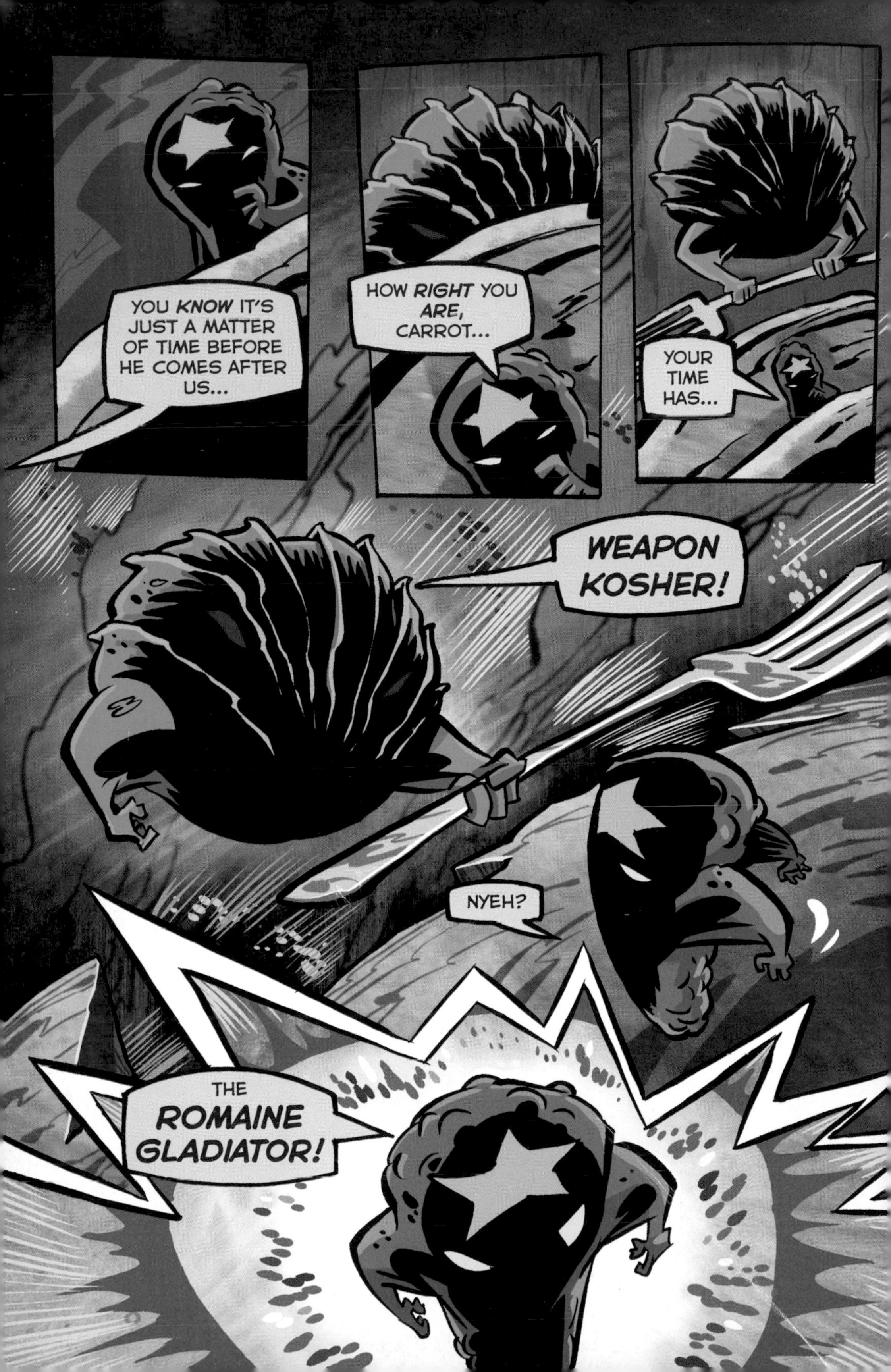
YOU *KNOW* IT'S JUST A MATTER OF TIME BEFORE HE COMES AFTER US...
HOW *RIGHT* YOU *ARE*, CARROT...
YOUR TIME HAS...
WEAPON KOSHER!
NYEH?
THE ***ROMAINE GLADIATOR!***

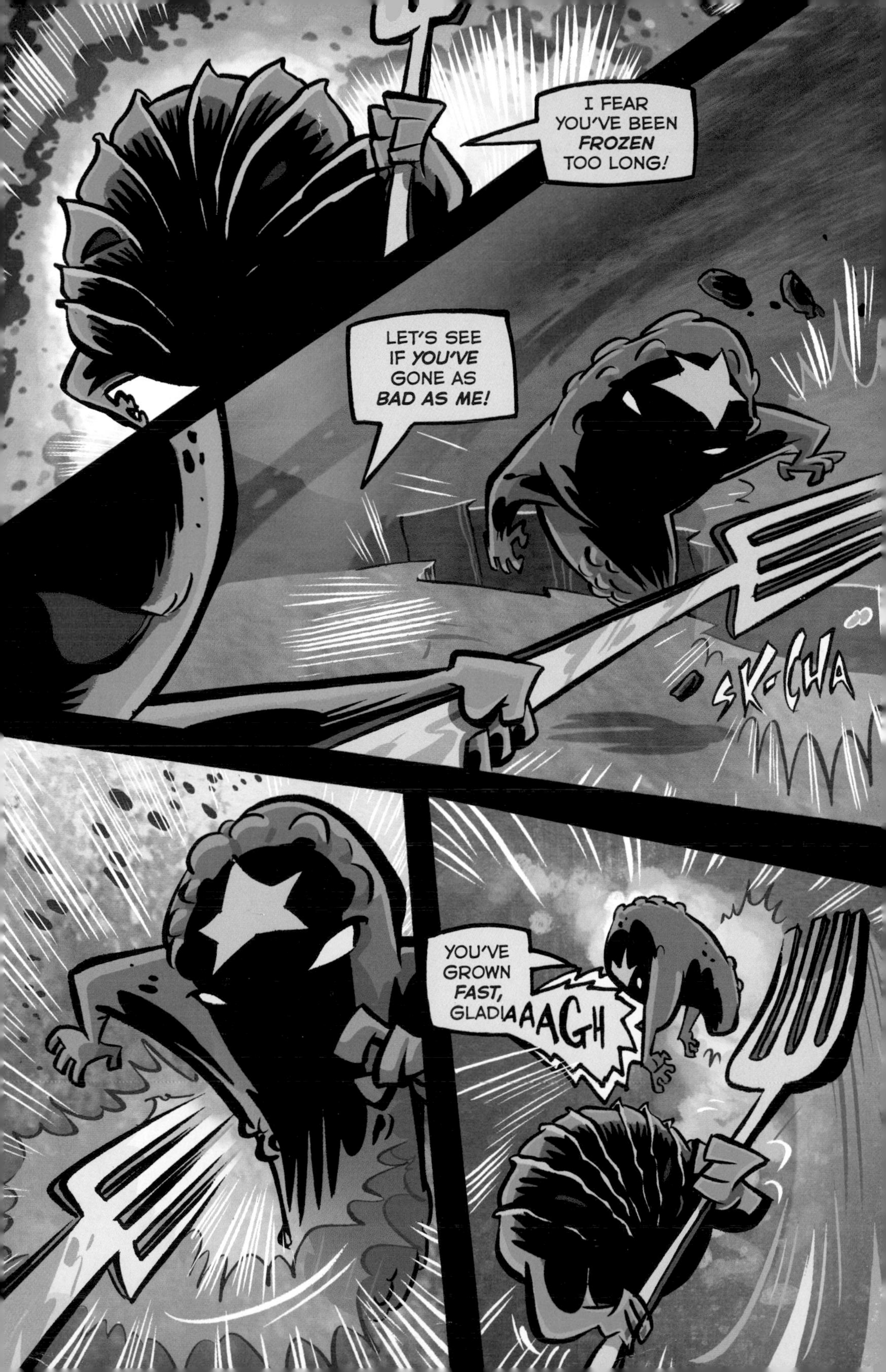
I FEAR YOU'VE BEEN *FROZEN* TOO LONG!
LET'S SEE IF *YOU'VE* GONE AS *BAD AS ME!*
SK-CHA
YOU'VE GROWN *FAST,* GLADIAAAGH

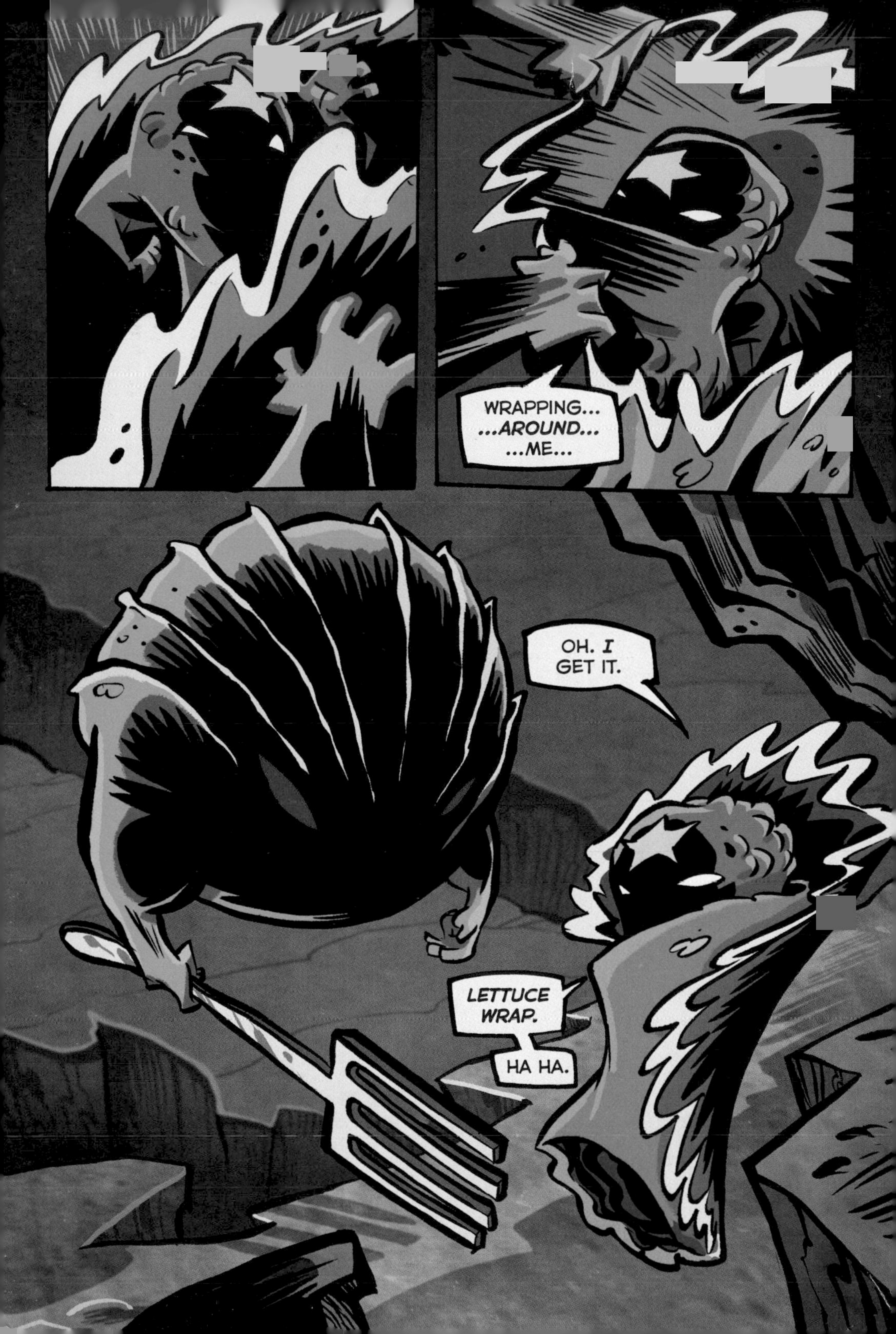
WRAPPING...
...AROUND...
...ME...
OH. I GET IT.
LETTUCE WRAP.
HA HA.

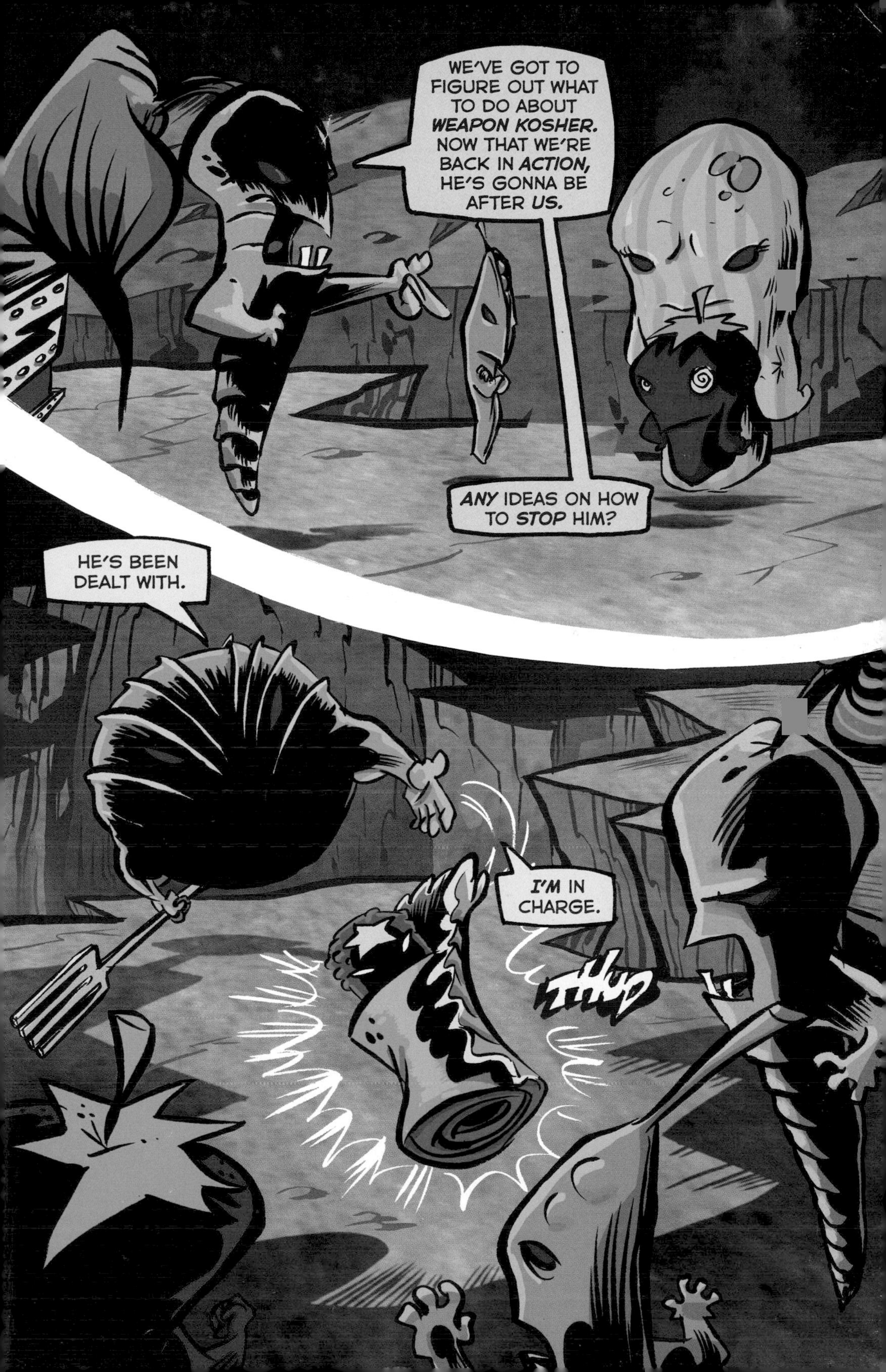
WE'VE GOT TO FIGURE OUT WHAT TO DO ABOUT WEAPON KOSHER. NOW THAT WE'RE BACK IN ACTION, HE'S GONNA BE AFTER US.
ANY IDEAS ON HOW TO STOP HIM?
HE'S BEEN DEALT WITH.
I'M IN CHARGE.
THUD

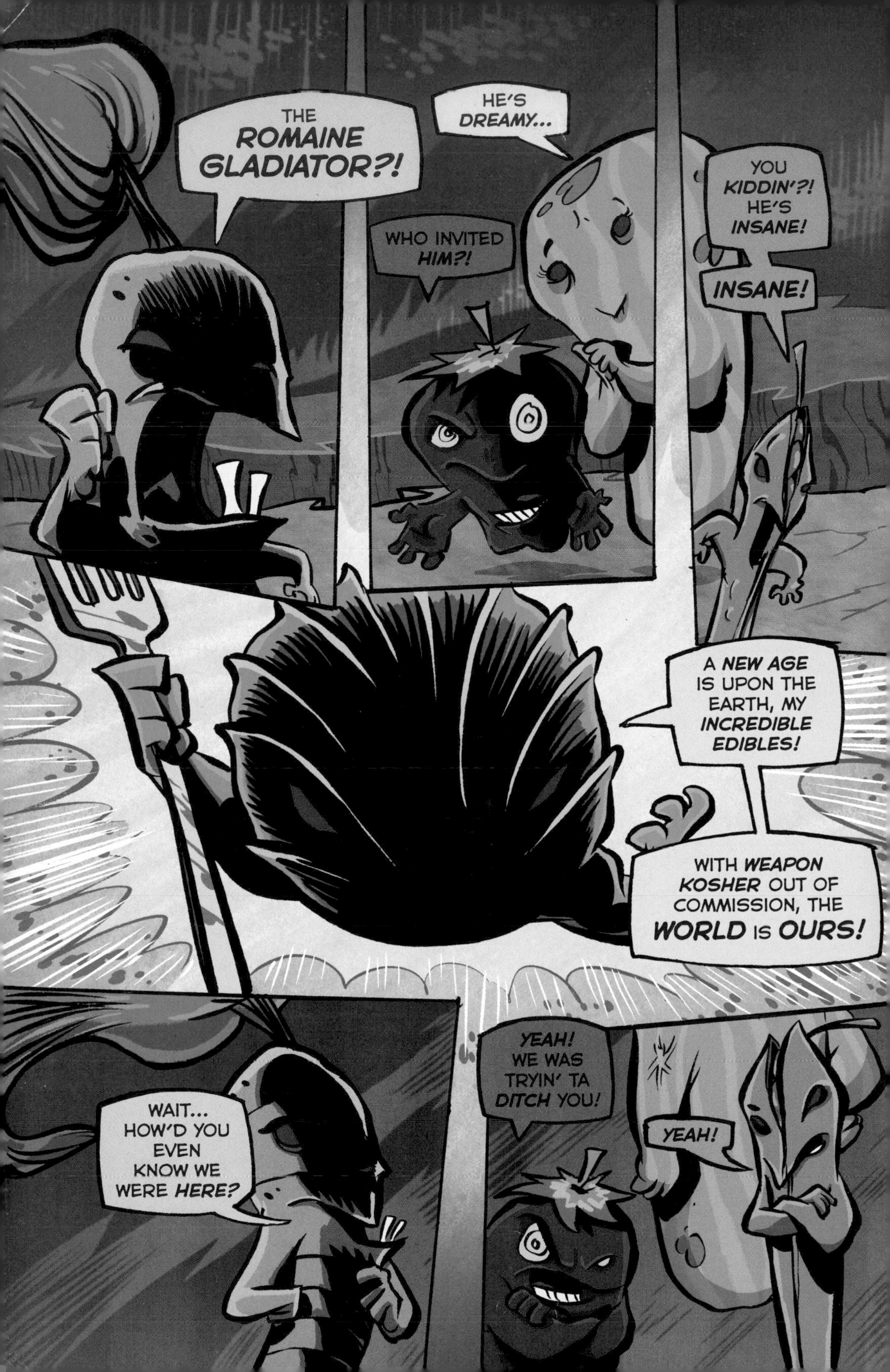
THE ROMAINE GLADIATOR?!
HE'S DREAMY...
WHO INVITED HIM?!
YOU KIDDIN'?! HE'S INSANE!
INSANE!
A NEW AGE IS UPON THE EARTH, MY INCREDIBLE EDIBLES!
WITH WEAPON KOSHER OUT OF COMMISSION, THE WORLD IS OURS!
WAIT... HOW'D YOU EVEN KNOW WE WERE HERE?
YEAH! WE WAS TRYIN' TA DITCH YOU!
YEAH!

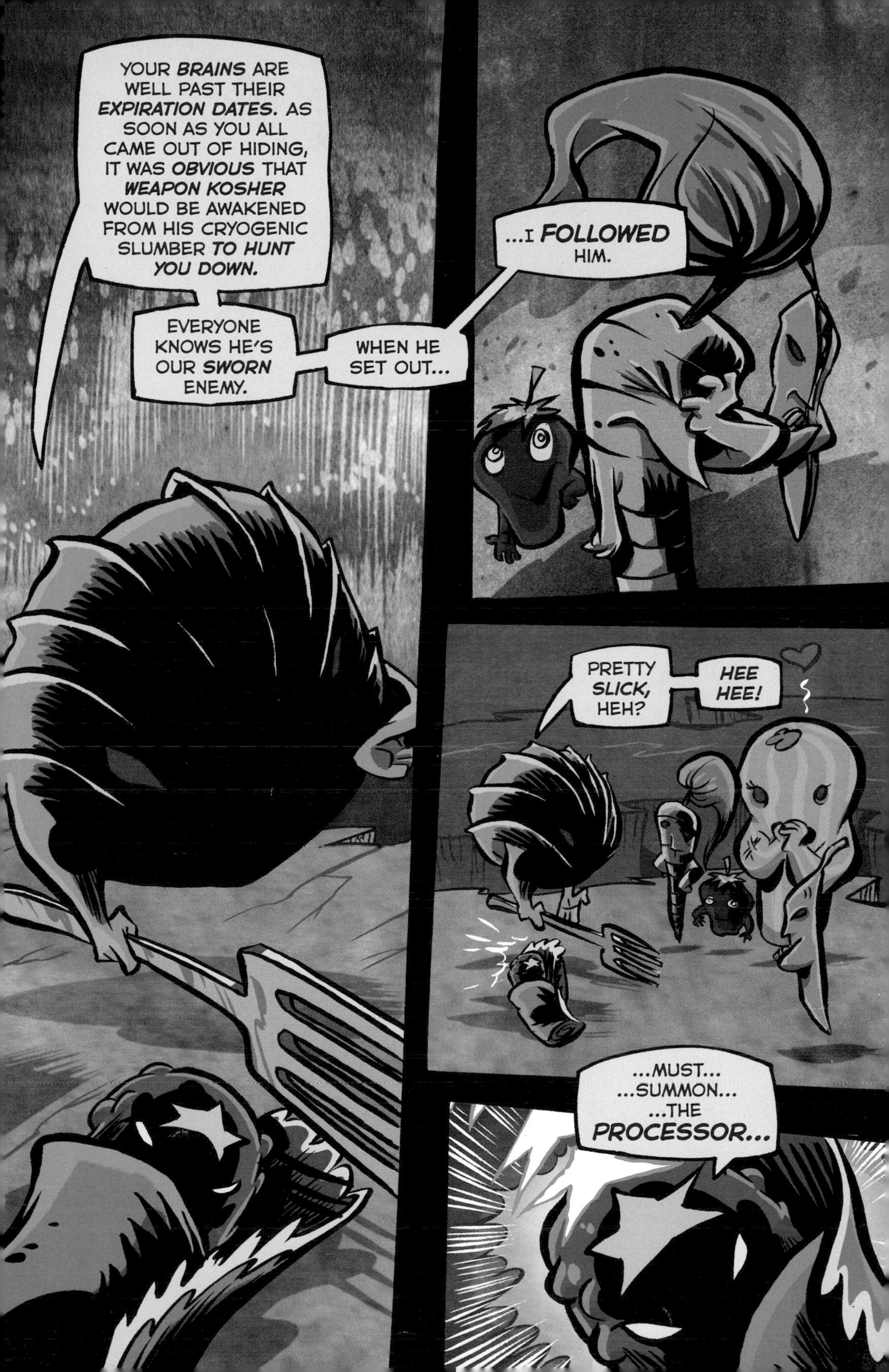
YOUR BRAINS ARE WELL PAST THEIR EXPIRATION DATES. AS SOON AS YOU ALL CAME OUT OF HIDING, IT WAS OBVIOUS THAT WEAPON KOSHER WOULD BE AWAKENED FROM HIS CRYOGENIC SLUMBER TO HUNT YOU DOWN.
EVERYONE KNOWS HE'S OUR SWORN ENEMY.
WHEN HE SET OUT...
...I FOLLOWED HIM.
PRETTY SLICK, HEH?
HEE HEE!
...MUST... ...SUMMON... ...THE PROCESSOR...

CHAPTER 3

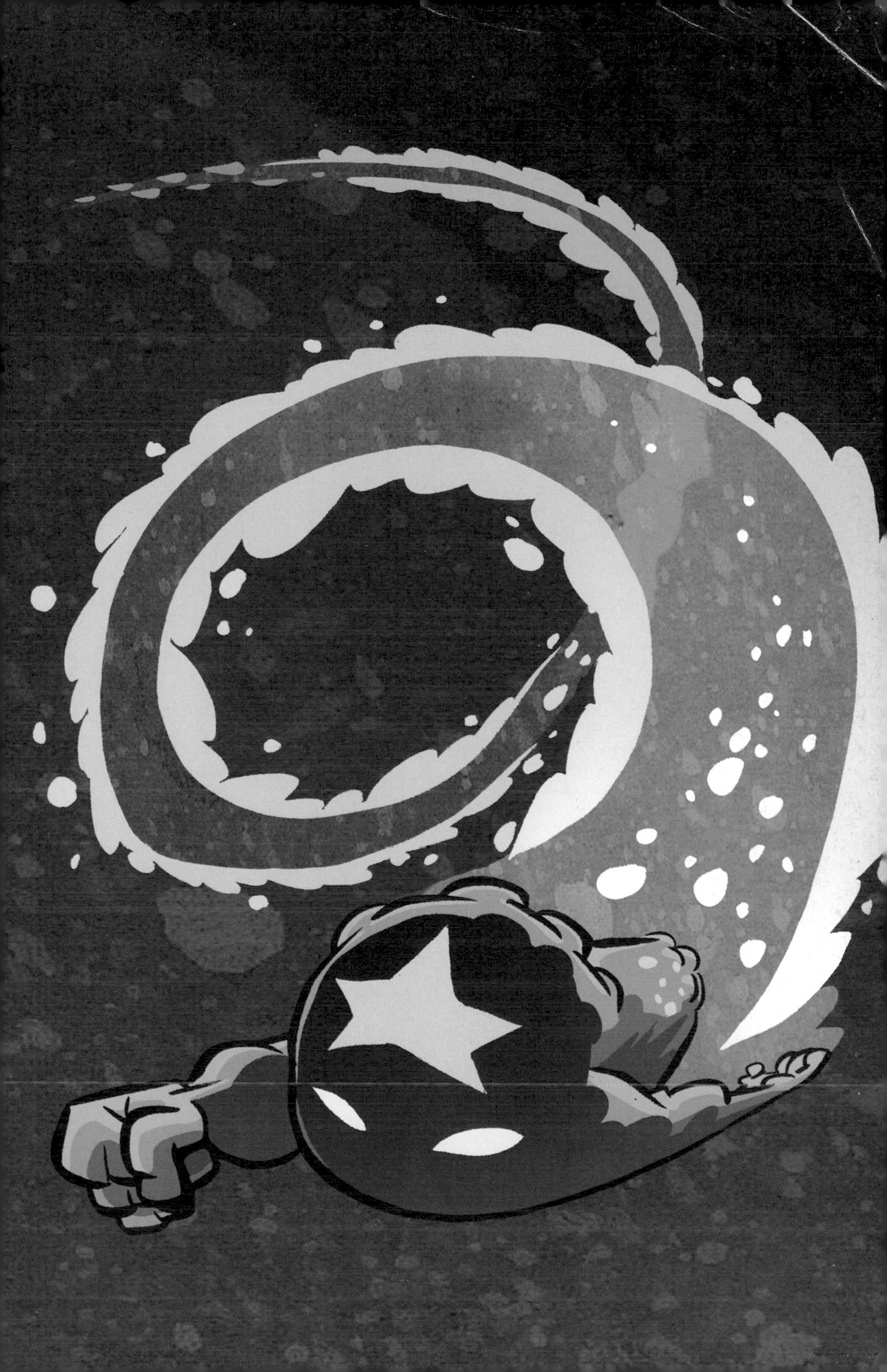

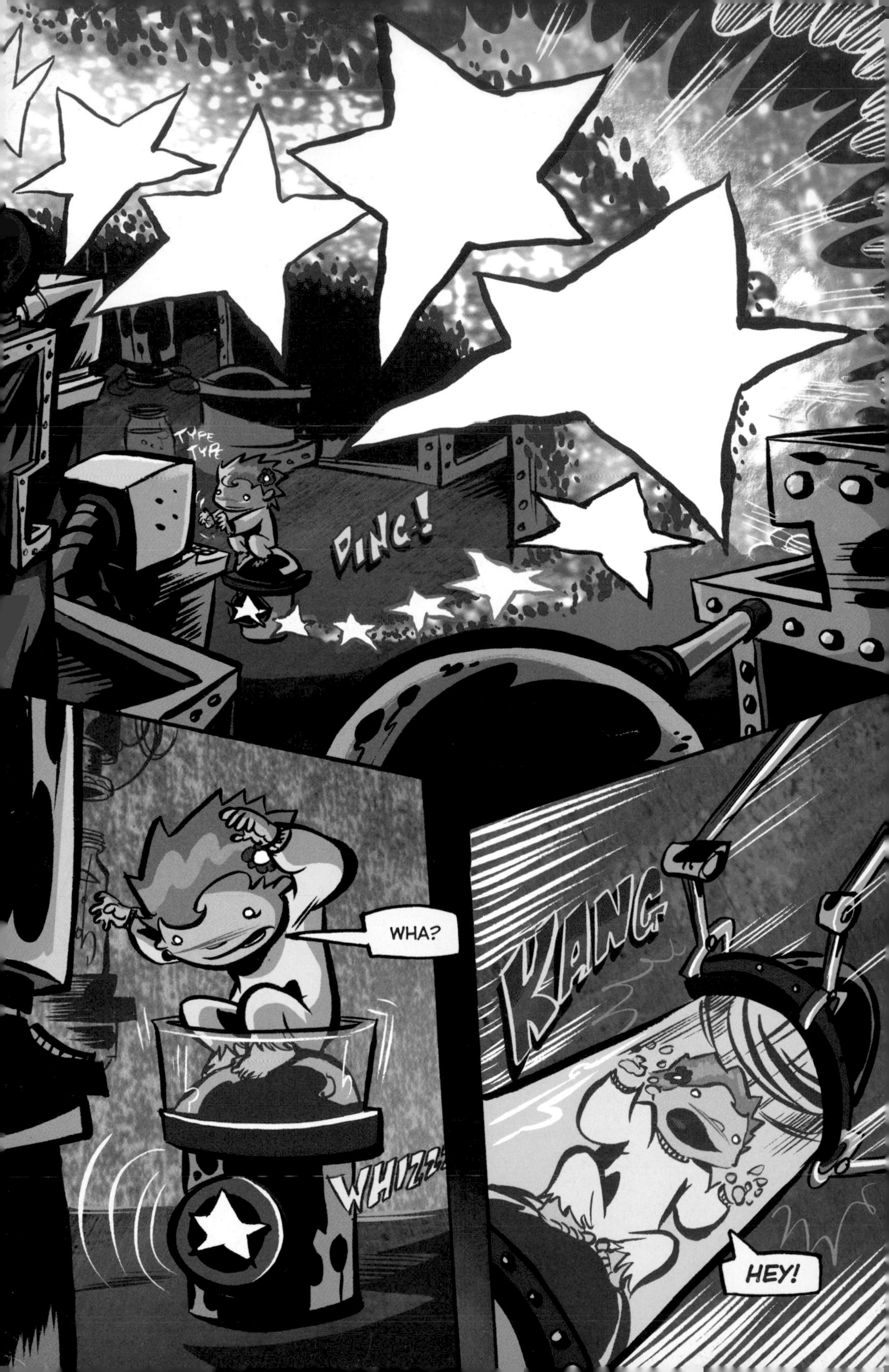
TYPE
TYPE
DING!
WHA?
KANG
WHIZZZ
HEY!

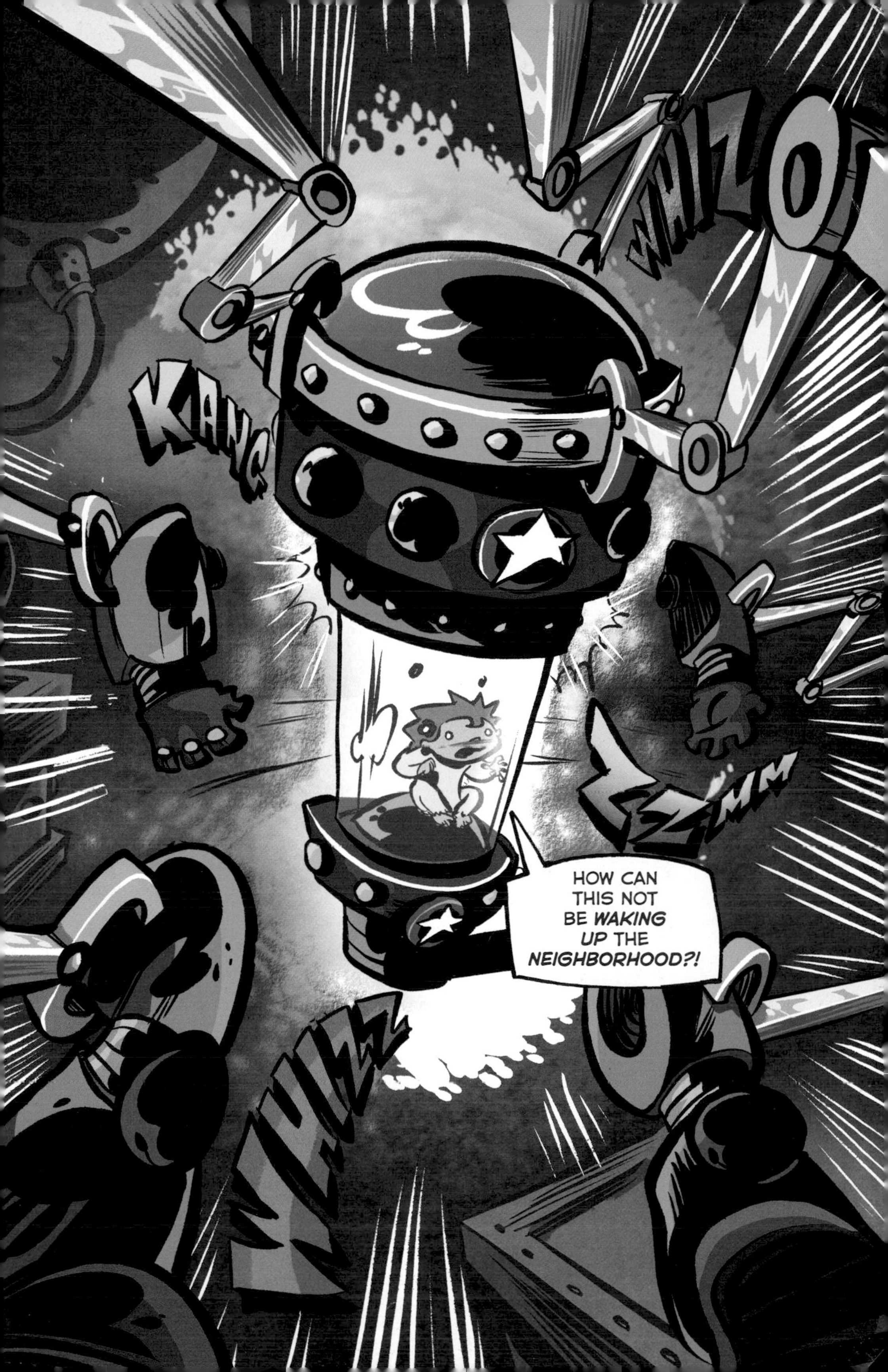
KLANG
WHIZLOT
HOW CAN THIS NOT BE *WAKING UP* THE *NEIGHBORHOOD?!*
ZZMM
WHIZZ

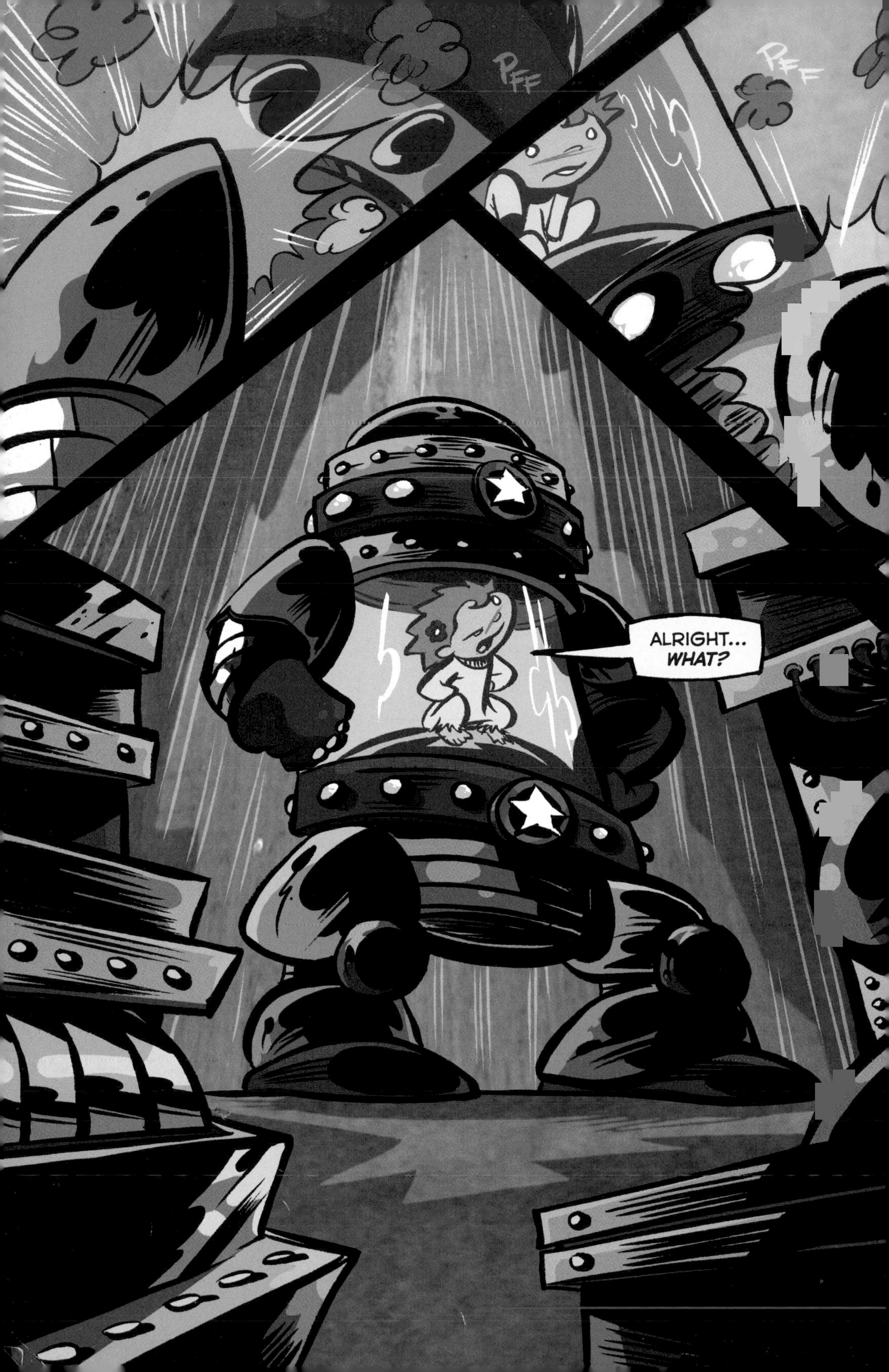
PFF
PFF
ALRIGHT... *WHAT?*

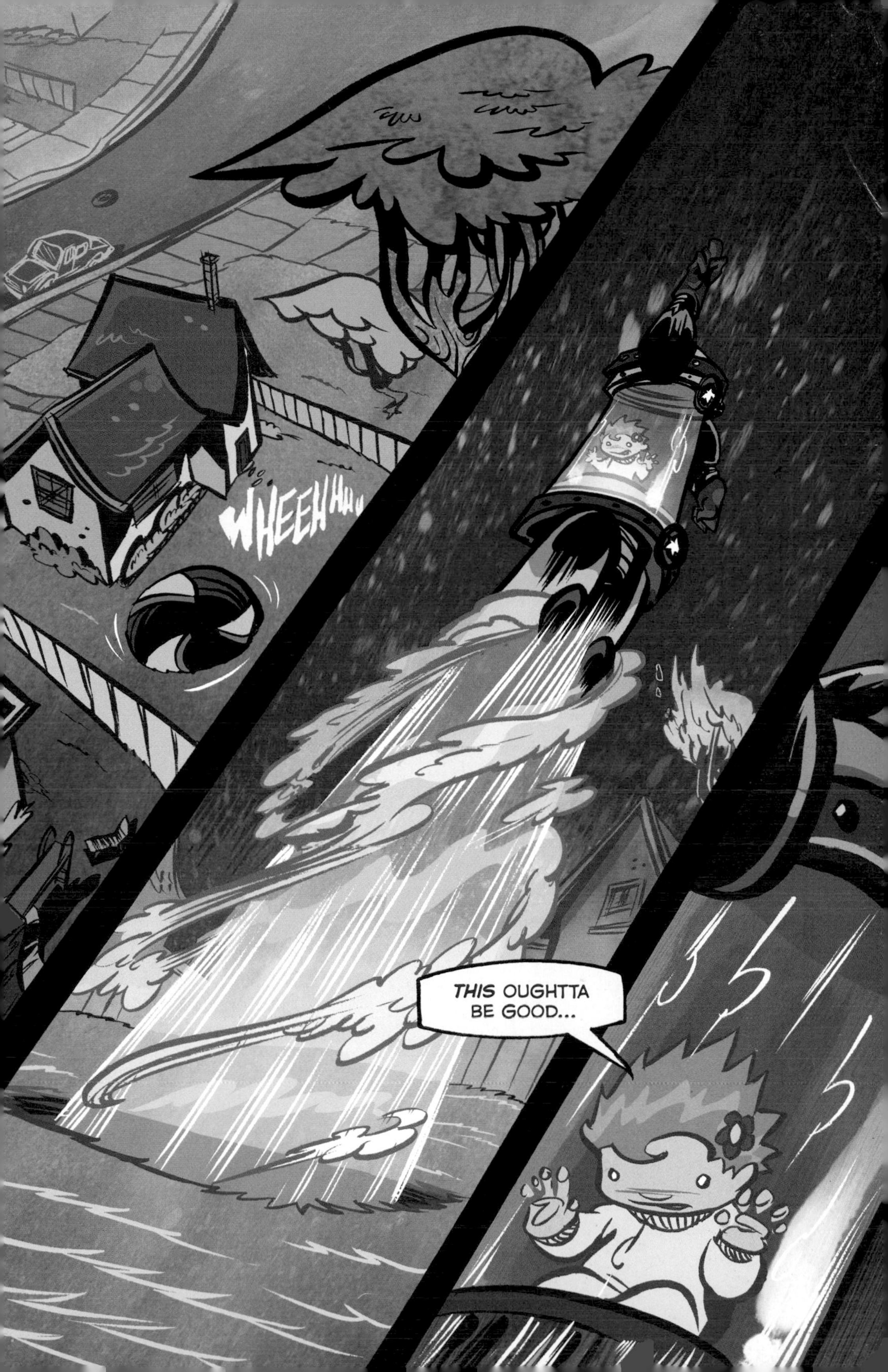
WHEEHuuu
THIS OUGHTTA BE GOOD...

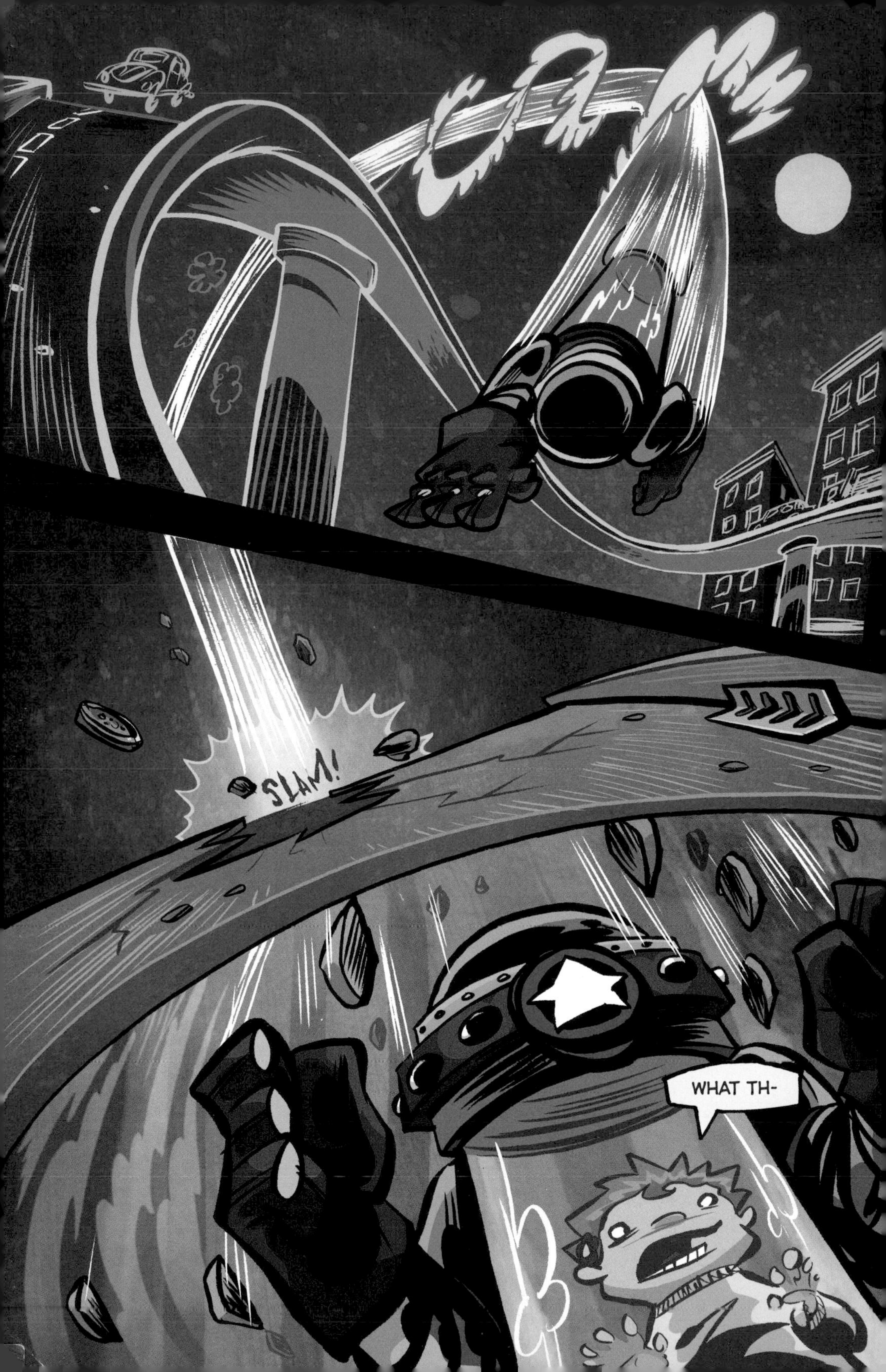
SLAM!
WHAT TH-

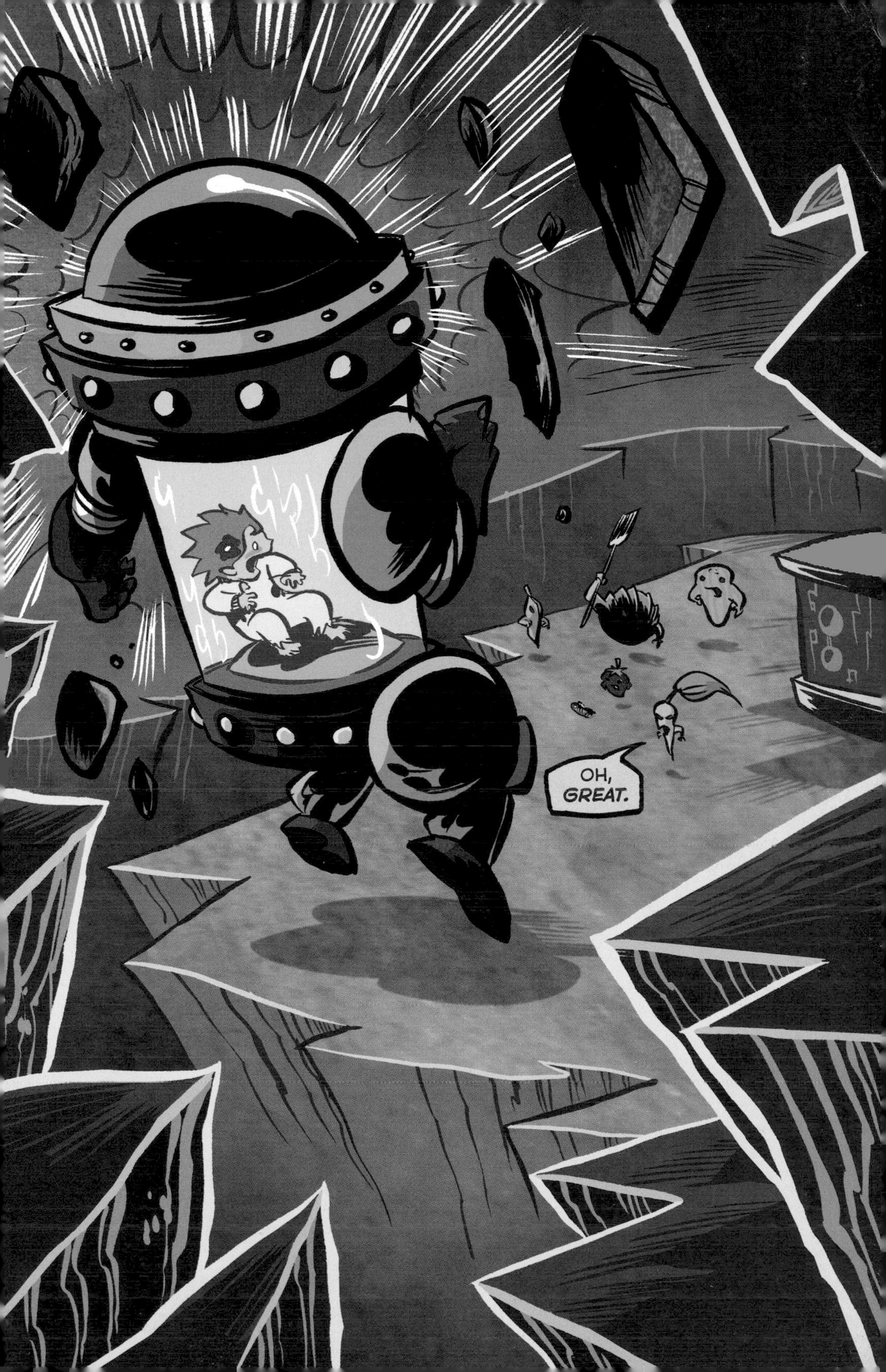
OH, GREAT.

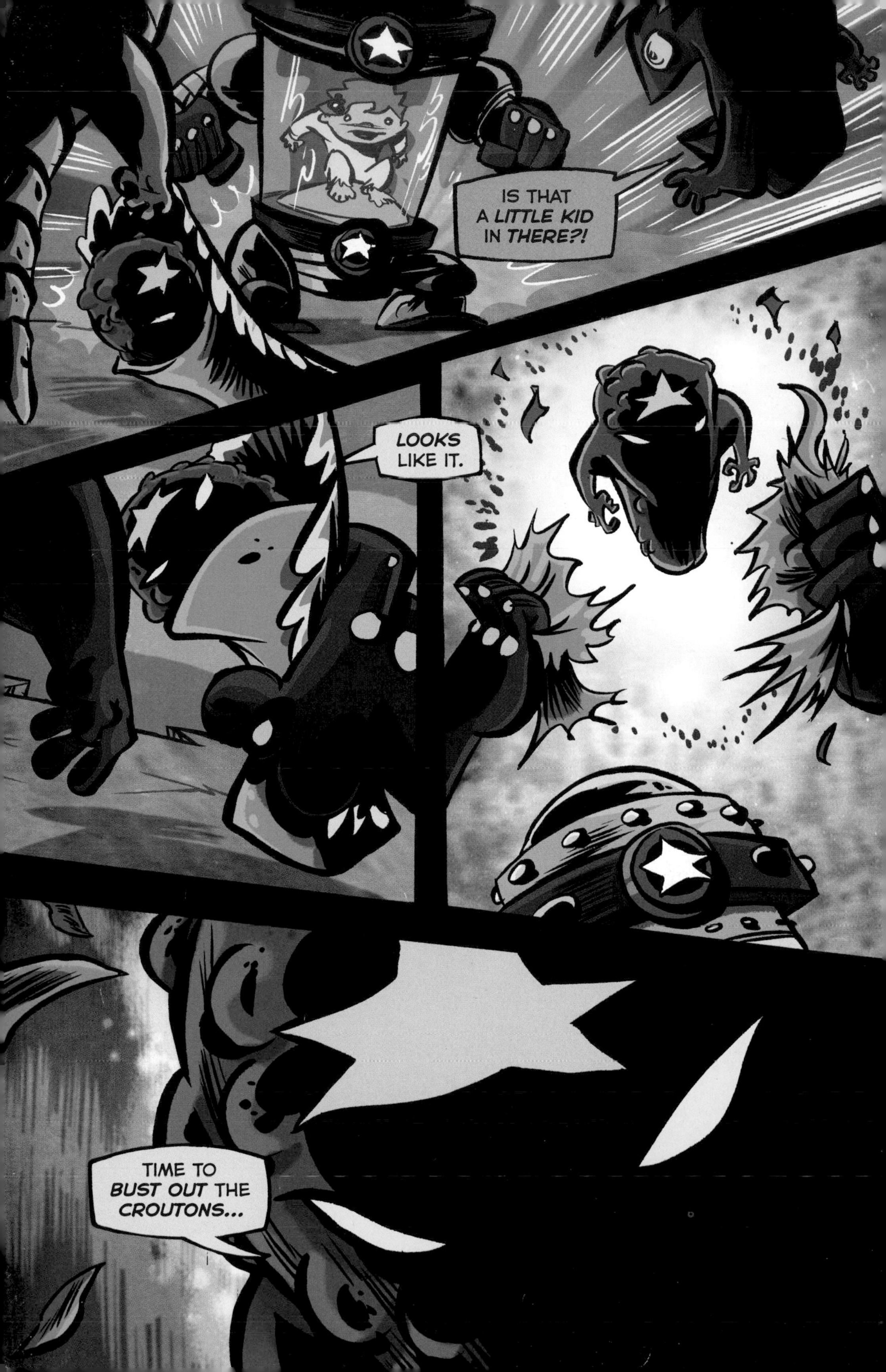
IS THAT A *LITTLE KID* IN *THERE?!*
LOOKS LIKE IT.
TIME TO *BUST OUT* THE *CROUTONS...*

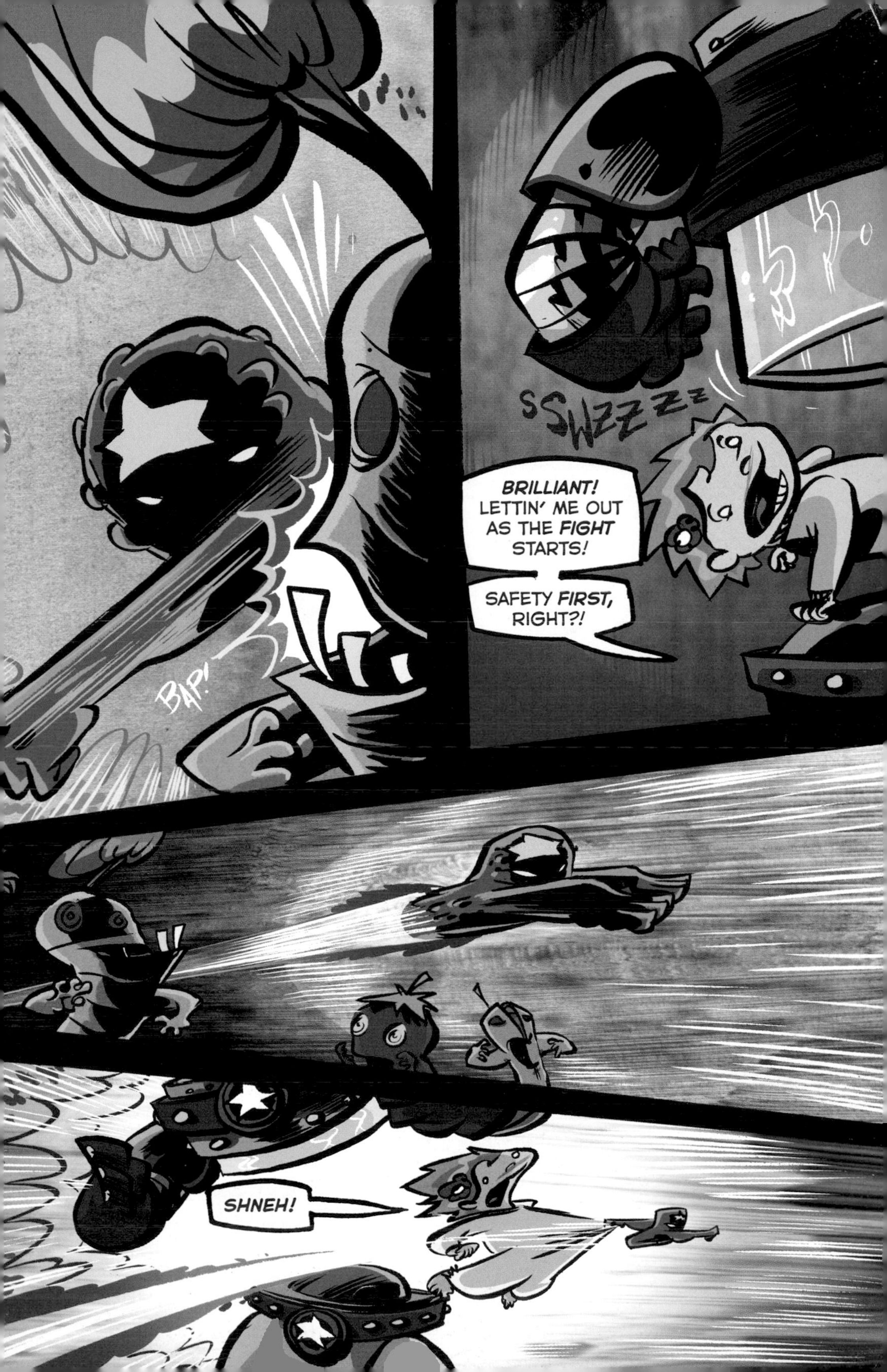
BAP!
SSWZZZZZ
BRILLIANT! LETTIN' ME OUT AS THE FIGHT STARTS!
SAFETY FIRST, RIGHT?!
SHNEH!

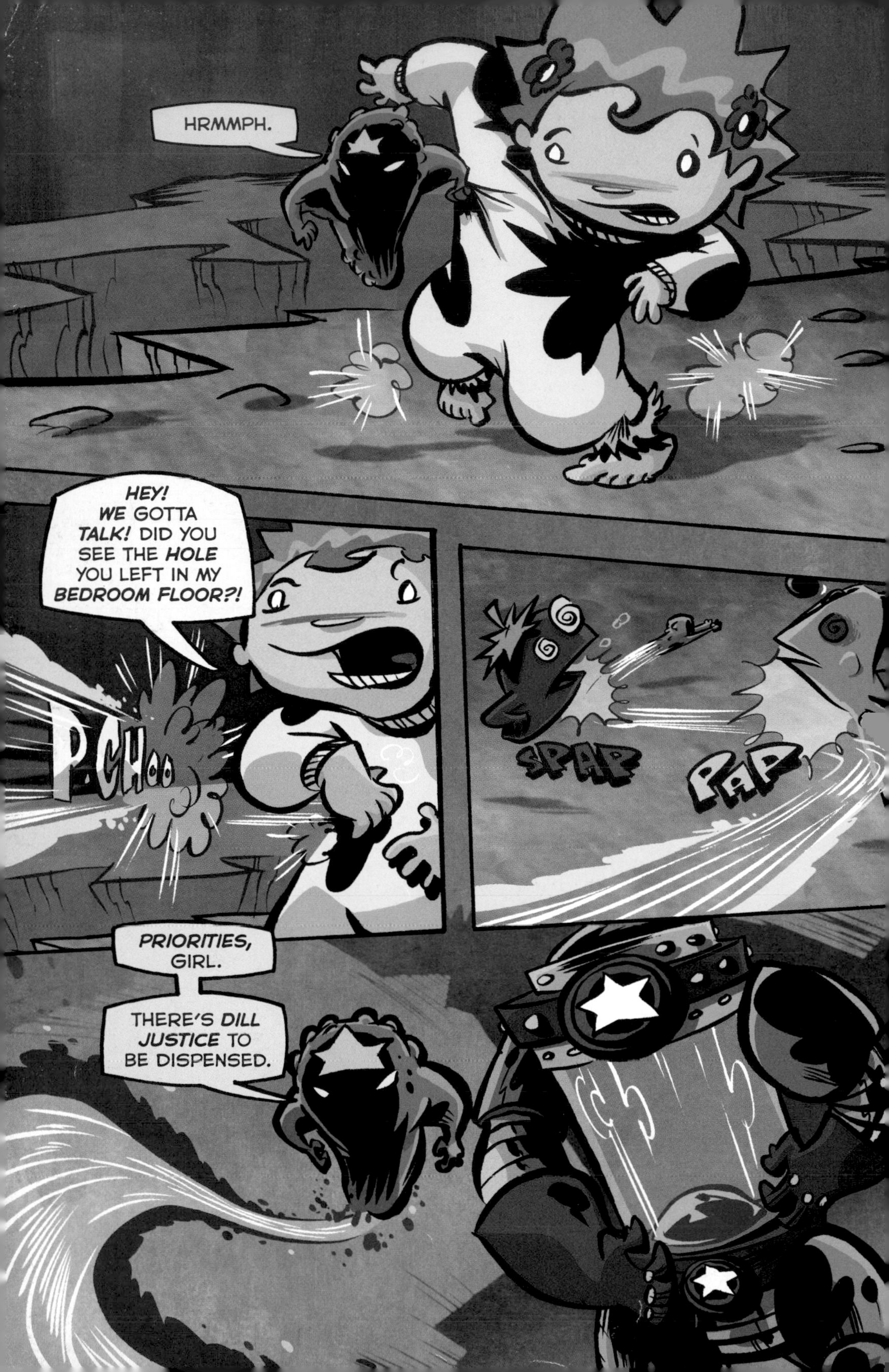
HRMMPH.
HEY! WE GOTTA TALK! DID YOU SEE THE HOLE YOU LEFT IN MY BEDROOM FLOOR?!
PCHOO
SPAP
PAP
PRIORITIES, GIRL.
THERE'S DILL JUSTICE TO BE DISPENSED.

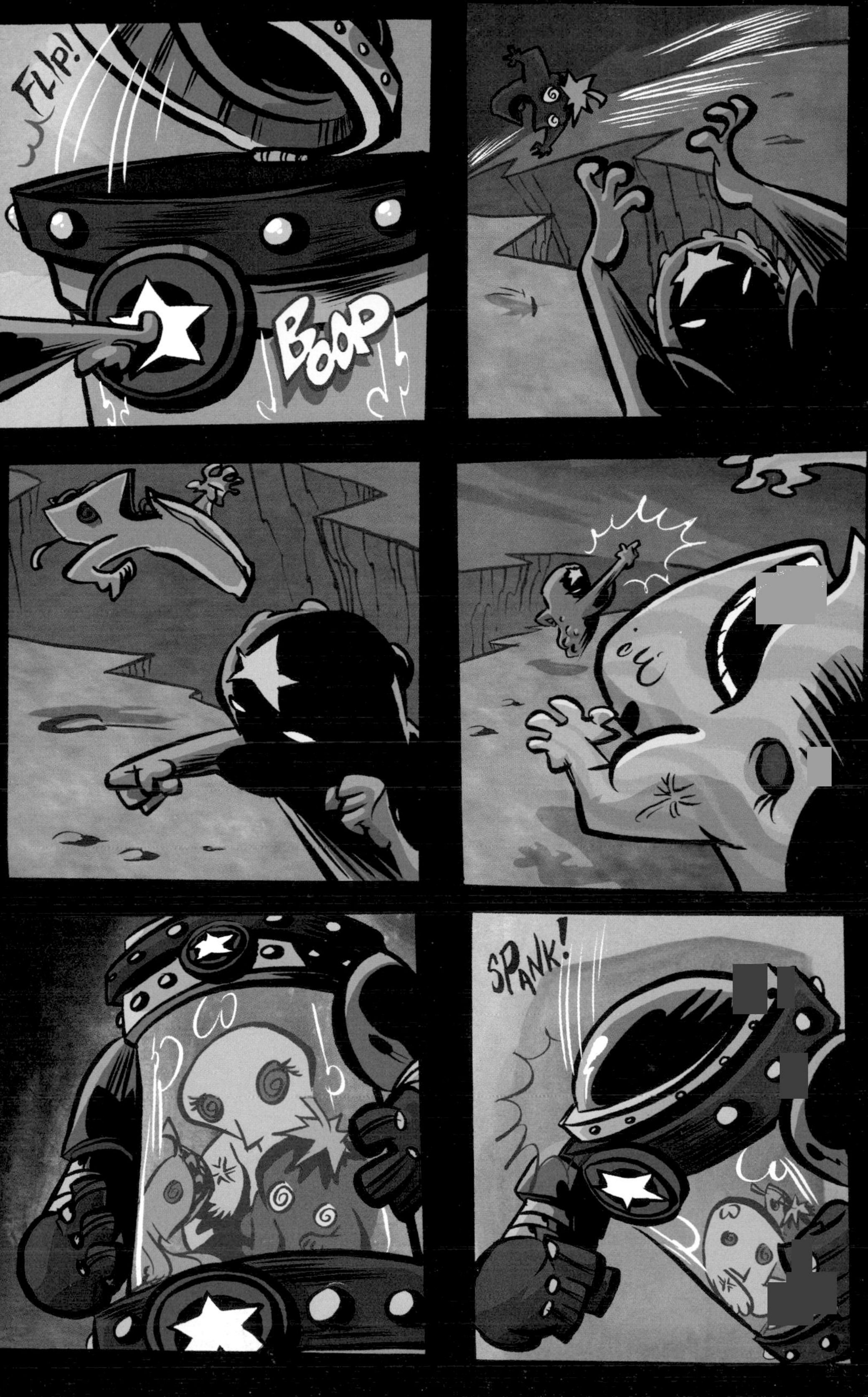
FLIP!
BOOP
SPANK!

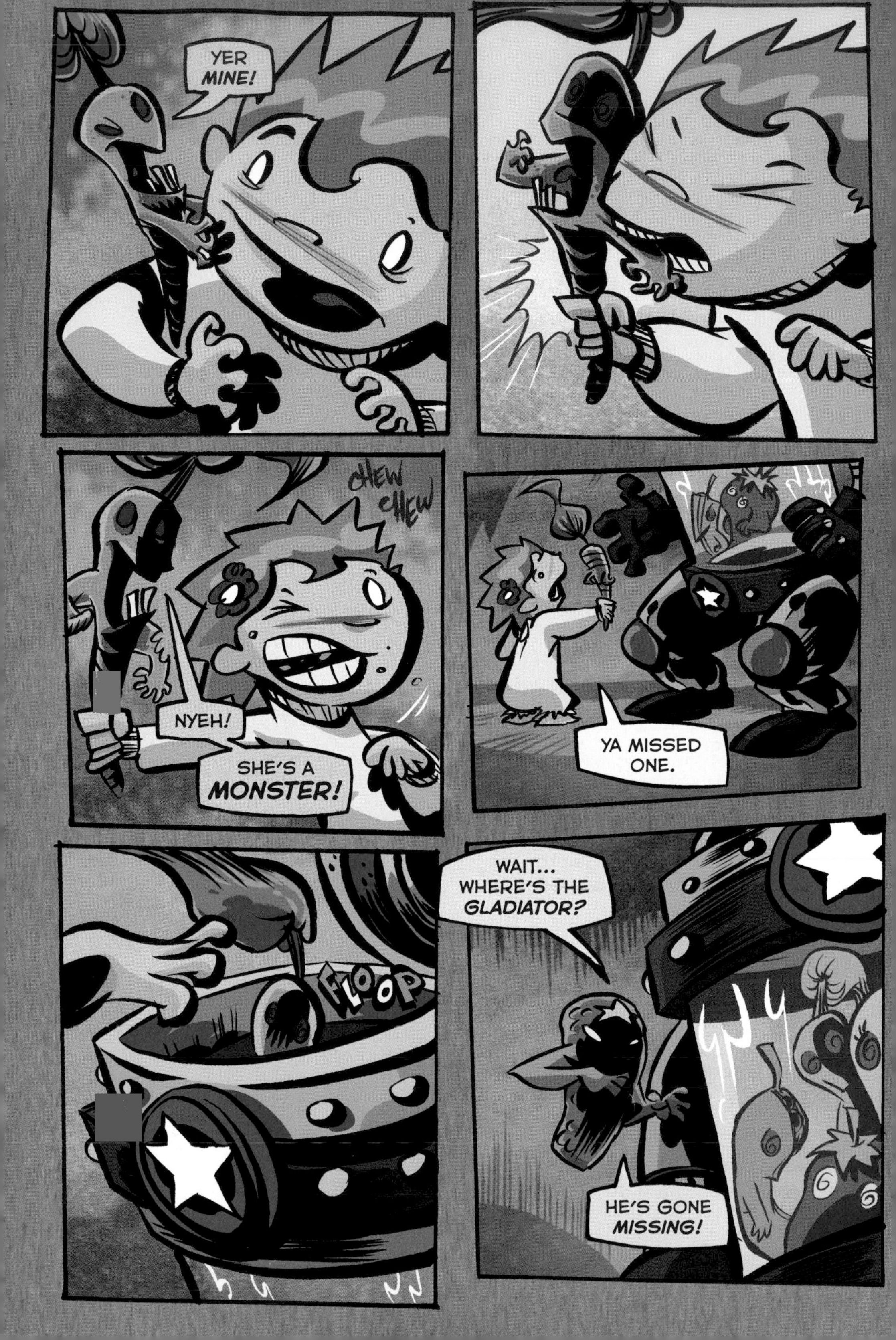
YER MINE!
CHEW CHEW
NYEH!
SHE'S A MONSTER!
YA MISSED ONE.
FLOOP
WAIT... WHERE'S THE GLADIATOR?
HE'S GONE MISSING!

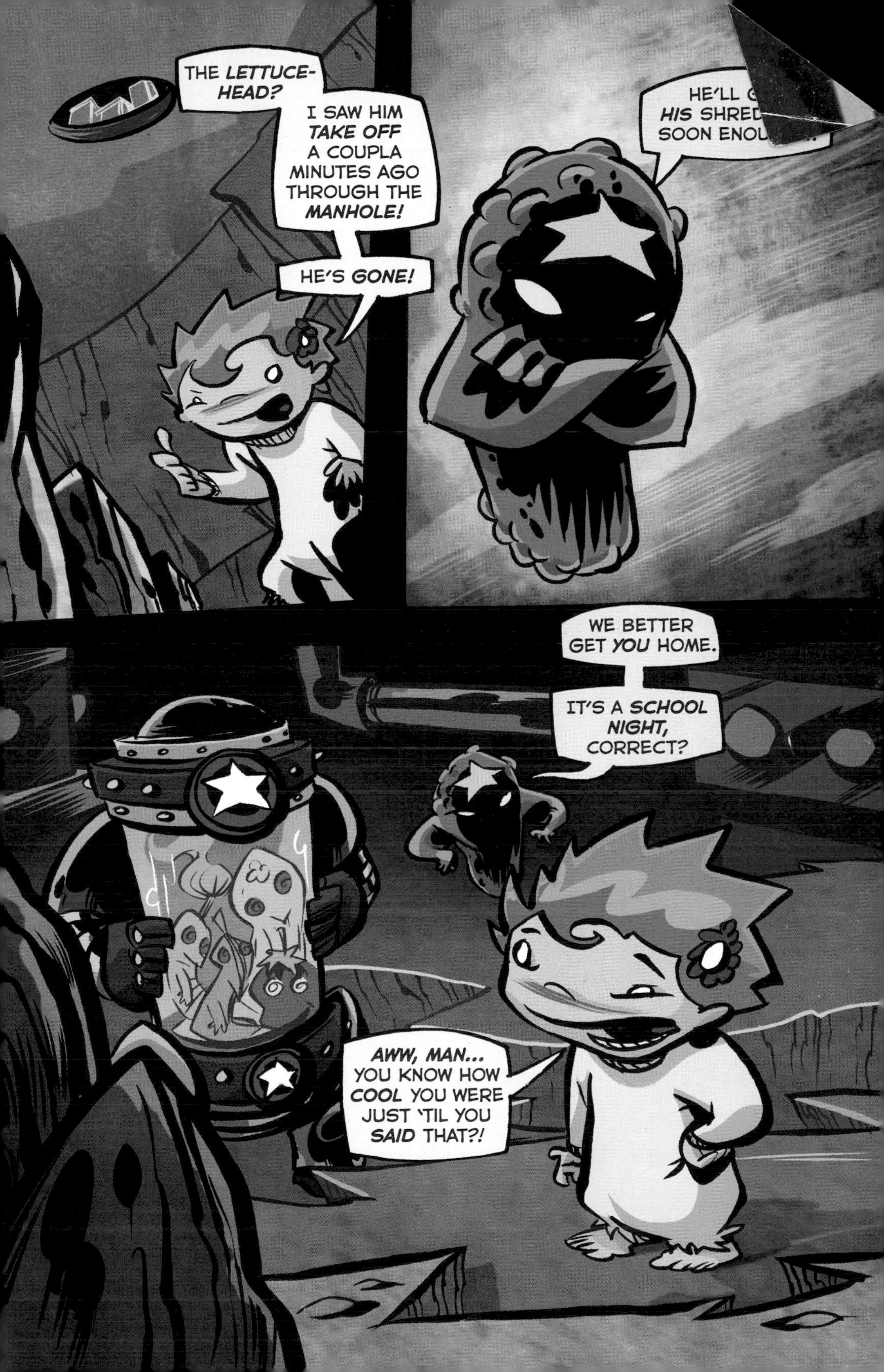

THE LETTUCE-HEAD?
I SAW HIM TAKE OFF A COUPLA MINUTES AGO THROUGH THE MANHOLE!
HE'S GONE!
HE'LL G HIS SHRED SOON ENOU
WE BETTER GET YOU HOME.
IT'S A SCHOOL NIGHT, CORRECT?
AWW, MAN... YOU KNOW HOW COOL YOU WERE JUST 'TIL YOU SAID THAT?!

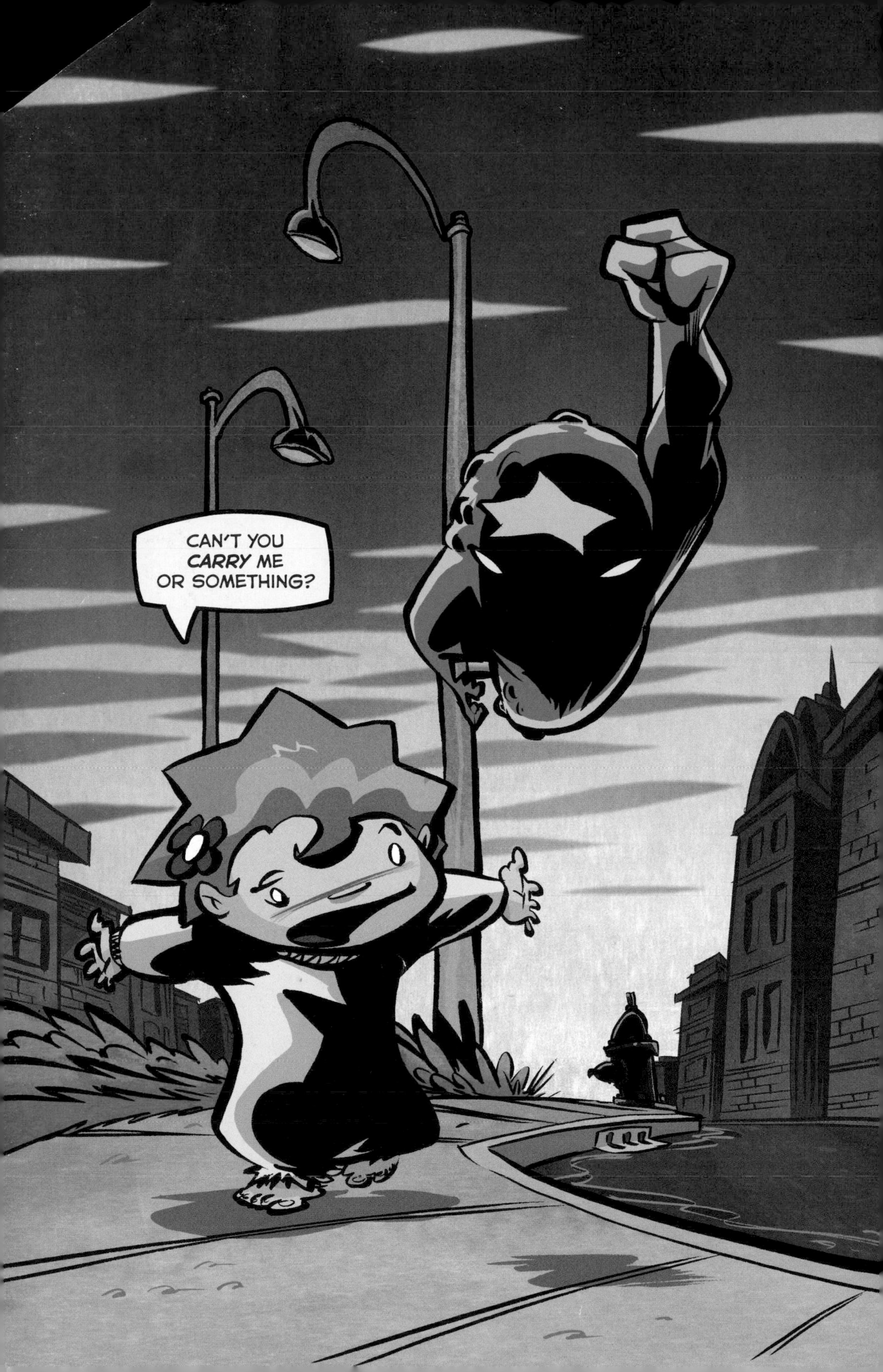
CAN'T YOU CARRY ME OR SOMETHING?

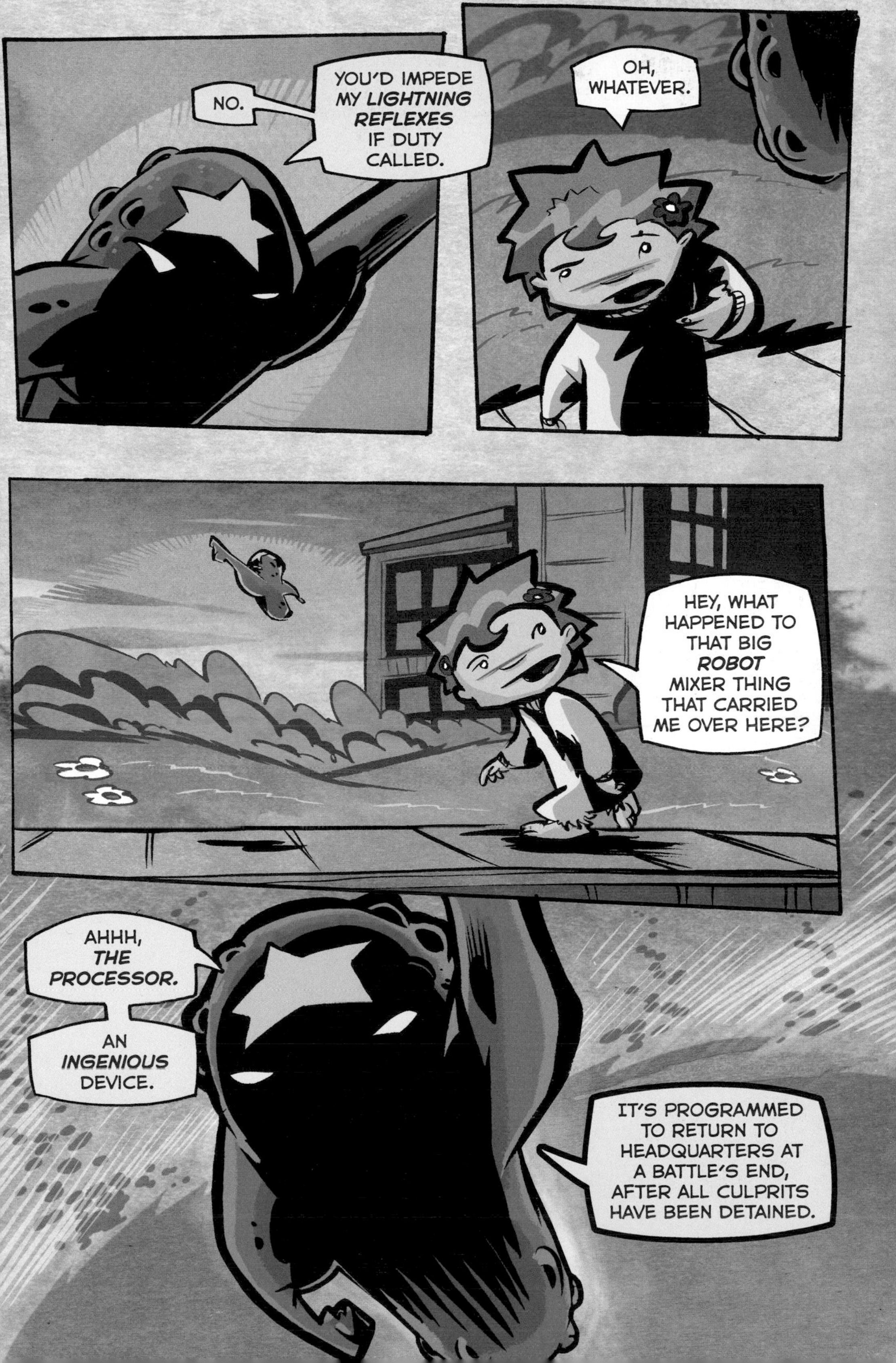
NO.
YOU'D IMPEDE MY LIGHTNING REFLEXES IF DUTY CALLED.
OH, WHATEVER.
HEY, WHAT HAPPENED TO THAT BIG ROBOT MIXER THING THAT CARRIED ME OVER HERE?
AHHH, THE PROCESSOR.
AN INGENIOUS DEVICE.
IT'S PROGRAMMED TO RETURN TO HEADQUARTERS AT A BATTLE'S END, AFTER ALL CULPRITS HAVE BEEN DETAINED.

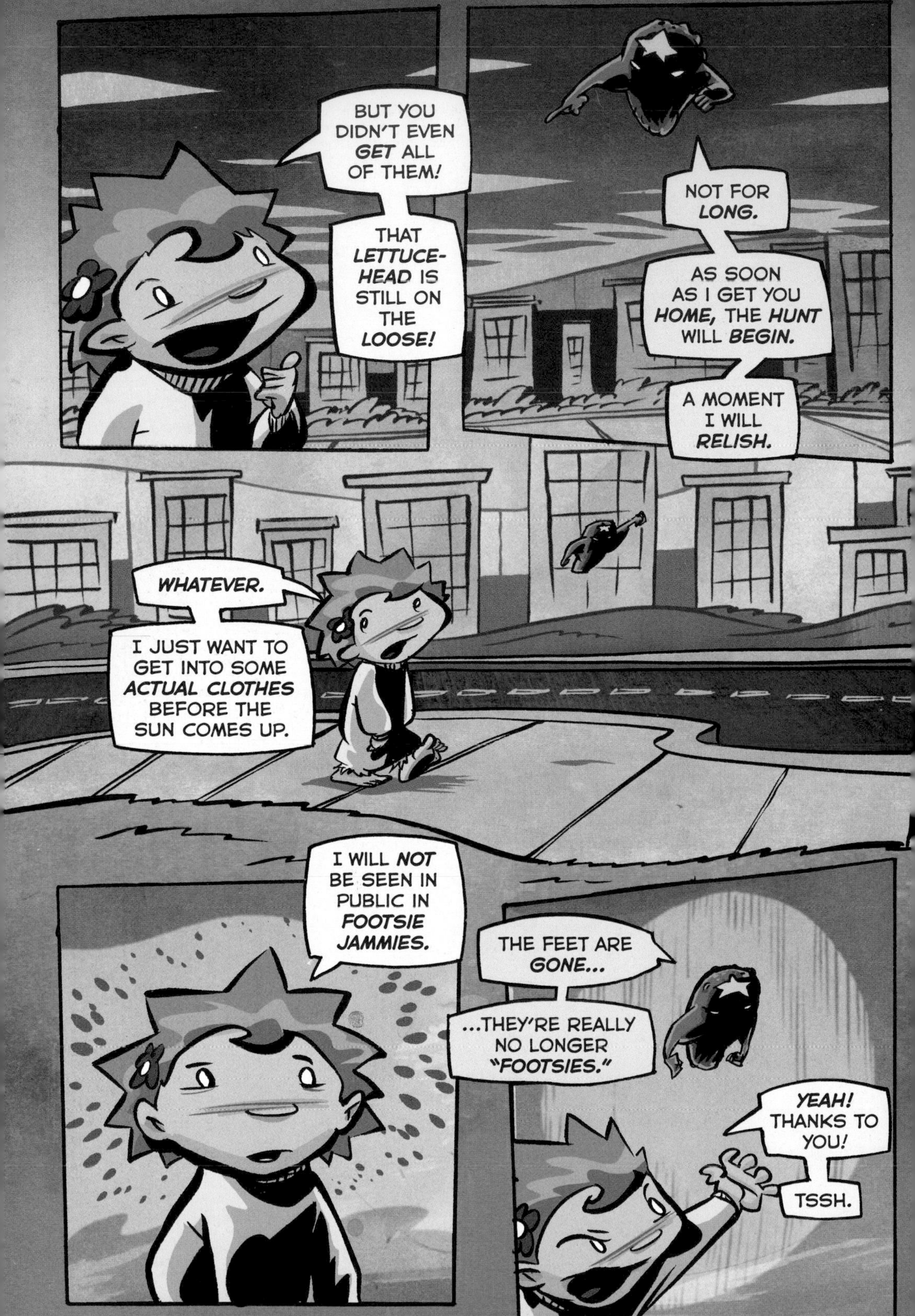
BUT YOU DIDN'T EVEN GET ALL OF THEM!
THAT LETTUCE-HEAD IS STILL ON THE LOOSE!
NOT FOR LONG.
AS SOON AS I GET YOU HOME, THE HUNT WILL BEGIN.
A MOMENT I WILL RELISH.
WHATEVER.
I JUST WANT TO GET INTO SOME ACTUAL CLOTHES BEFORE THE SUN COMES UP.
I WILL NOT BE SEEN IN PUBLIC IN FOOTSIE JAMMIES.
THE FEET ARE GONE...
...THEY'RE REALLY NO LONGER "FOOTSIES."
YEAH! THANKS TO YOU!
TSSH.

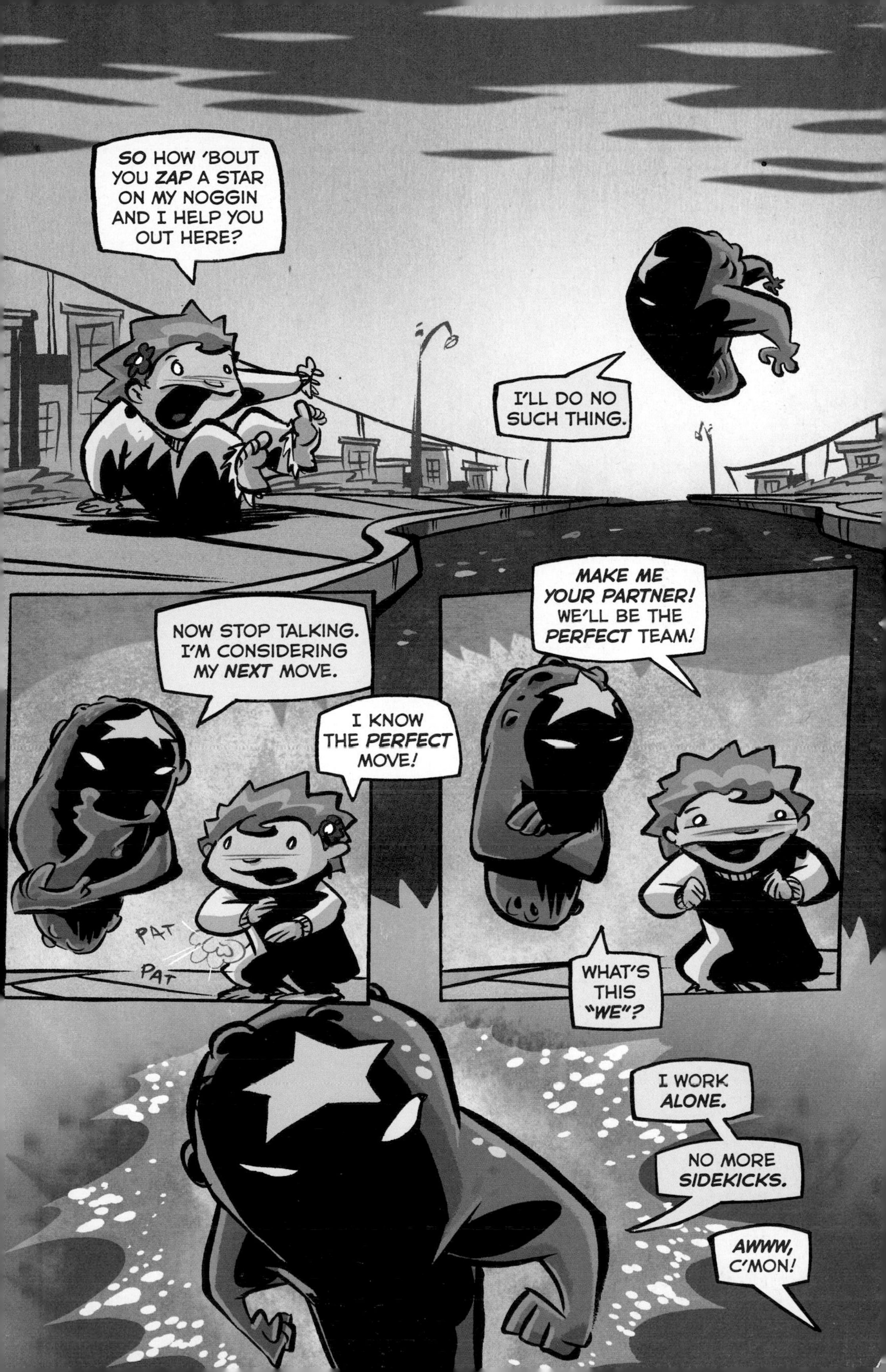
SO HOW 'BOUT YOU ZAP A STAR ON MY NOGGIN AND I HELP YOU OUT HERE?
I'LL DO NO SUCH THING.
NOW STOP TALKING. I'M CONSIDERING MY NEXT MOVE.
I KNOW THE PERFECT MOVE!
PAT
PAT
MAKE ME YOUR PARTNER! WE'LL BE THE PERFECT TEAM!
WHAT'S THIS "WE"?
I WORK ALONE.
NO MORE SIDEKICKS.
AWWW, C'MON!

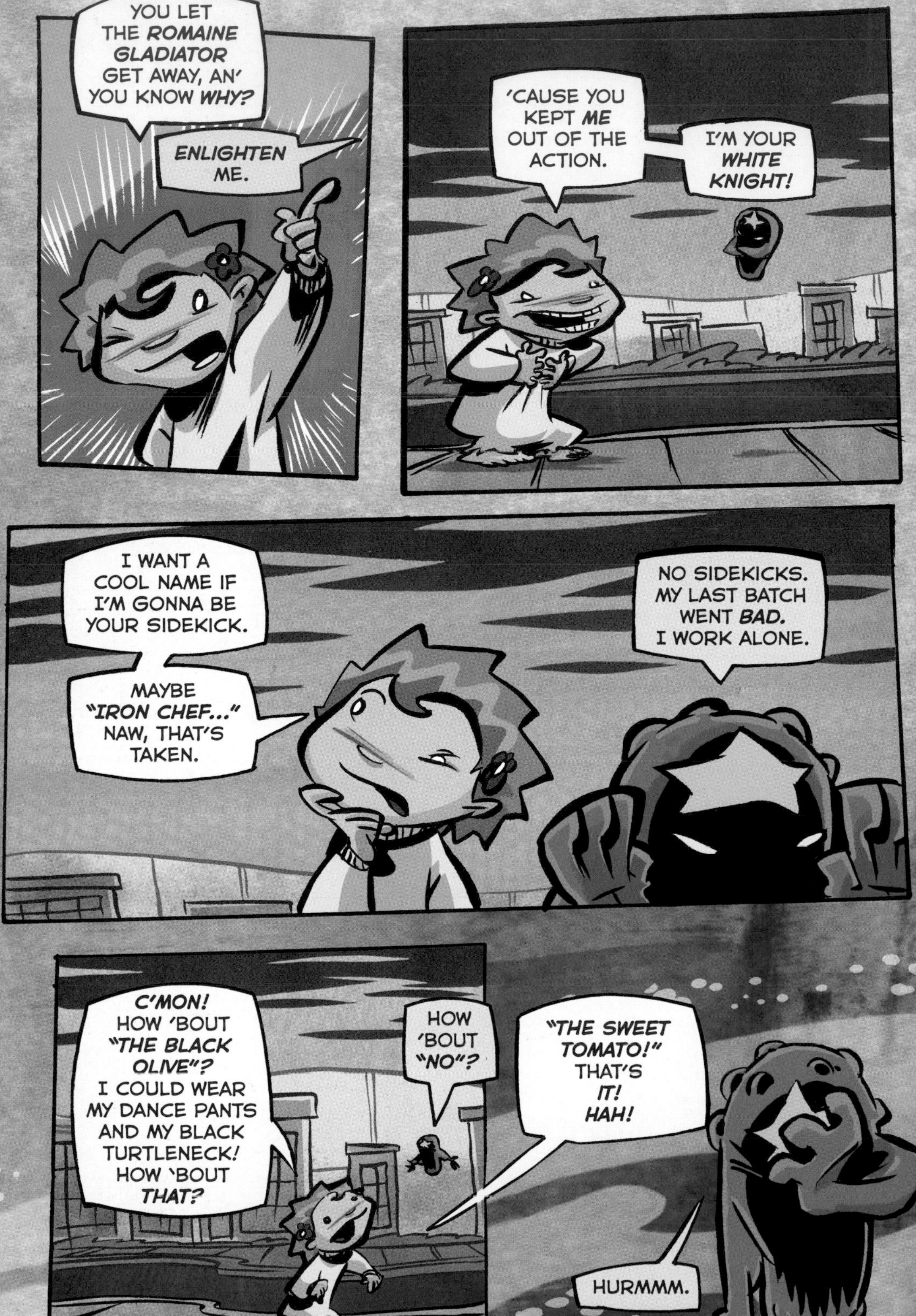
YOU LET THE ROMAINE GLADIATOR GET AWAY, AN' YOU KNOW WHY?
ENLIGHTEN ME.
'CAUSE YOU KEPT ME OUT OF THE ACTION.
I'M YOUR WHITE KNIGHT!
I WANT A COOL NAME IF I'M GONNA BE YOUR SIDEKICK.
MAYBE "IRON CHEF..." NAW, THAT'S TAKEN.
NO SIDEKICKS. MY LAST BATCH WENT BAD. I WORK ALONE.
C'MON! HOW 'BOUT "THE BLACK OLIVE"? I COULD WEAR MY DANCE PANTS AND MY BLACK TURTLENECK! HOW 'BOUT THAT?
HOW 'BOUT "NO"?
"THE SWEET TOMATO!" THAT'S IT! HAH!
HURMMM.

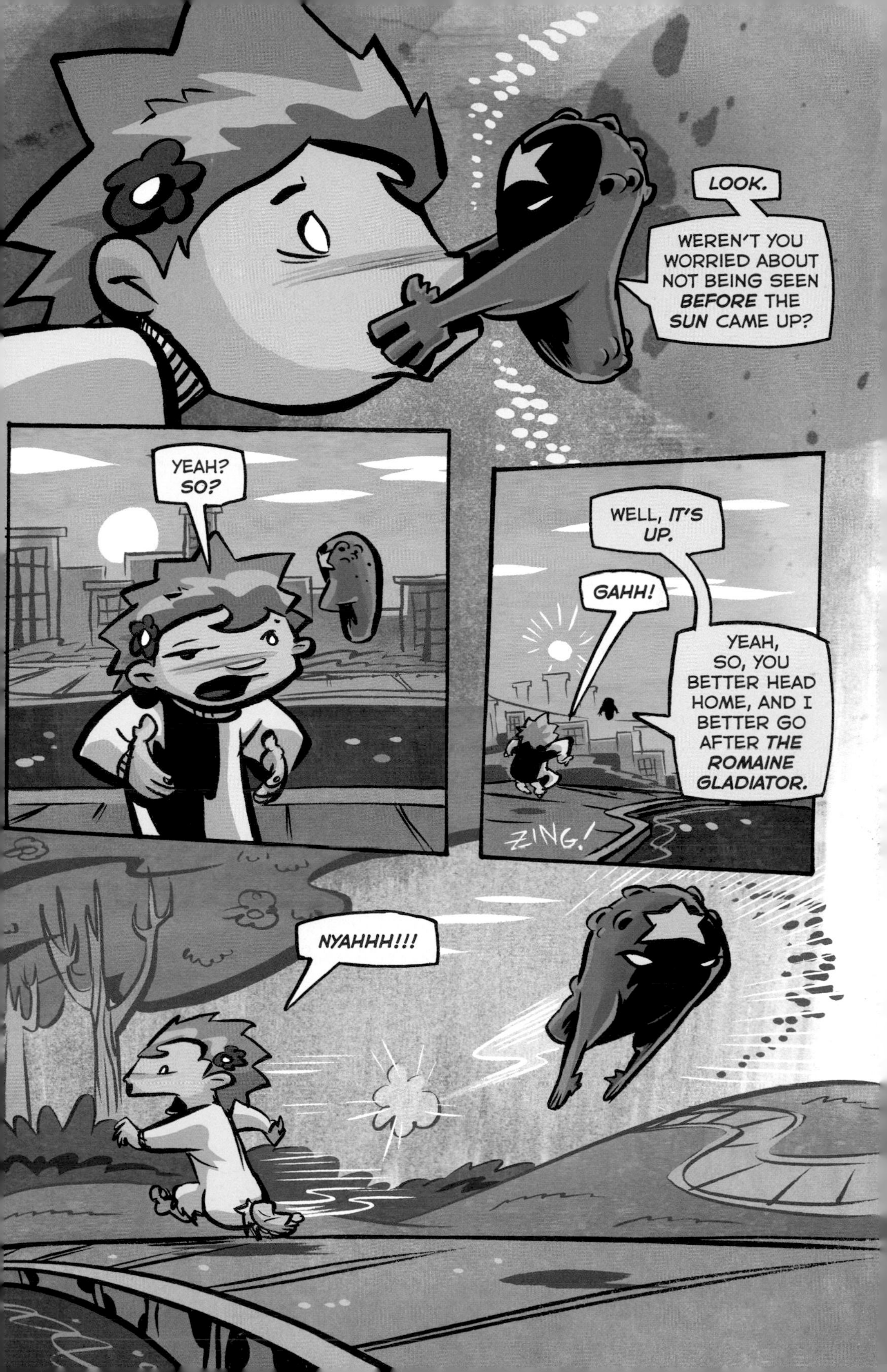
LOOK.
WEREN'T YOU WORRIED ABOUT NOT BEING SEEN *BEFORE* THE *SUN* CAME UP?
YEAH? SO?
WELL, *IT'S UP.*
GAHH!
YEAH, SO, YOU BETTER HEAD HOME, AND I BETTER GO AFTER *THE ROMAINE GLADIATOR.*
ZING!
NYAHHH!!!

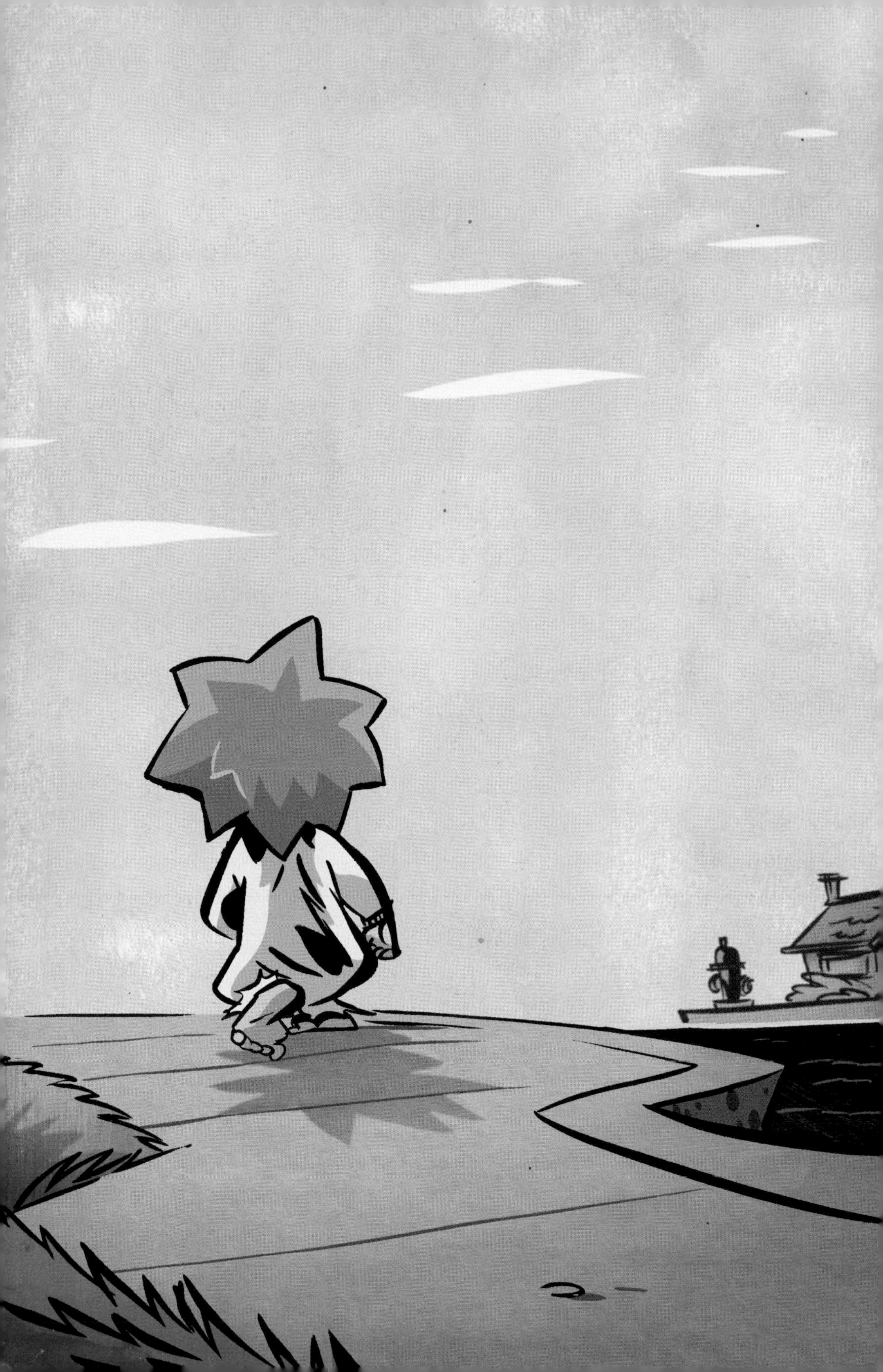

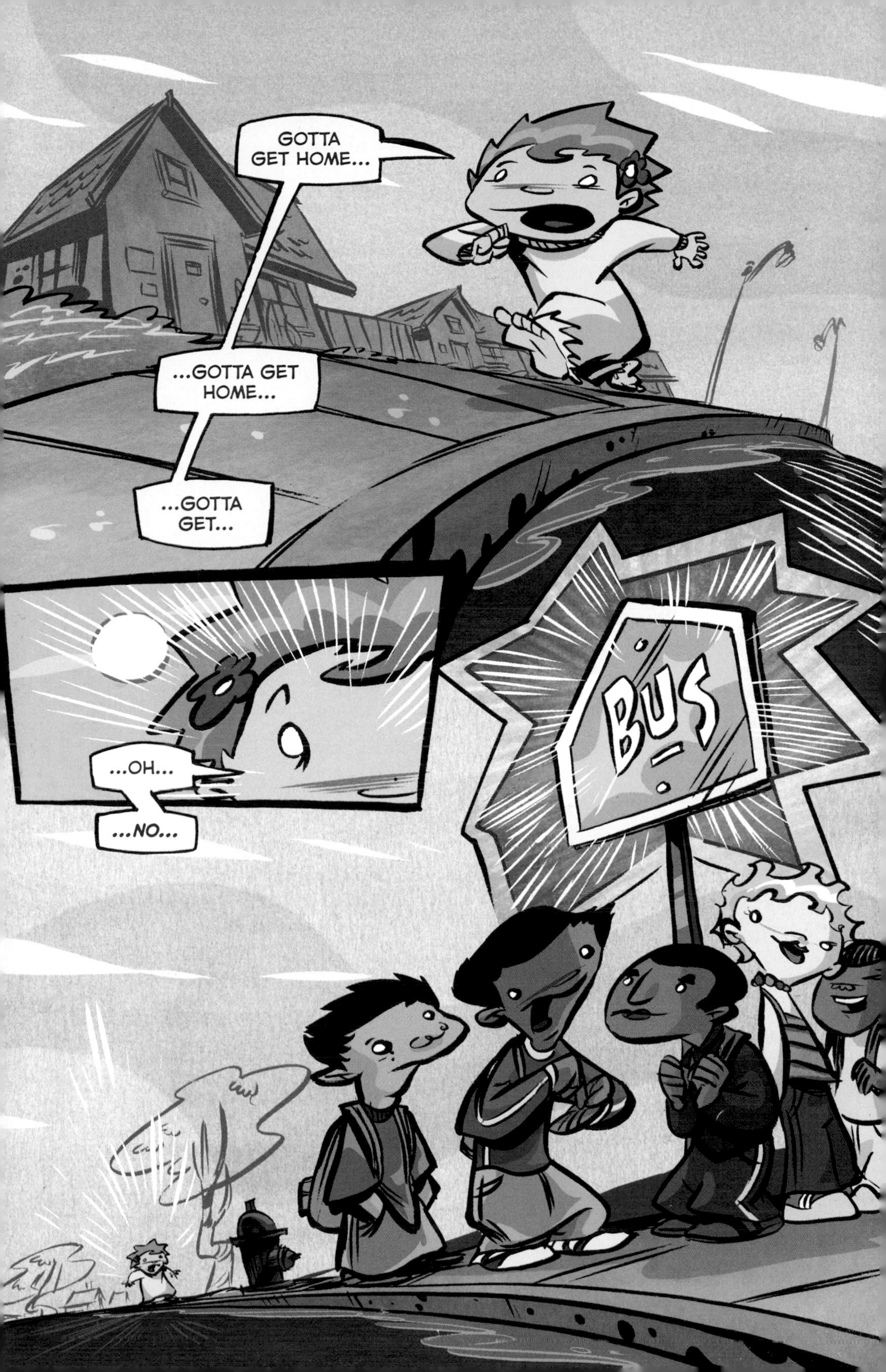
GOTTA GET HOME...
...GOTTA GET HOME...
...GOTTA GET...
...OH...
...NO...
BUS

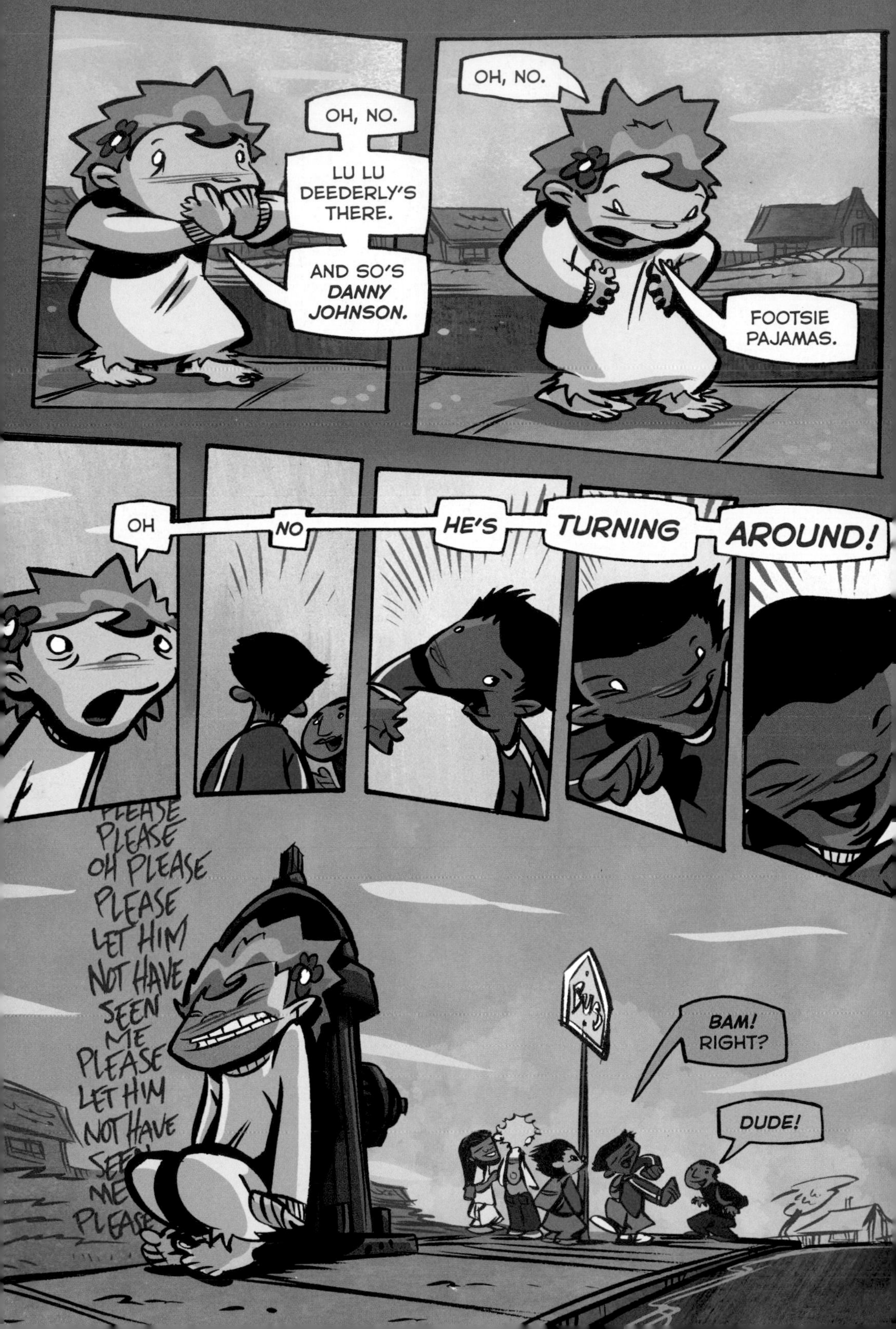
OH, NO.
LU LU DEEDERLY'S THERE.
AND SO'S *DANNY JOHNSON.*
OH, NO.
FOOTSIE PAJAMAS.
OH
NO
HE'S
TURNING
AROUND!
PLEASE PLEASE OH PLEASE PLEASE LET HIM NOT HAVE SEEN ME PLEASE LET HIM NOT HAVE SEEN ME PLEASE
BUS
BAM! RIGHT?
DUDE!

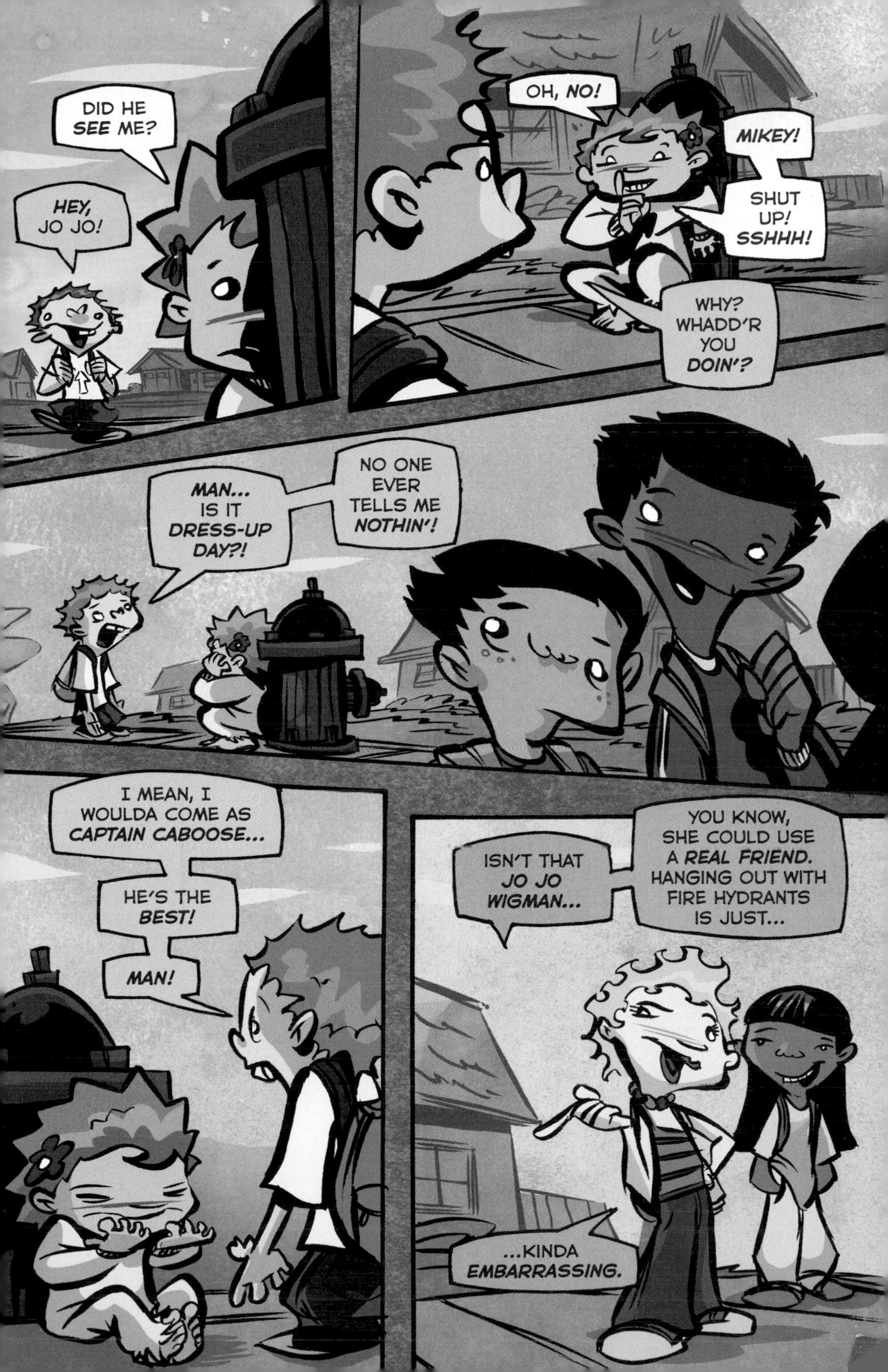
HEY, JO JO!
DID HE SEE ME?
OH, NO!
MIKEY!
SHUT UP! SSHHH!
WHY? WHADD'R YOU DOIN'?
MAN... IS IT DRESS-UP DAY?!
NO ONE EVER TELLS ME NOTHIN'!
I MEAN, I WOULDA COME AS CAPTAIN CABOOSE...
HE'S THE BEST!
MAN!
ISN'T THAT JO JO WIGMAN...
YOU KNOW, SHE COULD USE A REAL FRIEND. HANGING OUT WITH FIRE HYDRANTS IS JUST...
...KINDA EMBARRASSING.

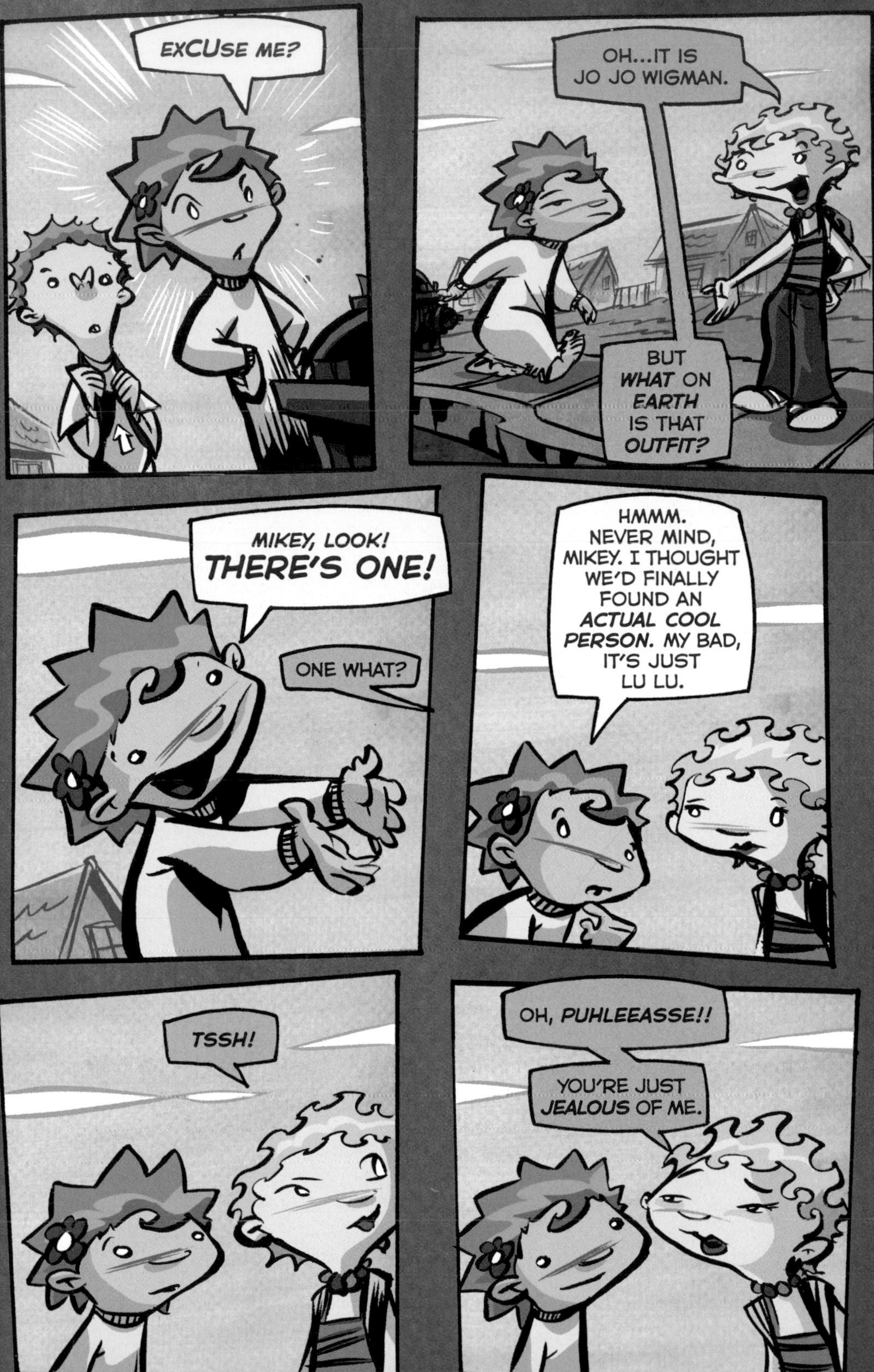

EXCUSE ME?
OH...IT IS JO JO WIGMAN.
BUT WHAT ON EARTH IS THAT OUTFIT?
MIKEY, LOOK! THERE'S ONE!
ONE WHAT?
HMMM. NEVER MIND, MIKEY. I THOUGHT WE'D FINALLY FOUND AN ACTUAL COOL PERSON. MY BAD, IT'S JUST LU LU.
TSSH!
OH, PUHLEEASSE!!
YOU'RE JUST JEALOUS OF ME.

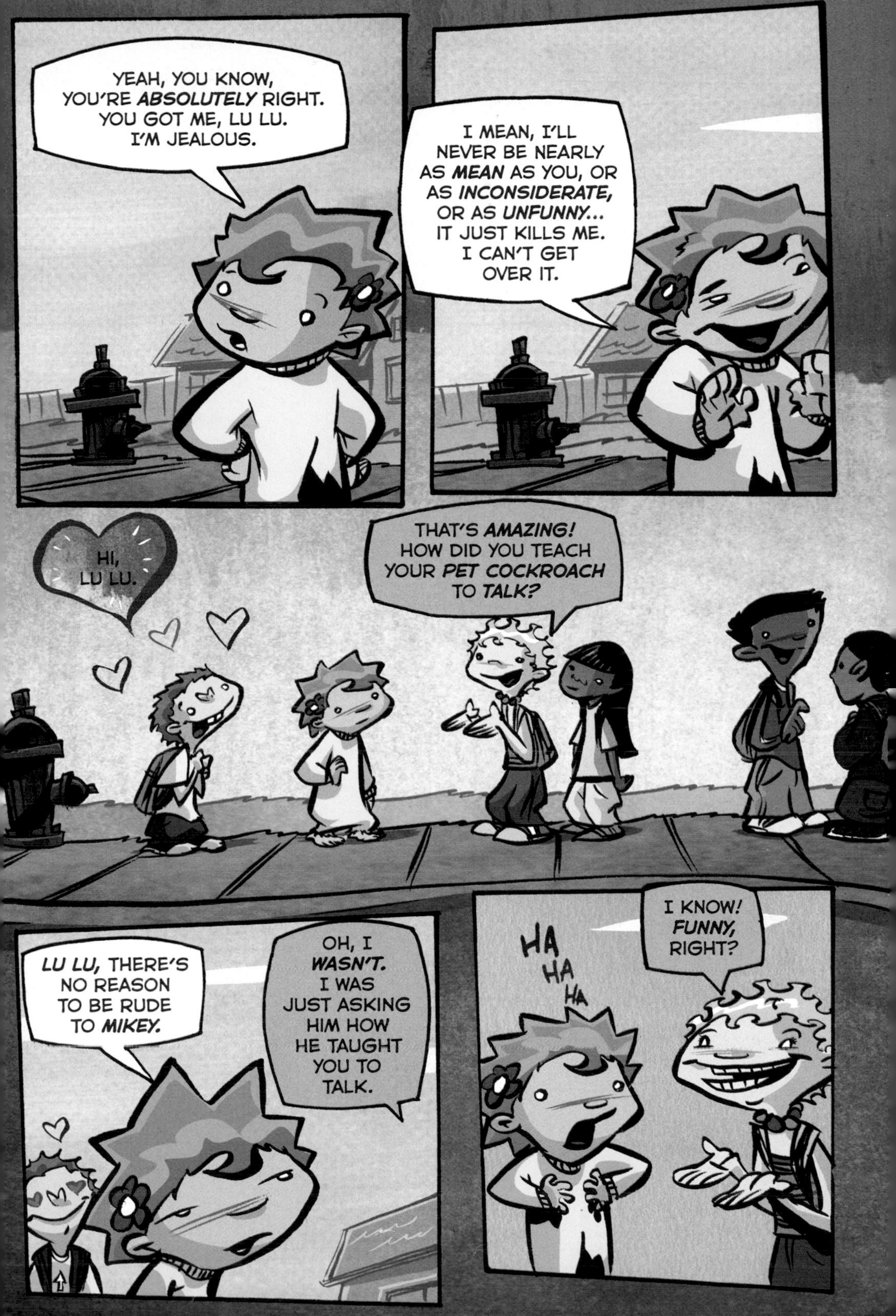
YEAH, YOU KNOW, YOU'RE *ABSOLUTELY* RIGHT. YOU GOT ME, LU LU. I'M JEALOUS.
I MEAN, I'LL NEVER BE NEARLY AS *MEAN* AS YOU, OR AS *INCONSIDERATE,* OR AS *UNFUNNY...* IT JUST KILLS ME. I CAN'T GET OVER IT.
HI, LU LU.
THAT'S *AMAZING!* HOW DID YOU TEACH YOUR *PET COCKROACH* TO *TALK?*
LU LU, THERE'S NO REASON TO BE RUDE TO *MIKEY.*
OH, I *WASN'T.* I WAS JUST ASKING HIM HOW HE TAUGHT YOU TO TALK.
HA HA HA
I KNOW! *FUNNY,* RIGHT?

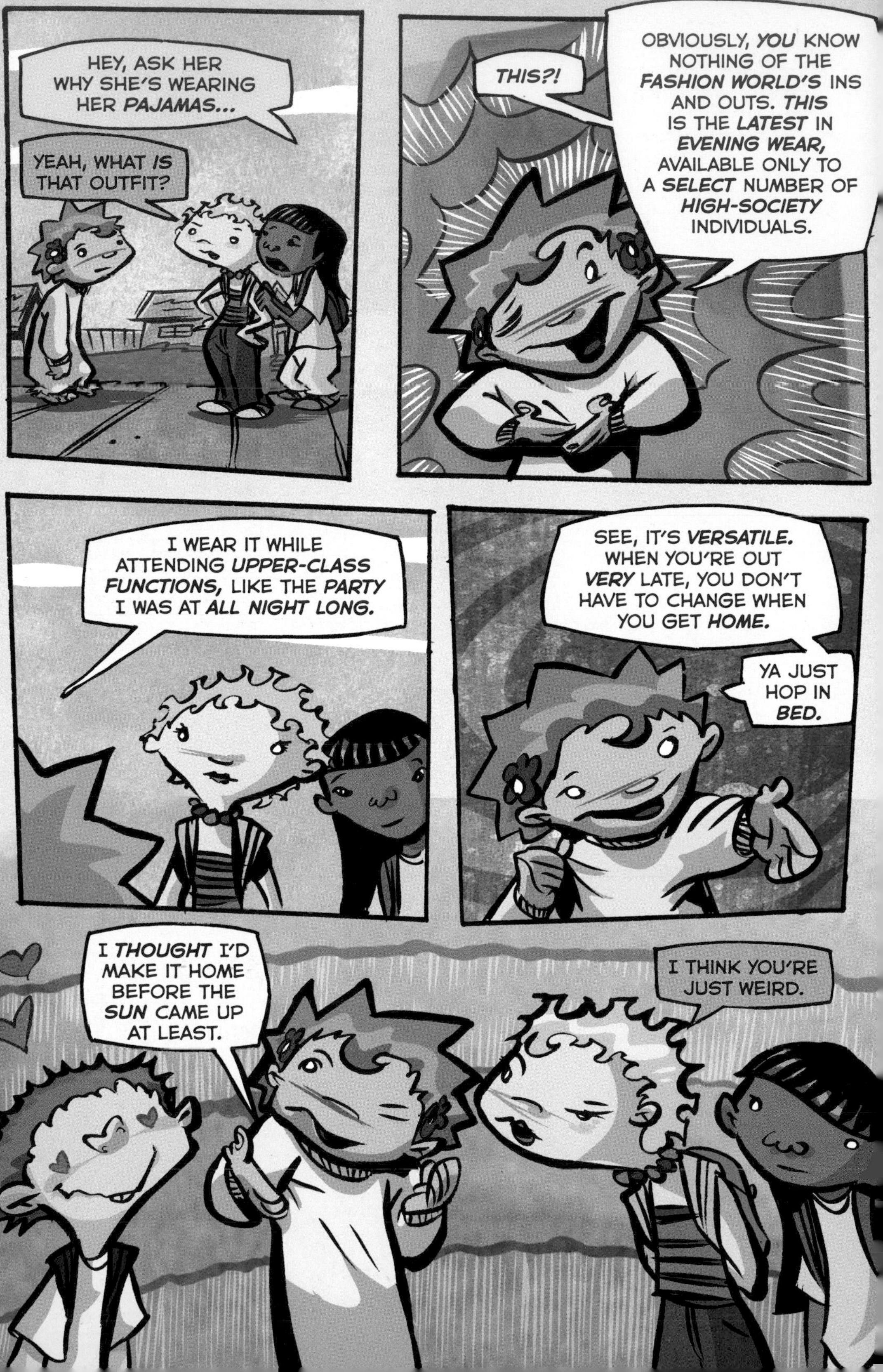
HEY, ASK HER WHY SHE'S WEARING HER PAJAMAS...
YEAH, WHAT IS THAT OUTFIT?
THIS?!
OBVIOUSLY, YOU KNOW NOTHING OF THE FASHION WORLD'S INS AND OUTS. THIS IS THE LATEST IN EVENING WEAR, AVAILABLE ONLY TO A SELECT NUMBER OF HIGH-SOCIETY INDIVIDUALS.
I WEAR IT WHILE ATTENDING UPPER-CLASS FUNCTIONS, LIKE THE PARTY I WAS AT ALL NIGHT LONG.
SEE, IT'S VERSATILE. WHEN YOU'RE OUT VERY LATE, YOU DON'T HAVE TO CHANGE WHEN YOU GET HOME.
YA JUST HOP IN BED.
I THOUGHT I'D MAKE IT HOME BEFORE THE SUN CAME UP AT LEAST.
I THINK YOU'RE JUST WEIRD.

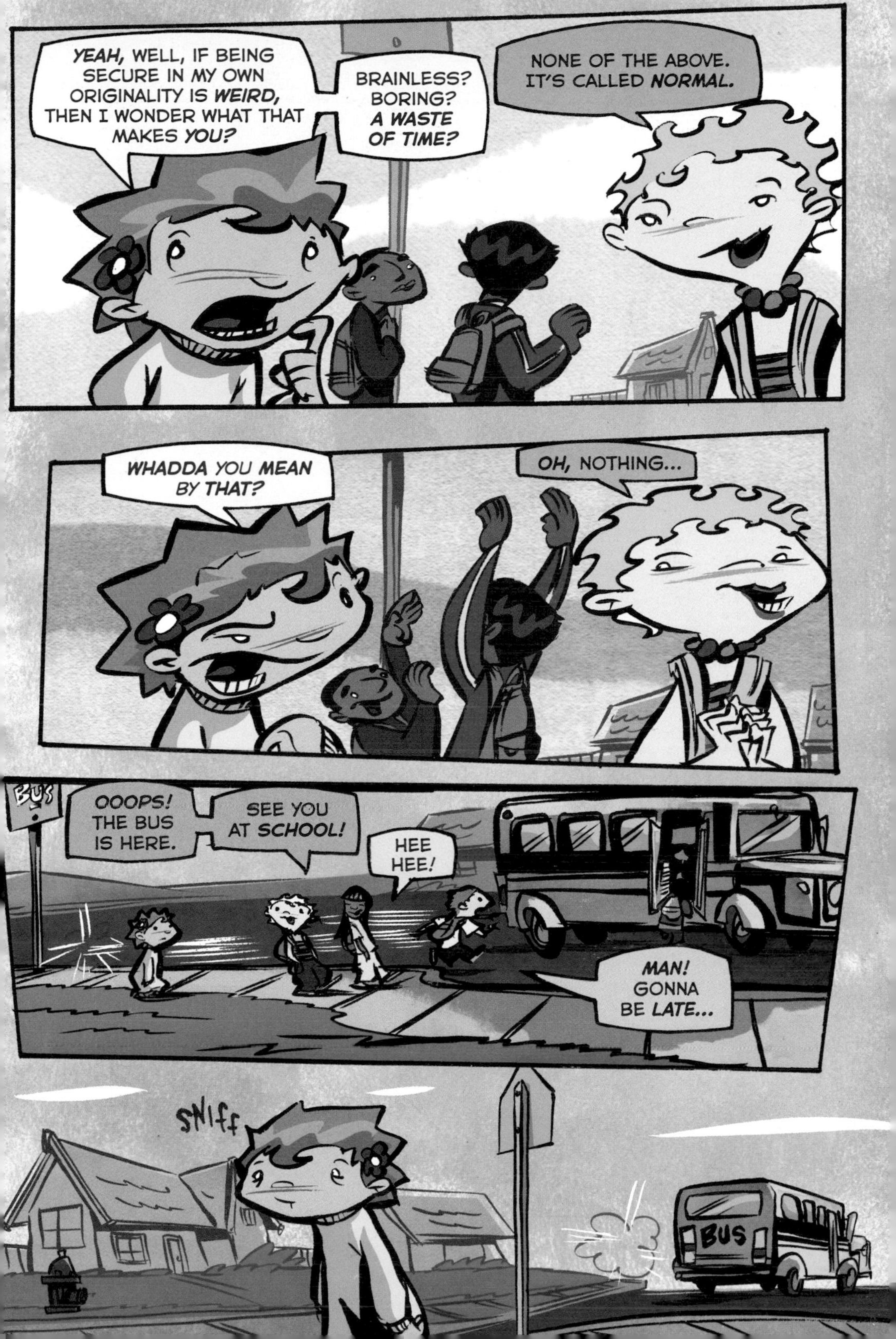

YEAH, WELL, IF BEING SECURE IN MY OWN ORIGINALITY IS WEIRD, THEN I WONDER WHAT THAT MAKES YOU?
BRAINLESS? BORING? A WASTE OF TIME?
NONE OF THE ABOVE. IT'S CALLED NORMAL.
WHADDA YOU MEAN BY THAT?
OH, NOTHING...
BUS
OOOPS! THE BUS IS HERE.
SEE YOU AT SCHOOL!
HEE HEE!
MAN! GONNA BE LATE...
SNIFF
BUS

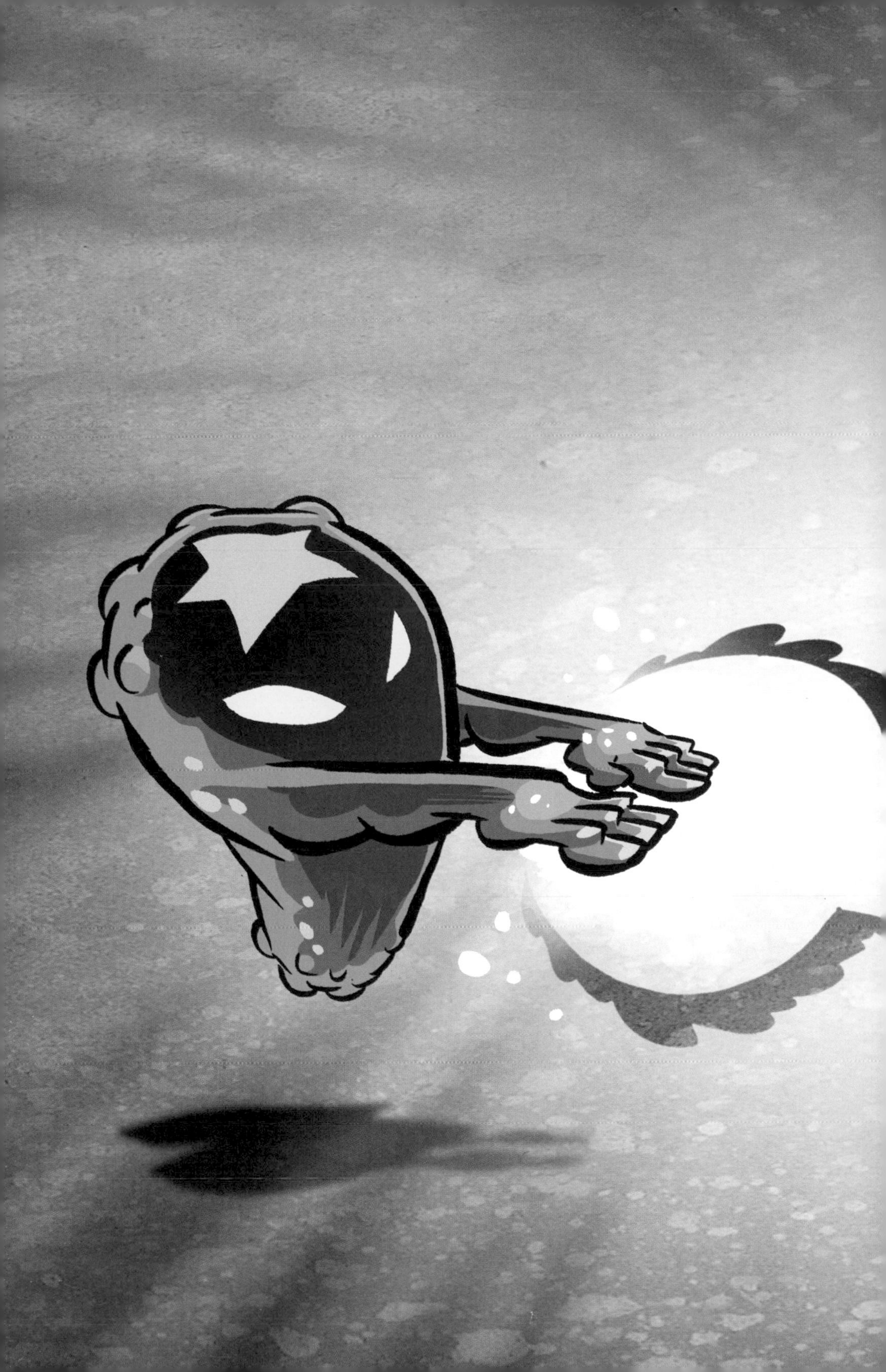

CHAPTER 4

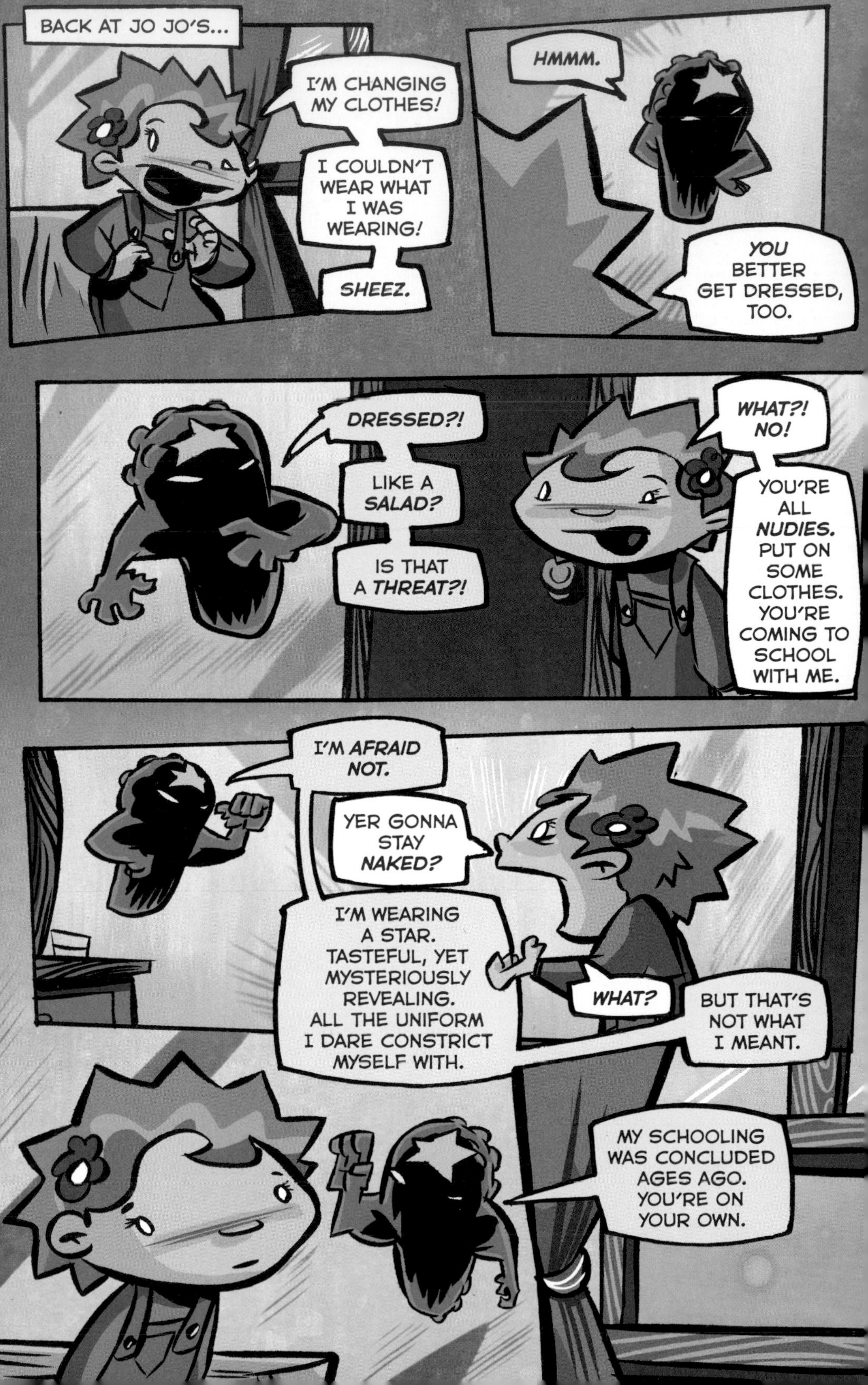
BACK AT JO JO'S...
I'M CHANGING MY CLOTHES!
I COULDN'T WEAR WHAT I WAS WEARING!
SHEEZ.
HMMM.
YOU BETTER GET DRESSED, TOO.
DRESSED?!
LIKE A SALAD?
IS THAT A THREAT?!
WHAT?! NO!
YOU'RE ALL NUDIES. PUT ON SOME CLOTHES. YOU'RE COMING TO SCHOOL WITH ME.
I'M AFRAID NOT.
YER GONNA STAY NAKED?
I'M WEARING A STAR. TASTEFUL, YET MYSTERIOUSLY REVEALING. ALL THE UNIFORM I DARE CONSTRICT MYSELF WITH.
WHAT?
BUT THAT'S NOT WHAT I MEANT.
MY SCHOOLING WAS CONCLUDED AGES AGO. YOU'RE ON YOUR OWN.

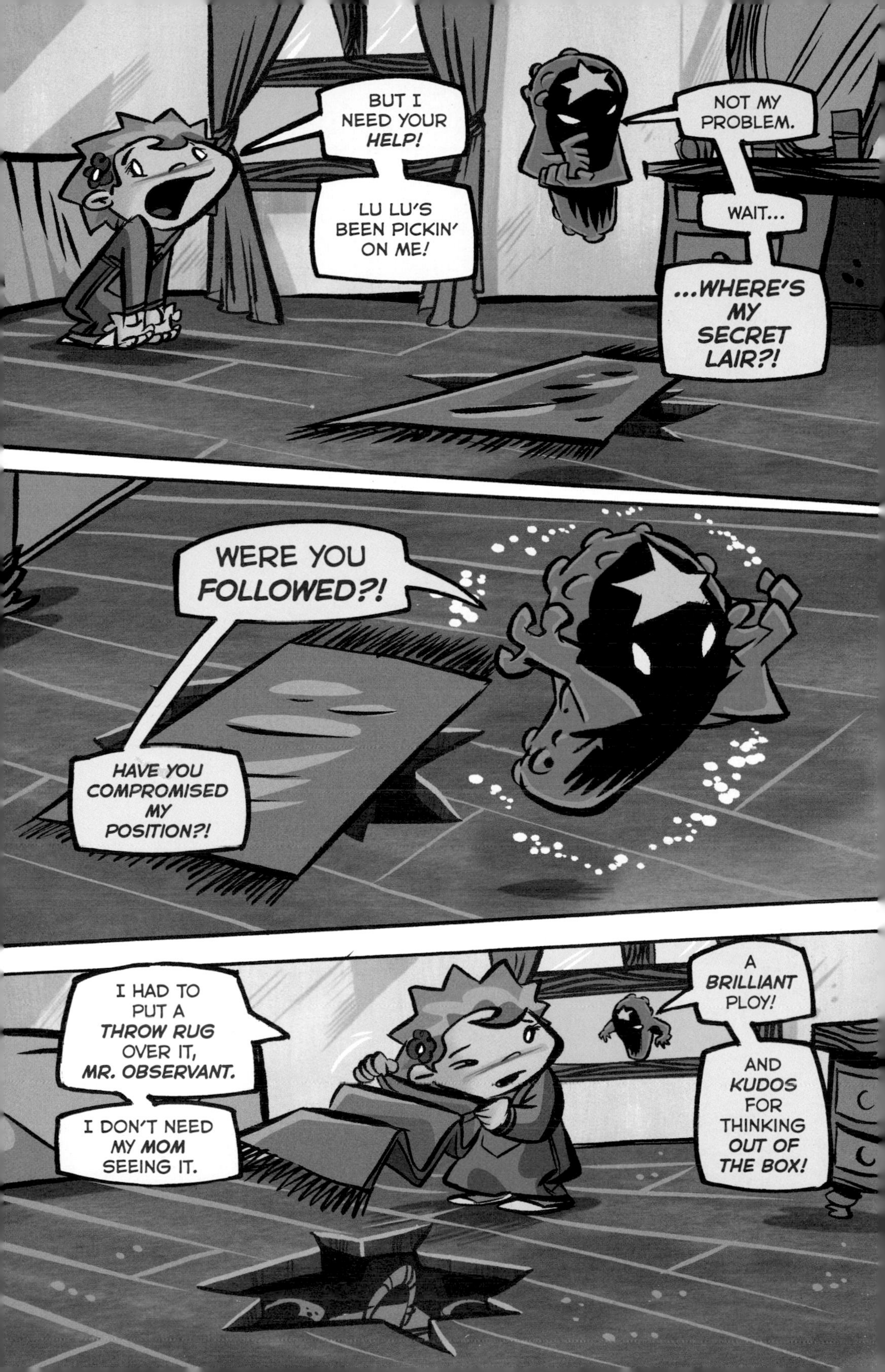
BUT I NEED YOUR *HELP!*
LU LU'S BEEN PICKIN' ON ME!
NOT MY PROBLEM.
WAIT...
...WHERE'S MY SECRET LAIR?!
WERE YOU *FOLLOWED?!*
HAVE YOU COMPROMISED MY POSITION?!
I HAD TO PUT A *THROW RUG* OVER IT, *MR. OBSERVANT.*
I DON'T NEED MY *MOM* SEEING IT.
A *BRILLIANT* PLOY!
AND *KUDOS* FOR THINKING *OUT OF THE BOX!*

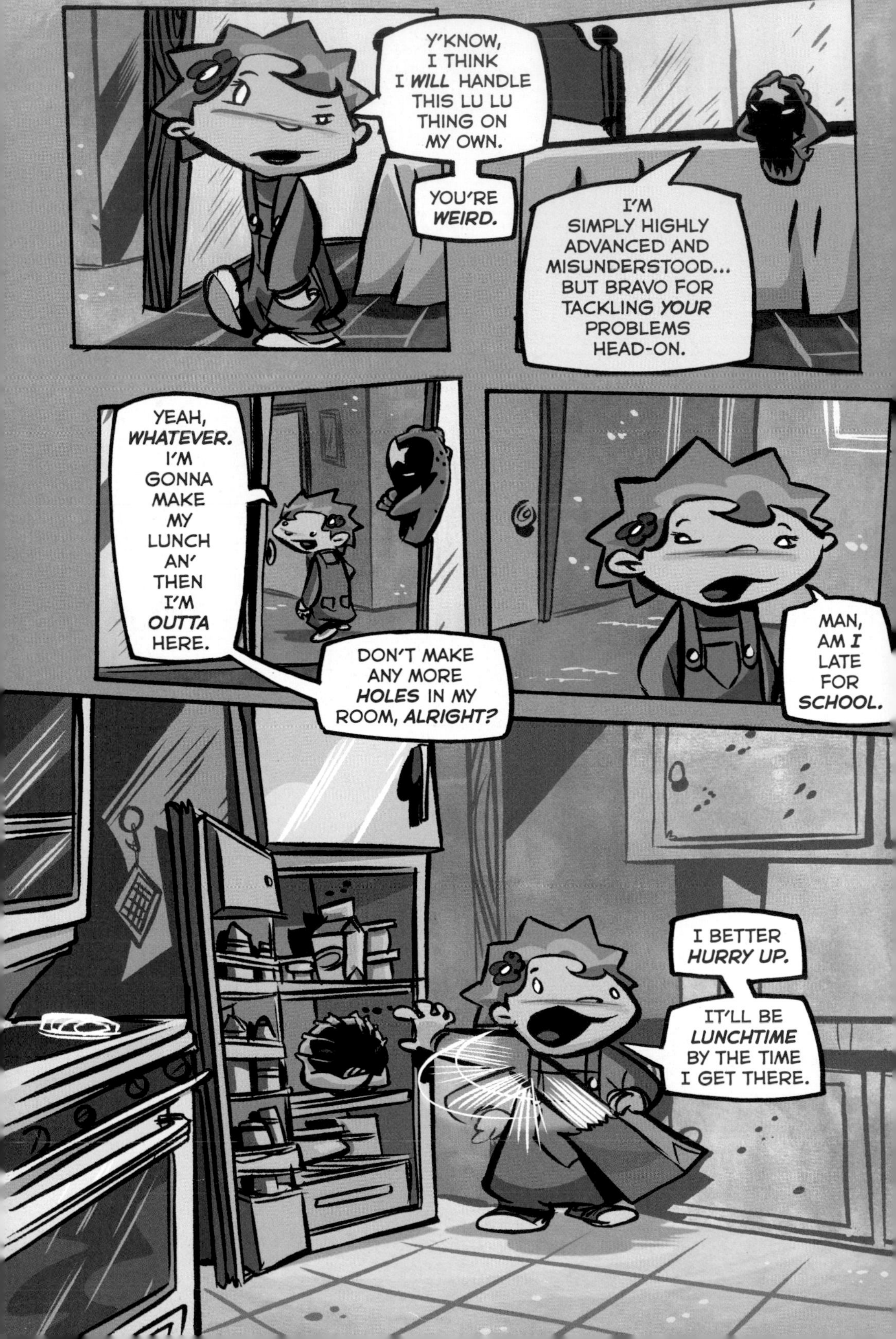
Y'KNOW, I THINK I *WILL* HANDLE THIS LU LU THING ON MY OWN.
YOU'RE *WEIRD.*
I'M SIMPLY HIGHLY ADVANCED AND MISUNDERSTOOD... BUT BRAVO FOR TACKLING *YOUR* PROBLEMS HEAD-ON.
YEAH, *WHATEVER.* I'M GONNA MAKE MY LUNCH AN' THEN I'M *OUTTA* HERE.
DON'T MAKE ANY MORE *HOLES* IN MY ROOM, *ALRIGHT?*
MAN, AM *I* LATE FOR *SCHOOL.*
I BETTER *HURRY UP.*
IT'LL BE *LUNCHTIME* BY THE TIME I GET THERE.

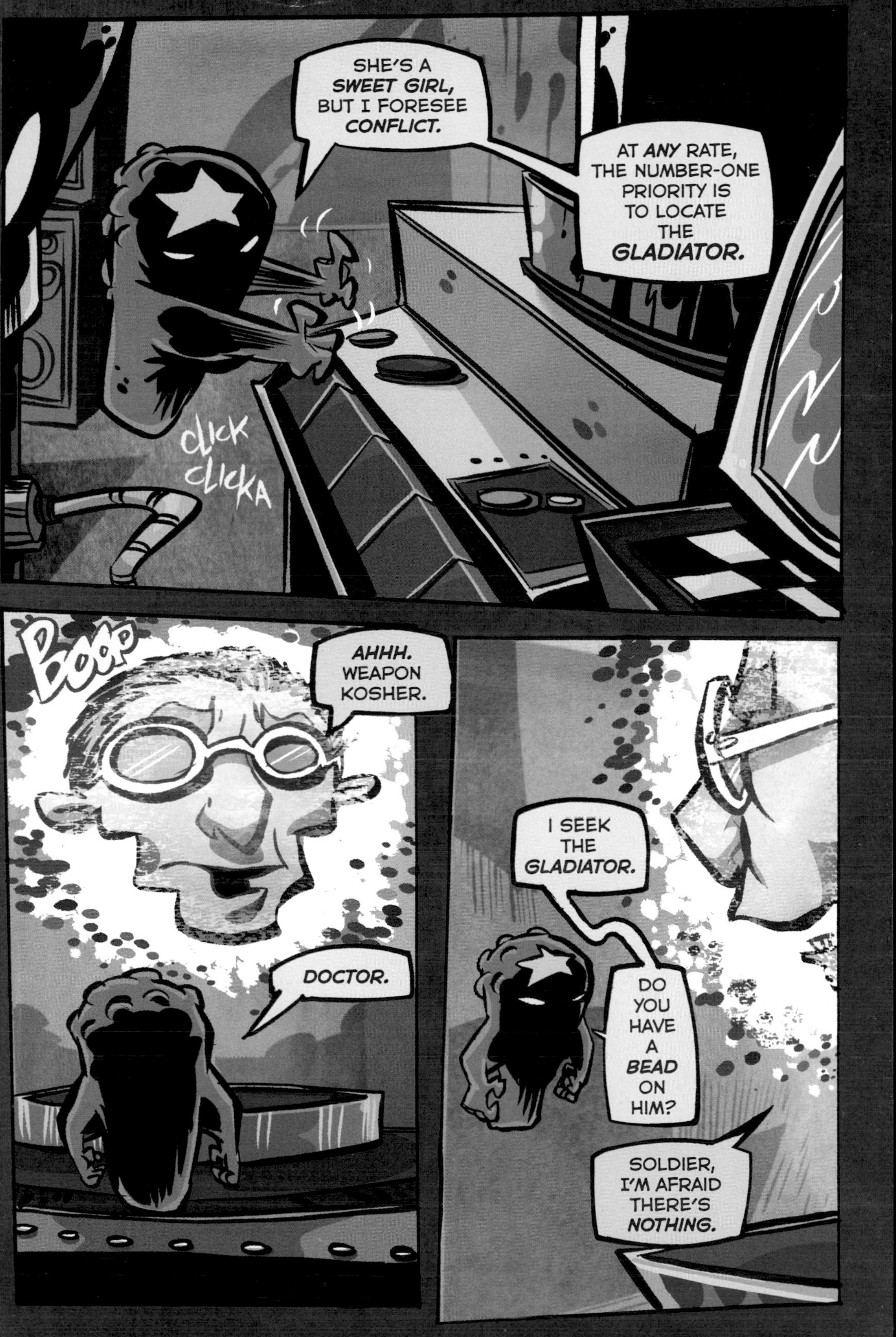

SHE'S A SWEET GIRL, BUT I FORESEE CONFLICT.
AT ANY RATE, THE NUMBER-ONE PRIORITY IS TO LOCATE THE GLADIATOR.
CLICK CLICKA
BOOP
AHHH. WEAPON KOSHER.
DOCTOR.
I SEEK THE GLADIATOR.
DO YOU HAVE A BEAD ON HIM?
SOLDIER, I'M AFRAID THERE'S NOTHING.

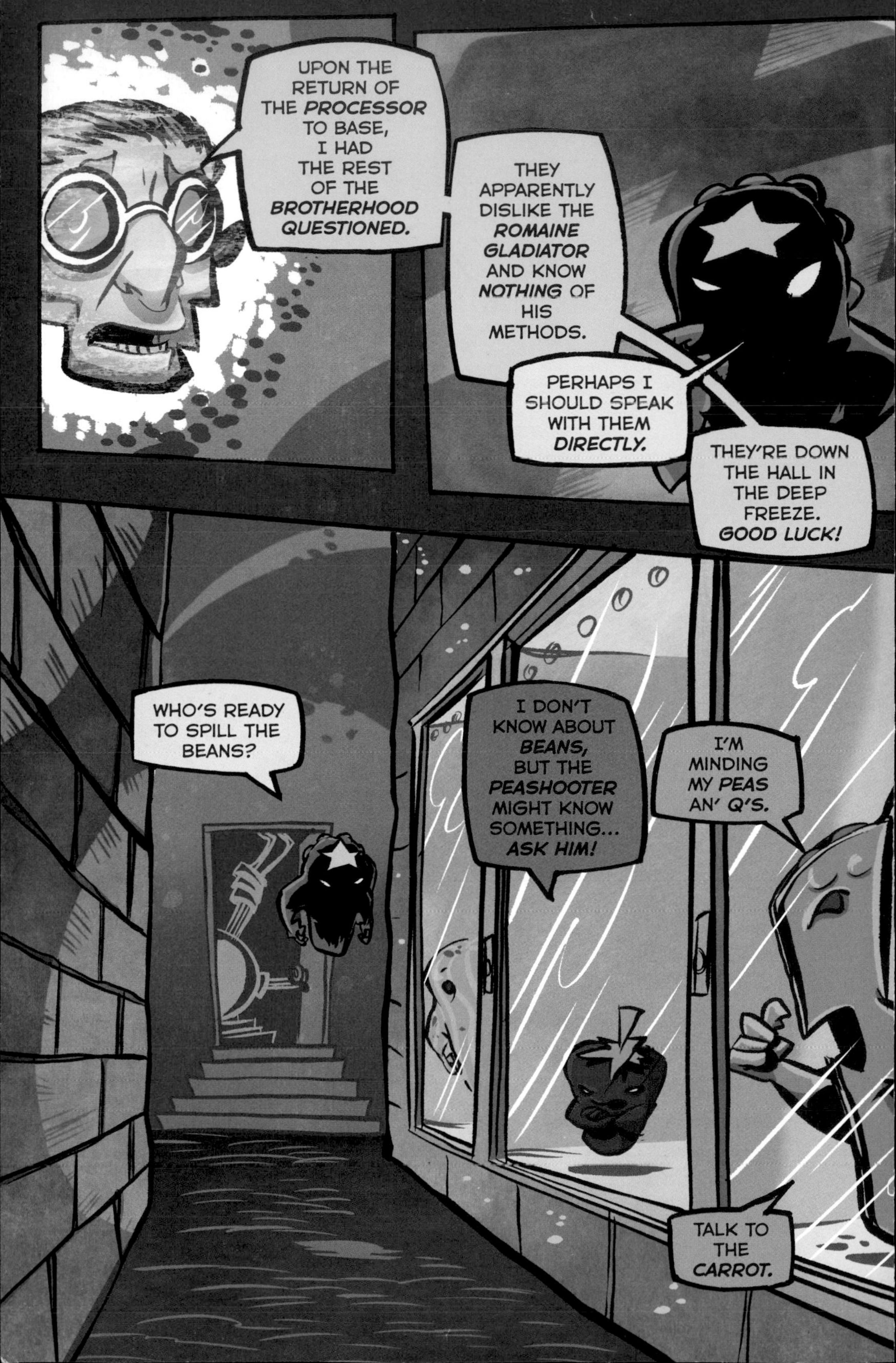
UPON THE RETURN OF THE *PROCESSOR* TO BASE, I HAD THE REST OF THE *BROTHERHOOD QUESTIONED.*
THEY APPARENTLY DISLIKE THE *ROMAINE GLADIATOR* AND KNOW *NOTHING* OF HIS METHODS.
PERHAPS I SHOULD SPEAK WITH THEM *DIRECTLY.*
THEY'RE DOWN THE HALL IN THE DEEP FREEZE. *GOOD LUCK!*
WHO'S READY TO SPILL THE BEANS?
I DON'T KNOW ABOUT *BEANS,* BUT THE *PEASHOOTER* MIGHT KNOW SOMETHING... *ASK HIM!*
I'M MINDING MY *PEAS* AN' *Q'S.*
TALK TO THE *CARROT.*

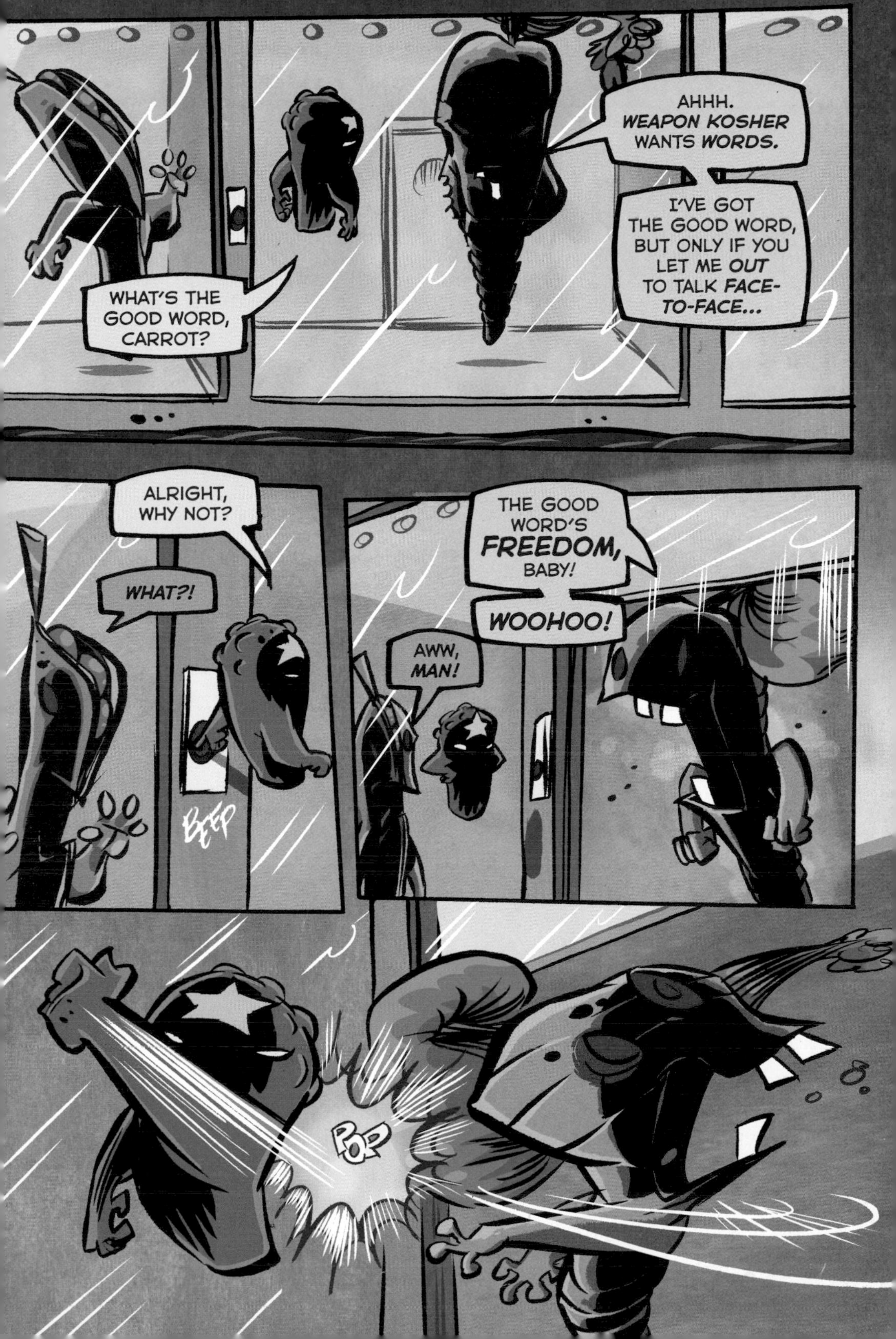
AHHH. WEAPON KOSHER WANTS WORDS.
I'VE GOT THE GOOD WORD, BUT ONLY IF YOU LET ME OUT TO TALK FACE-TO-FACE...
WHAT'S THE GOOD WORD, CARROT?
ALRIGHT, WHY NOT?
WHAT?!
BEEP
THE GOOD WORD'S FREEDOM, BABY!
WOOHOO!
AWW, MAN!
POP

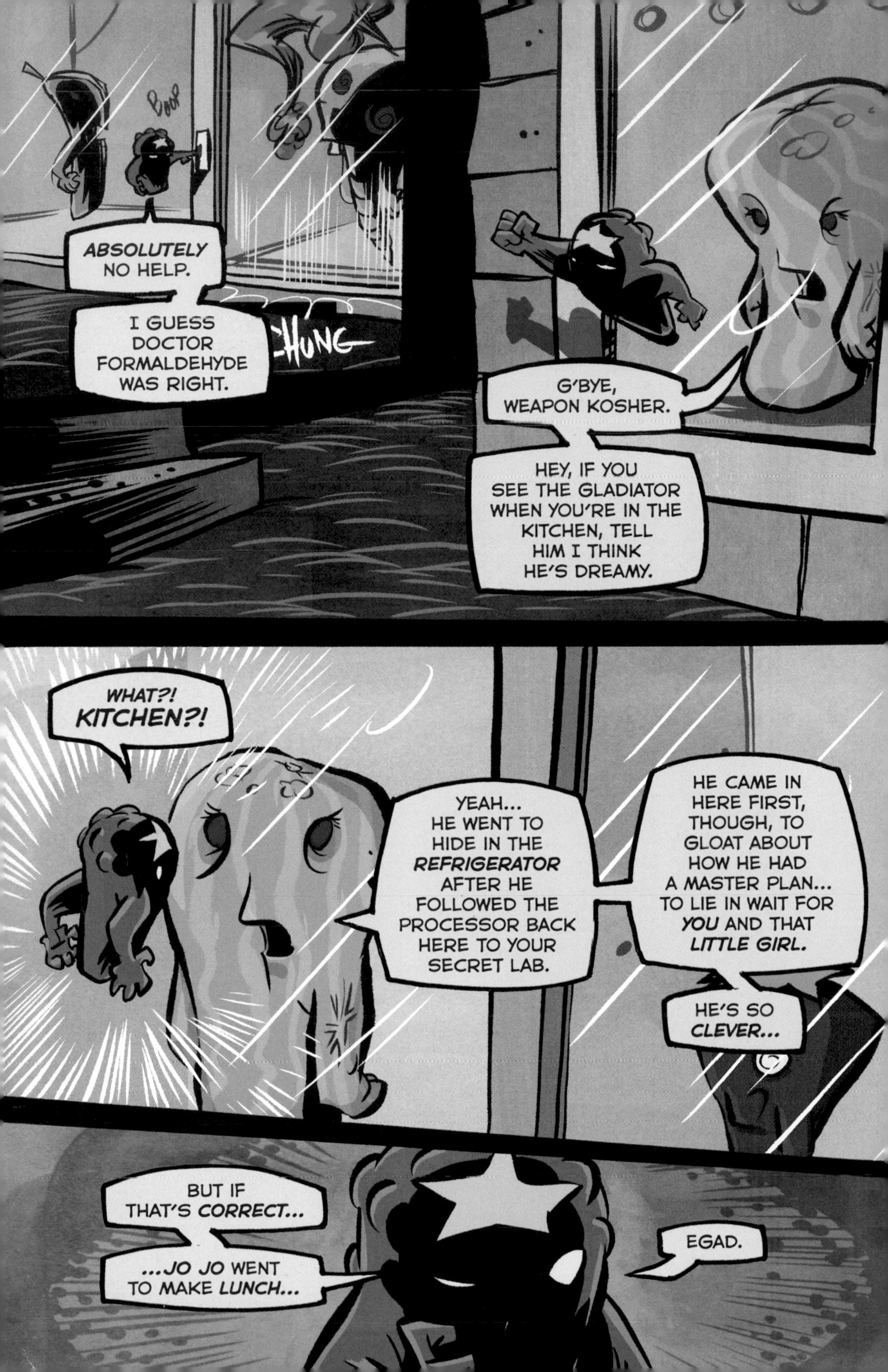
BOOP
ABSOLUTELY NO HELP.
I GUESS DOCTOR FORMALDEHYDE WAS RIGHT.
CHUNG
G'BYE, WEAPON KOSHER.
HEY, IF YOU SEE THE GLADIATOR WHEN YOU'RE IN THE KITCHEN, TELL HIM I THINK HE'S DREAMY.
WHAT?! KITCHEN?!
YEAH... HE WENT TO HIDE IN THE *REFRIGERATOR* AFTER HE FOLLOWED THE PROCESSOR BACK HERE TO YOUR SECRET LAB.
HE CAME IN HERE FIRST, THOUGH, TO GLOAT ABOUT HOW HE HAD A MASTER PLAN... TO LIE IN WAIT FOR *YOU* AND THAT *LITTLE GIRL.*
HE'S SO *CLEVER...*
BUT IF THAT'S *CORRECT...*
...JO JO WENT TO MAKE *LUNCH...*
EGAD.

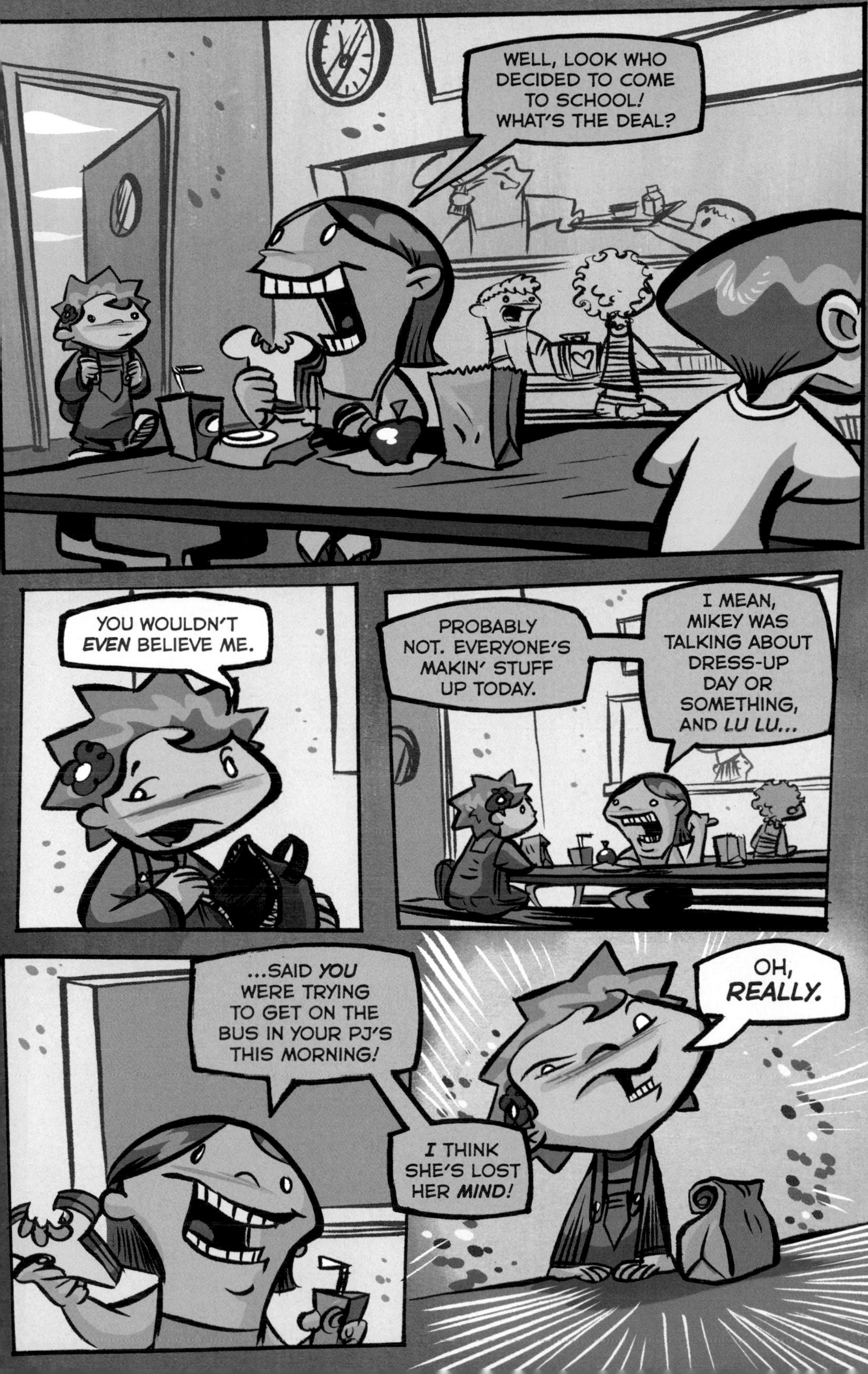
WELL, LOOK WHO DECIDED TO COME TO SCHOOL! WHAT'S THE DEAL?
YOU WOULDN'T *EVEN* BELIEVE ME.
PROBABLY NOT. EVERYONE'S MAKIN' STUFF UP TODAY.
I MEAN, MIKEY WAS TALKING ABOUT DRESS-UP DAY OR SOMETHING, AND *LU LU...*
...SAID *YOU* WERE TRYING TO GET ON THE BUS IN YOUR PJ'S THIS MORNING!
I THINK SHE'S LOST HER *MIND!*
OH, ***REALLY.***

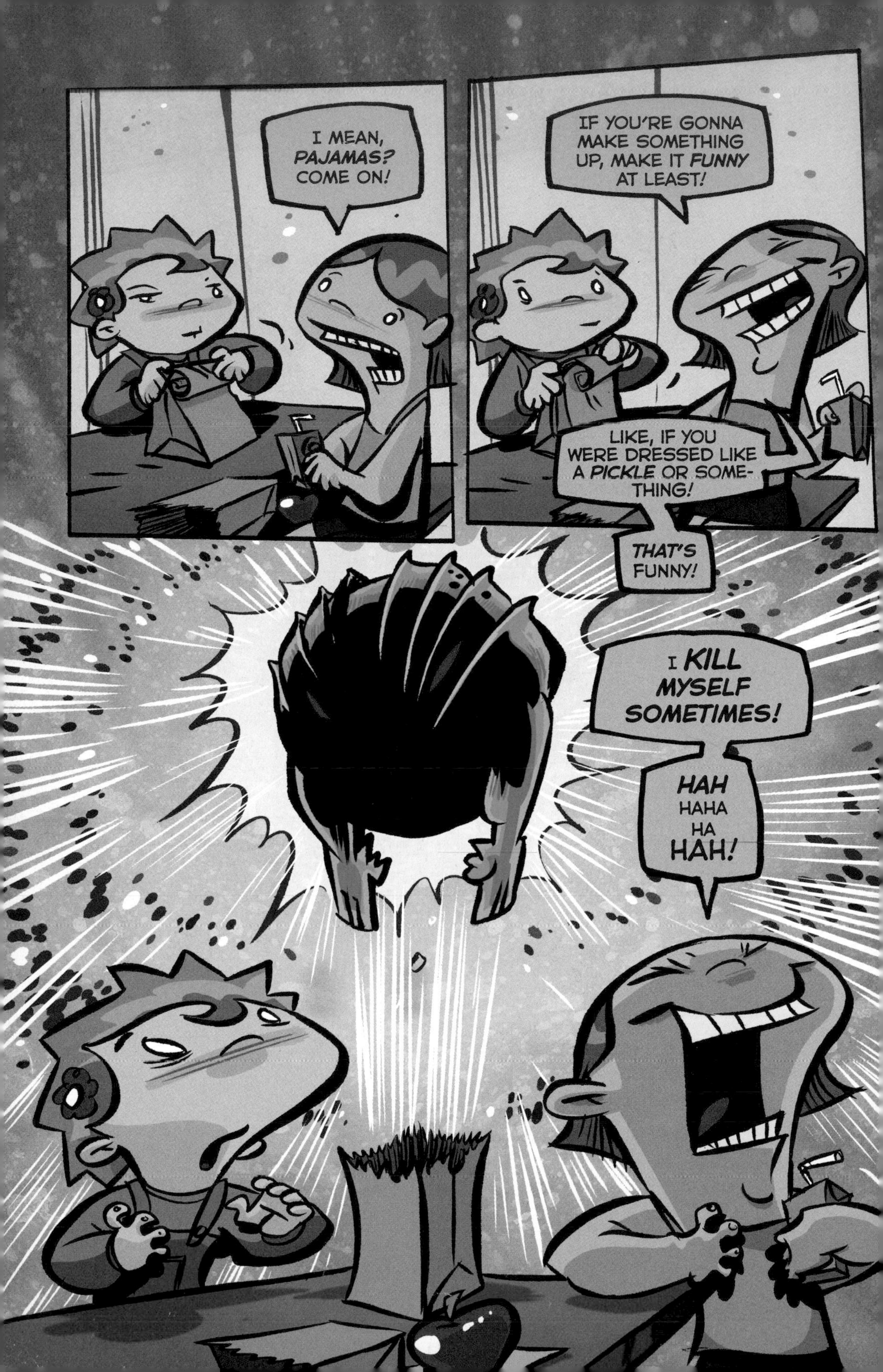
I MEAN, *PAJAMAS?* COME ON!
IF YOU'RE GONNA MAKE SOMETHING UP, MAKE IT *FUNNY* AT LEAST!
LIKE, IF YOU WERE DRESSED LIKE A *PICKLE* OR SOME-THING!
THAT'S FUNNY!
I **KILL MYSELF SOMETIMES!**
HAH HAHA HA **HAH!**

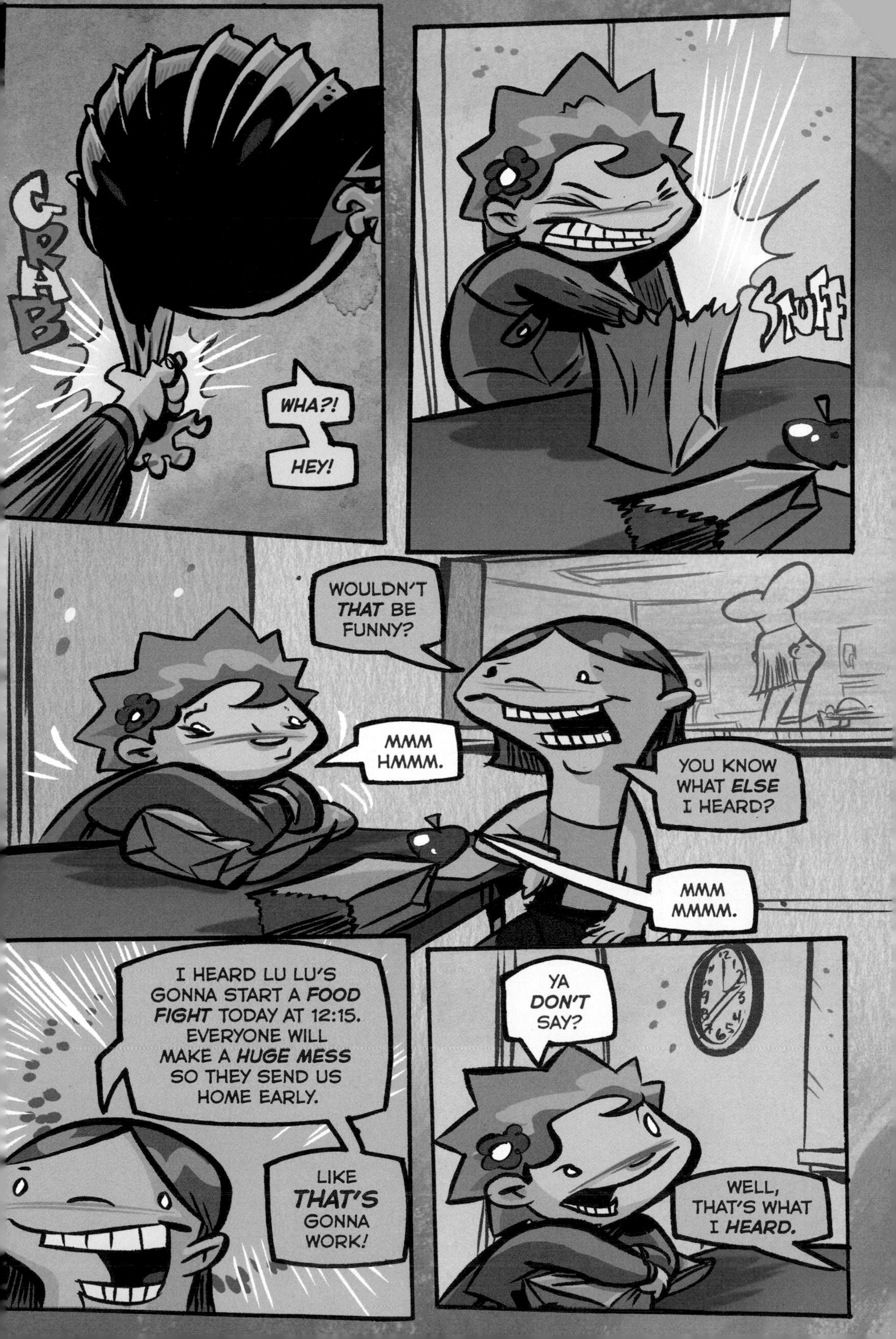
GRABB
WHA?!
HEY!
STUFF
WOULDN'T *THAT* BE FUNNY?
MMM HMMM.
YOU KNOW WHAT *ELSE* I HEARD?
MMM MMMM.
I HEARD LU LU'S GONNA START A *FOOD FIGHT* TODAY AT 12:15. EVERYONE WILL MAKE A *HUGE MESS* SO THEY SEND US HOME EARLY.
LIKE *THAT'S* GONNA WORK!
YA *DON'T* SAY?
WELL, THAT'S WHAT I *HEARD.*

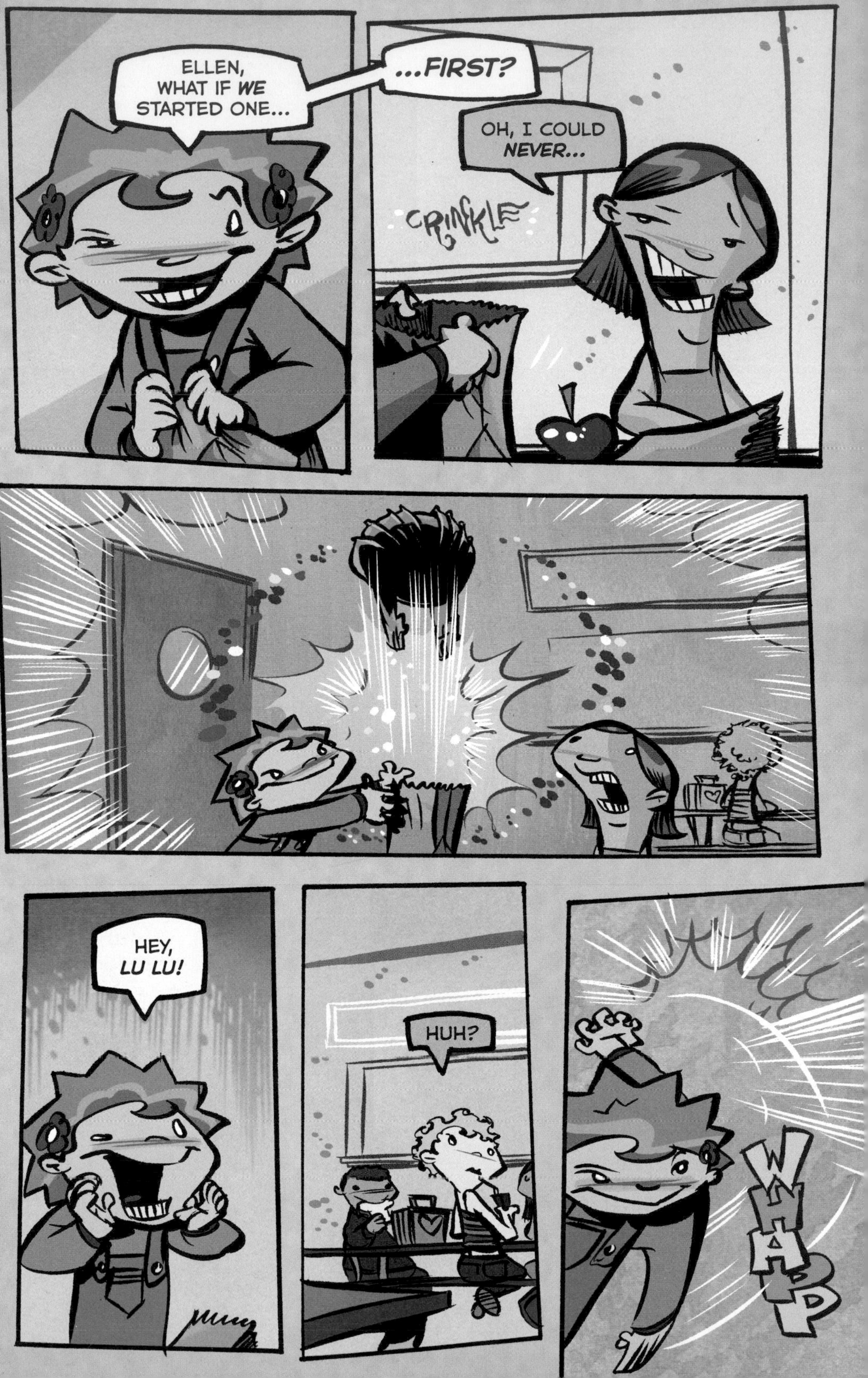
ELLEN, WHAT IF WE STARTED ONE...
...FIRST?
OH, I COULD NEVER...
CRINKLE
HEY, LU LU!
HUH?
WHAP

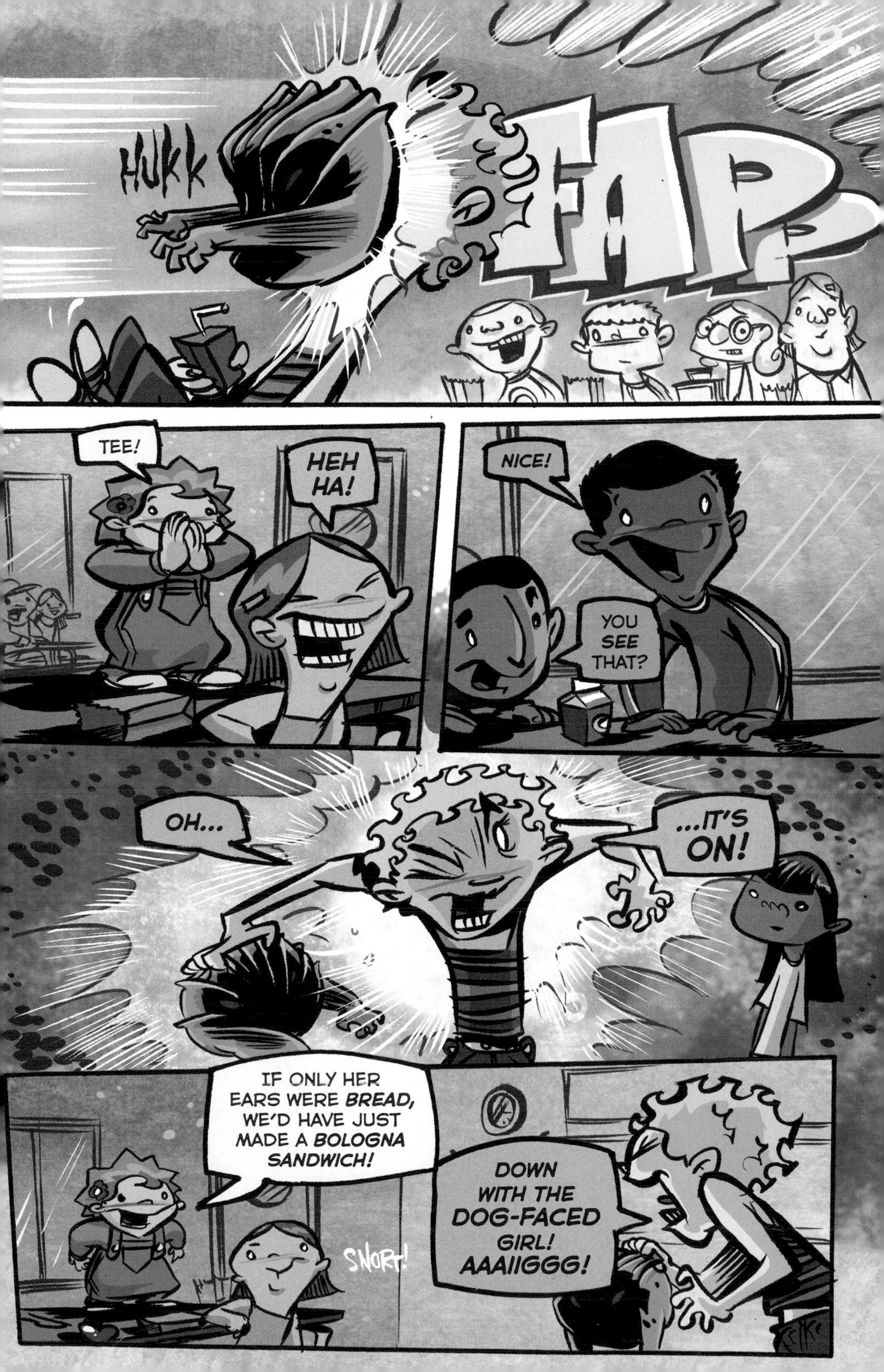
HUKK
FAP
TEE!
HEH HA!
NICE!
YOU SEE THAT?
OH...
...IT'S ON!
IF ONLY HER EARS WERE BREAD, WE'D HAVE JUST MADE A BOLOGNA SANDWICH!
SNORT!
DOWN WITH THE DOG-FACED GIRL! AAAIIGGG!

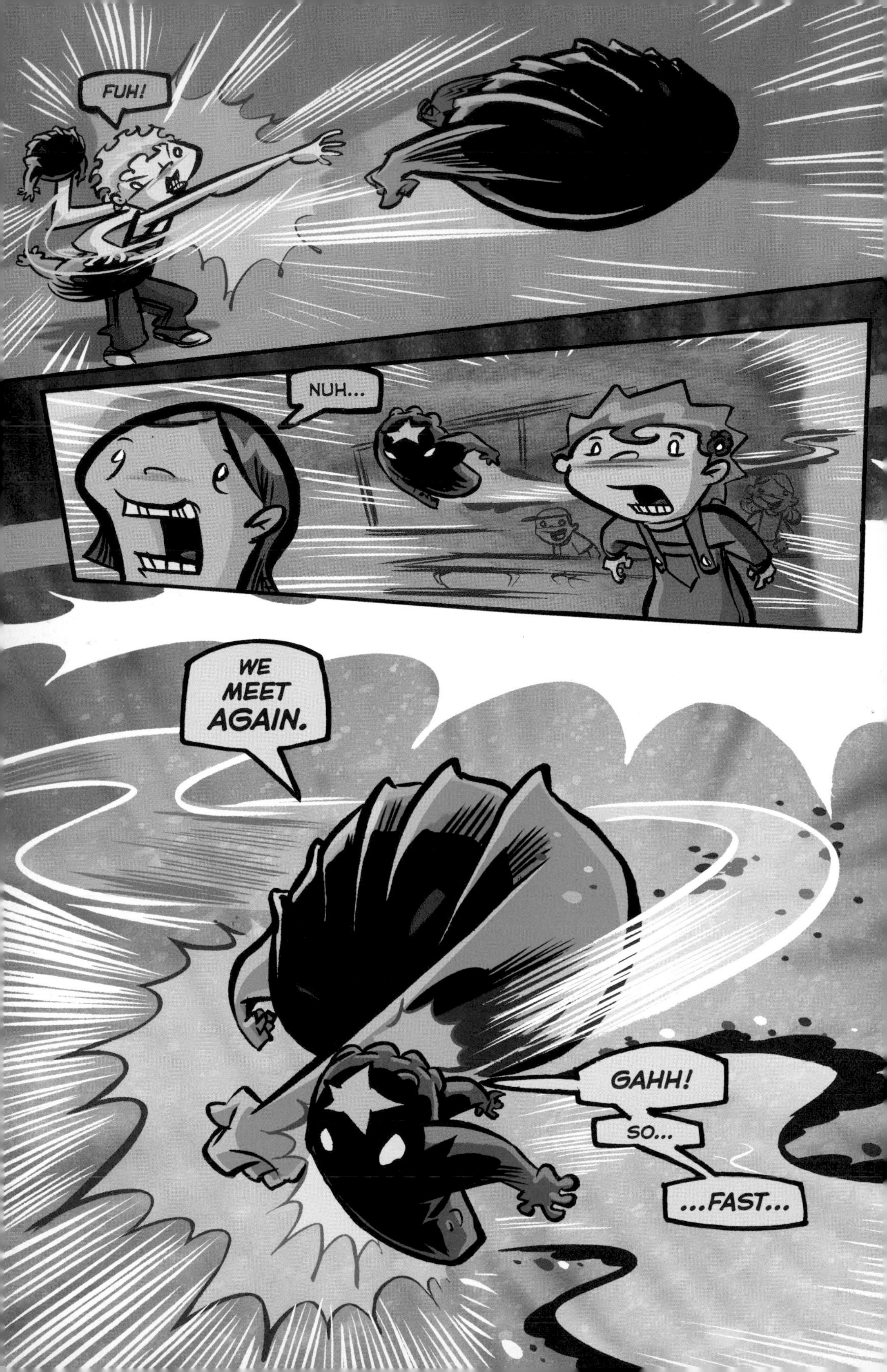
FUH!
NUH...
WE MEET AGAIN.
GAHH!
SO...
...FAST...

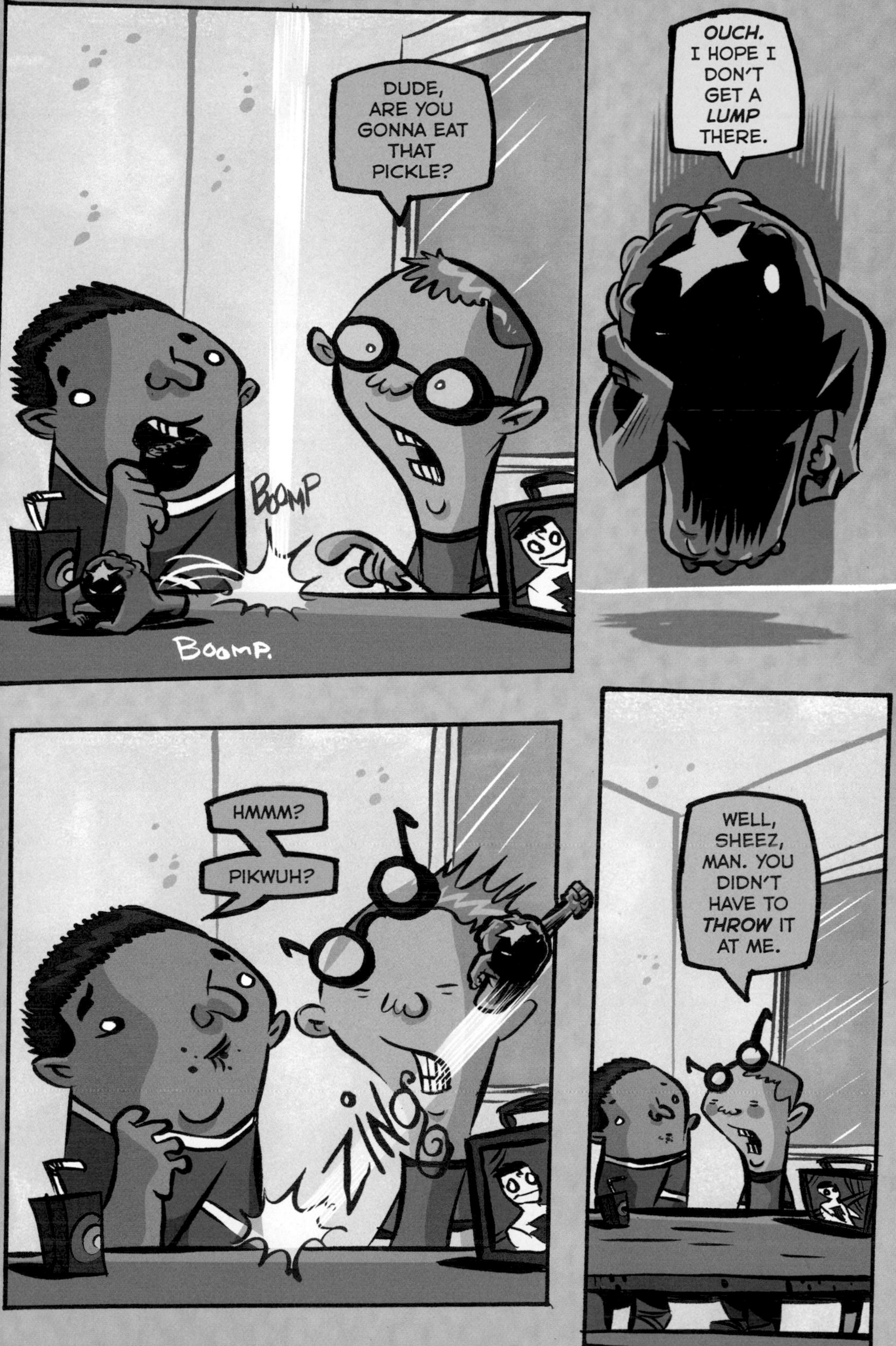
DUDE, ARE YOU GONNA EAT THAT PICKLE?
BOOMP
BOOMP.
OUCH. I HOPE I DON'T GET A LUMP THERE.
HMMM?
PIKWUH?
ZING
WELL, SHEEZ, MAN. YOU DIDN'T HAVE TO THROW IT AT ME.

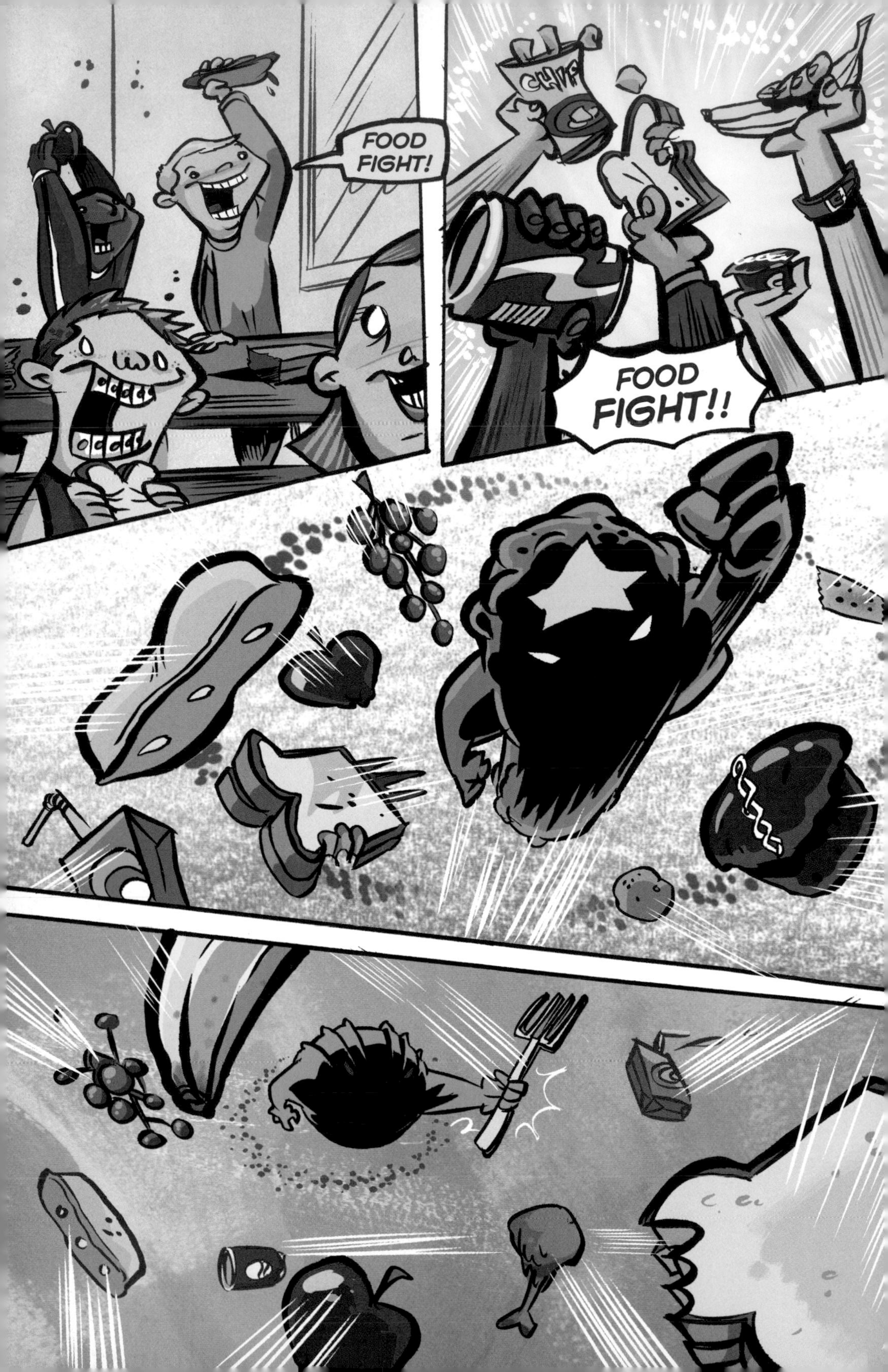
FOOD FIGHT!
FOOD FIGHT!!

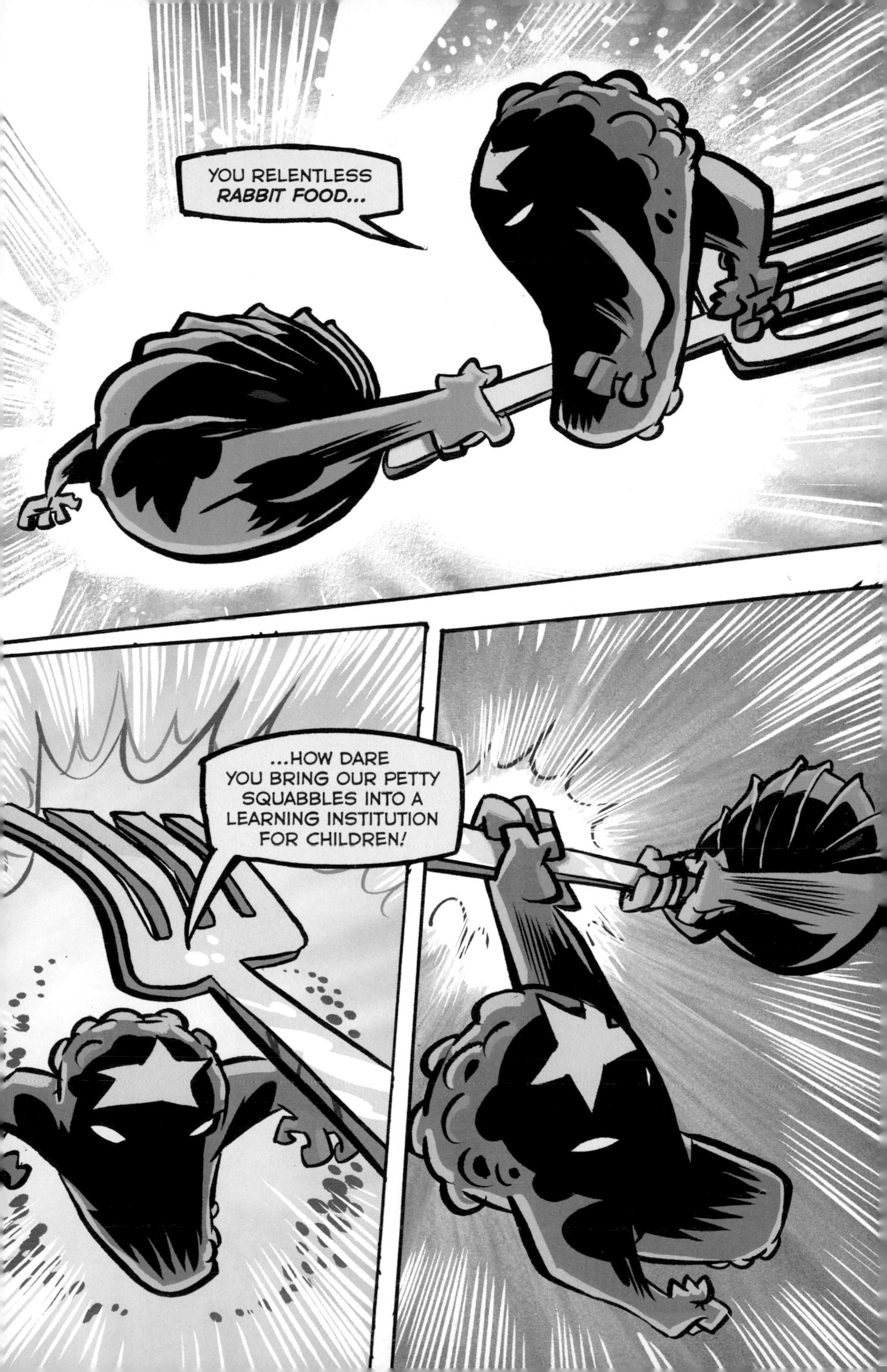
YOU RELENTLESS *RABBIT FOOD*...
...HOW DARE YOU BRING OUR PETTY SQUABBLES INTO A LEARNING INSTITUTION FOR CHILDREN!

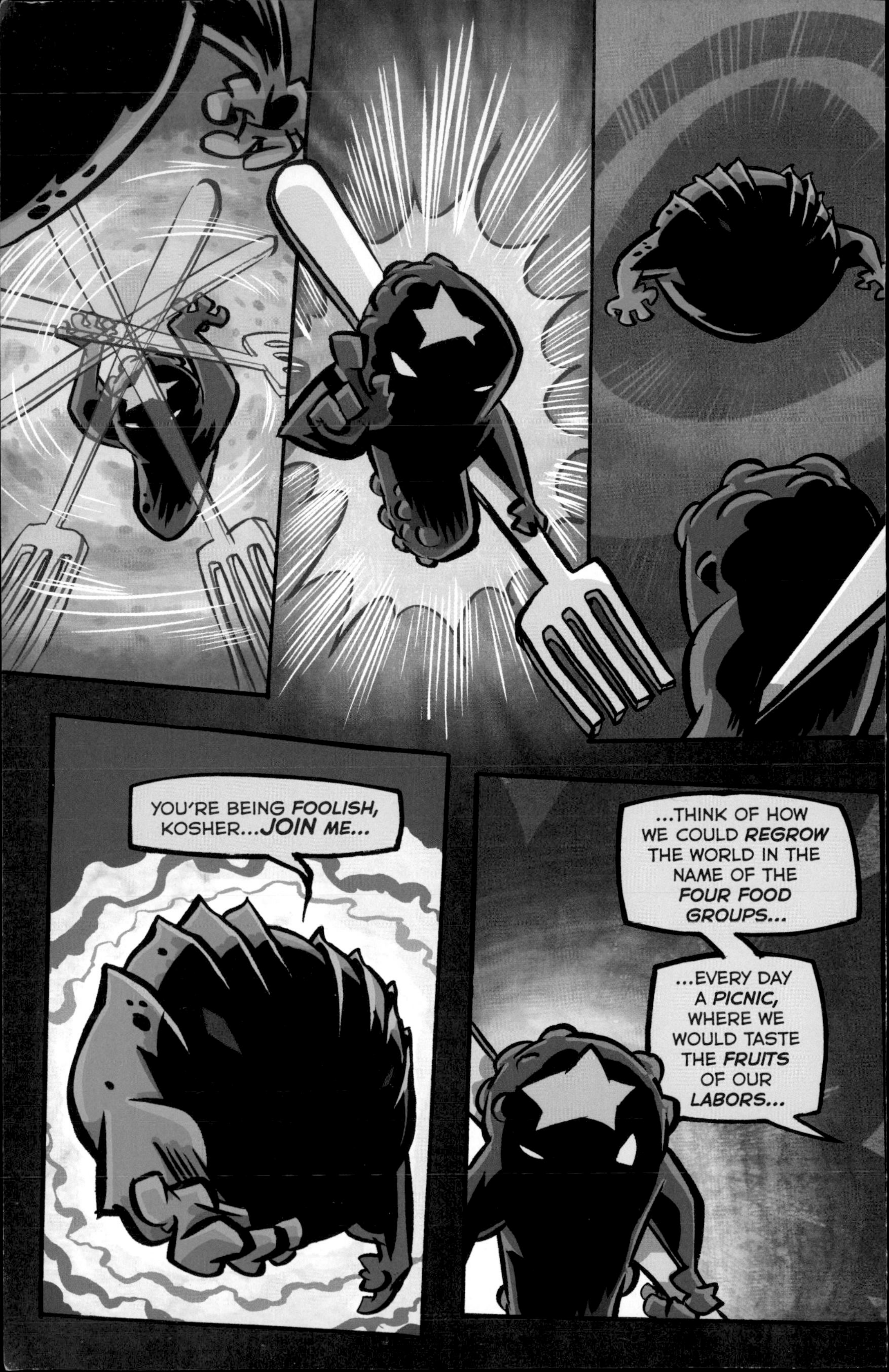
YOU'RE BEING FOOLISH, KOSHER...JOIN ME...
...THINK OF HOW WE COULD REGROW THE WORLD IN THE NAME OF THE FOUR FOOD GROUPS...
...EVERY DAY A PICNIC, WHERE WE WOULD TASTE THE FRUITS OF OUR LABORS...

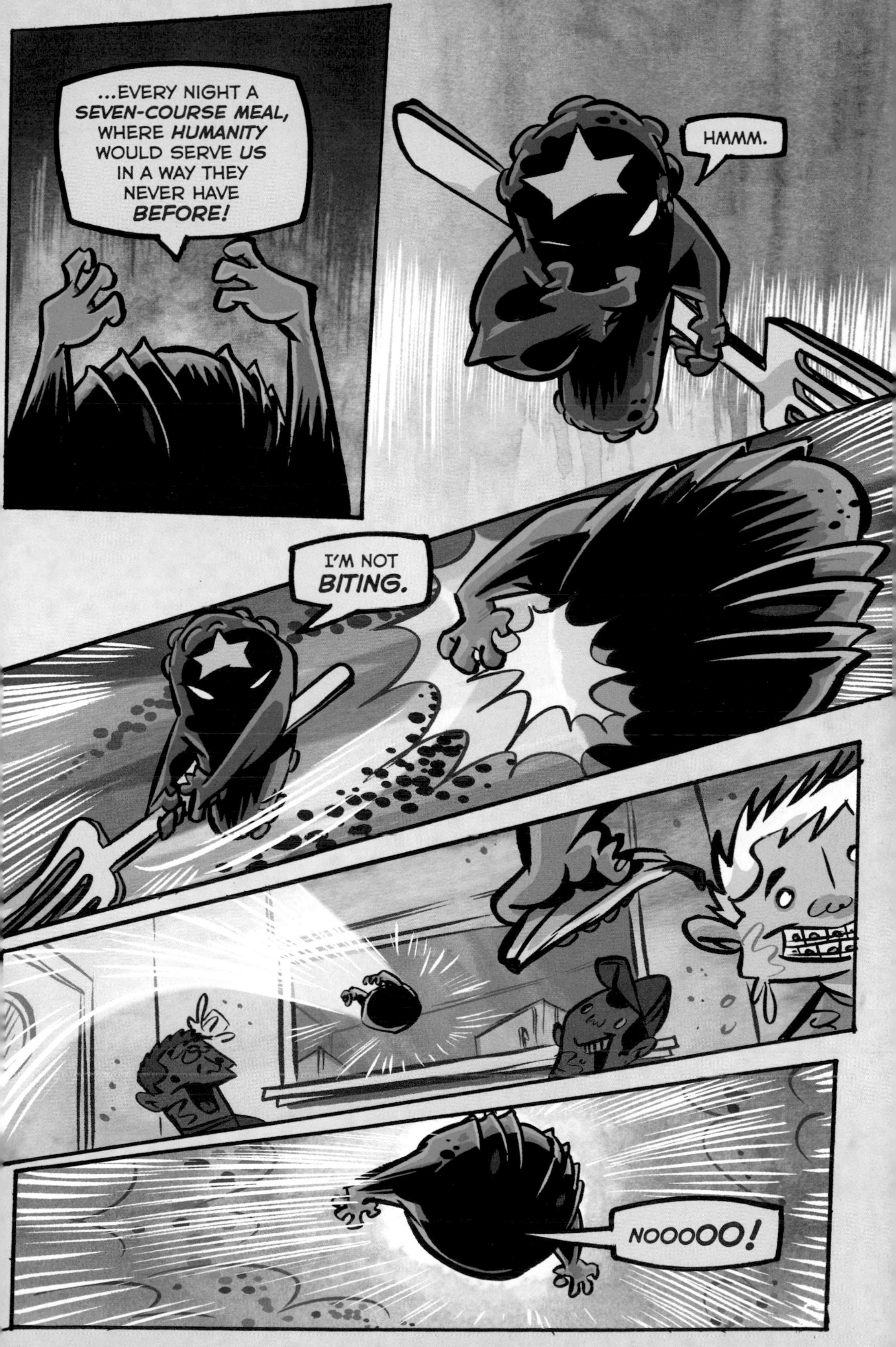
...EVERY NIGHT A SEVEN-COURSE MEAL, WHERE HUMANITY WOULD SERVE US IN A WAY THEY NEVER HAVE BEFORE!
HMMM.
I'M NOT BITING.
NOOOOO!

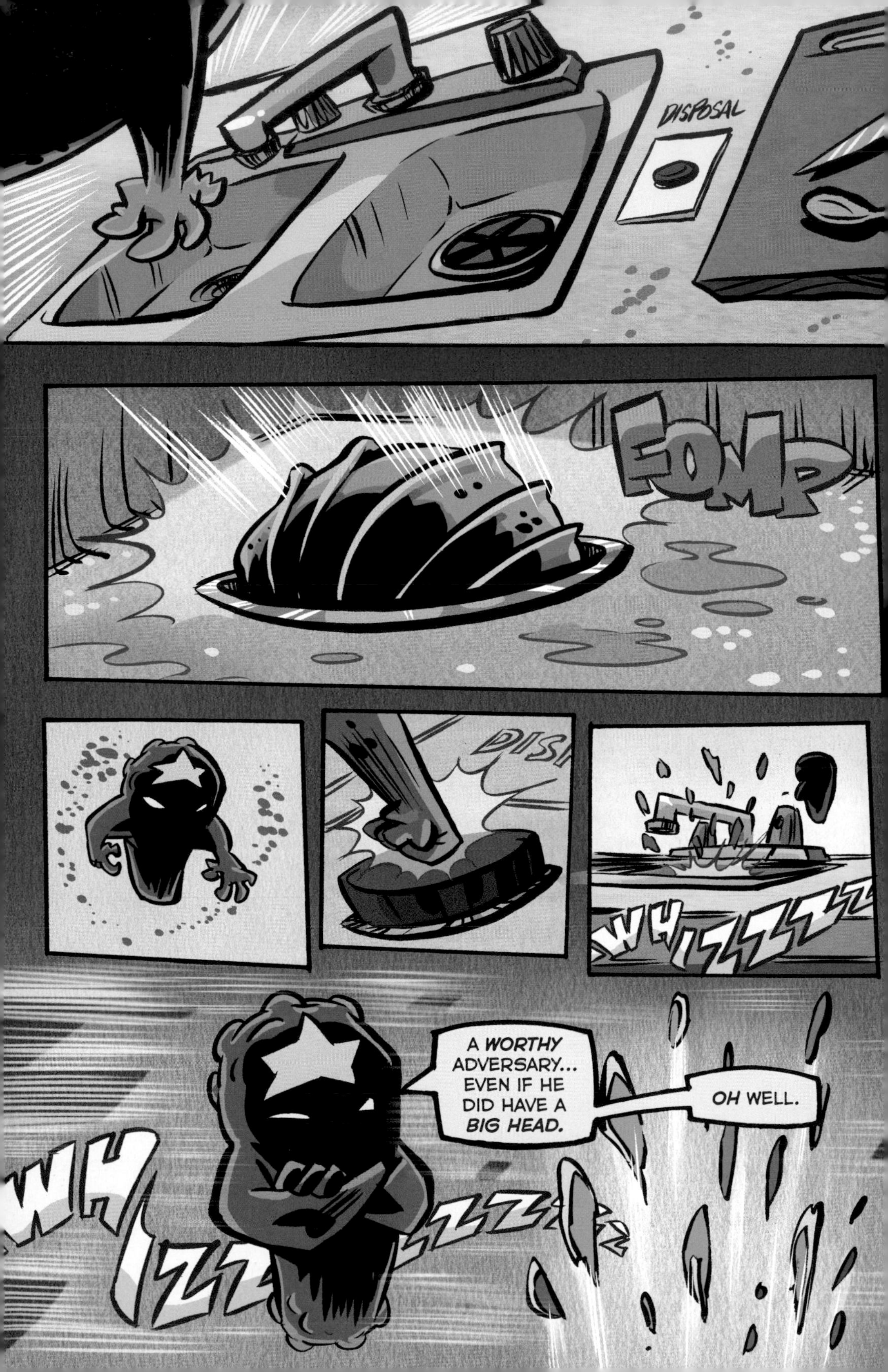
DISPOSAL
EOMP
DISP
WHIZZZZZ
A WORTHY ADVERSARY... EVEN IF HE DID HAVE A BIG HEAD.
OH WELL.
WHIZZZZZZZ

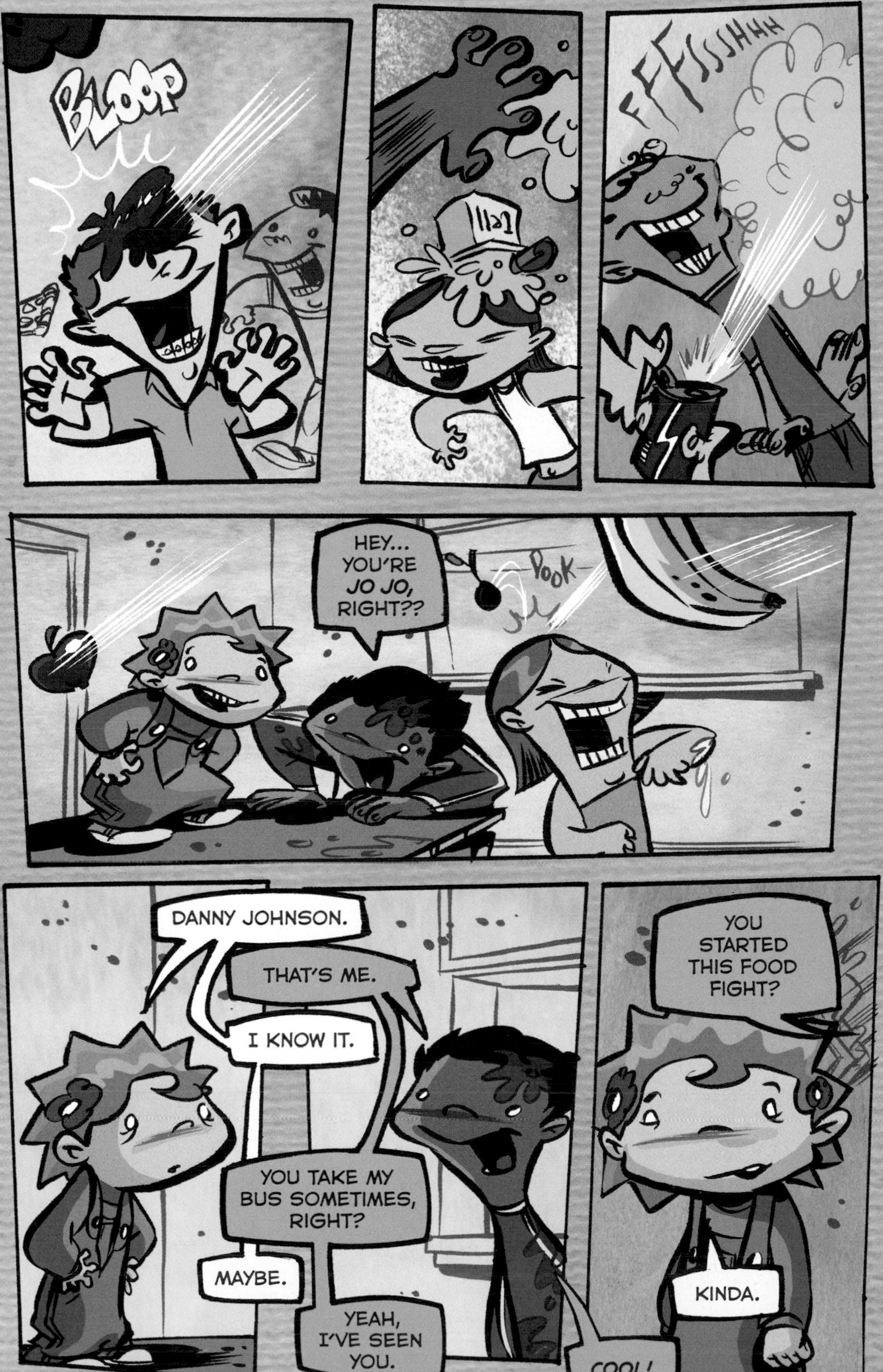
BLOOP
FFFSSSHHH
HEY... YOU'RE JO JO, RIGHT??
POOK
DANNY JOHNSON.
THAT'S ME.
I KNOW IT.
YOU TAKE MY BUS SOMETIMES, RIGHT?
MAYBE.
YEAH, I'VE SEEN YOU.
COOL!
YOU STARTED THIS FOOD FIGHT?
KINDA.

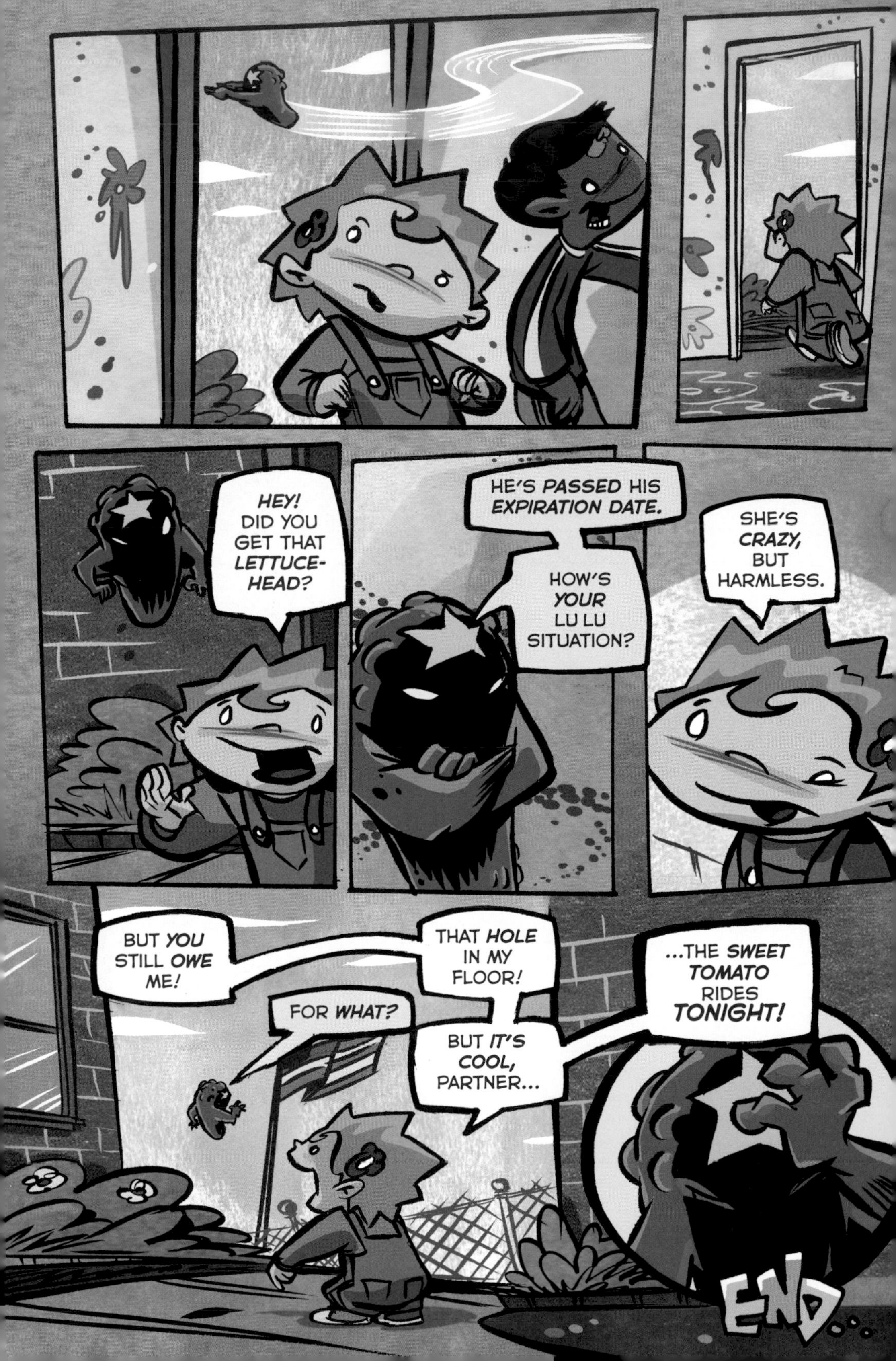
HEY! DID YOU GET THAT LETTUCE-HEAD?
HE'S PASSED HIS EXPIRATION DATE.
HOW'S YOUR LU LU SITUATION?
SHE'S CRAZY, BUT HARMLESS.
BUT YOU STILL OWE ME!
FOR WHAT?
THAT HOLE IN MY FLOOR!
BUT IT'S COOL, PARTNER...
...THE SWEET TOMATO RIDES TONIGHT!
END...

MAGIC PICKLE & THE LOCONUT IN NUTTIN' BUT CRAZY*

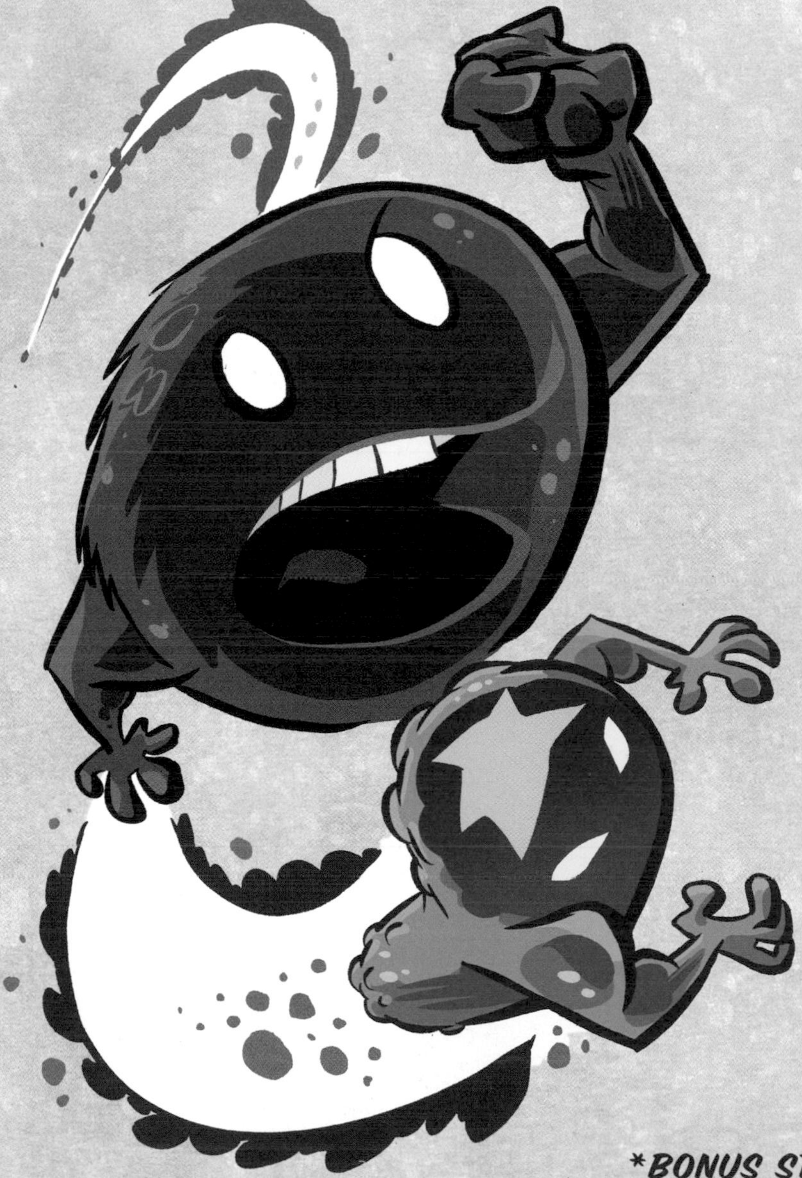

*BONUS STORY

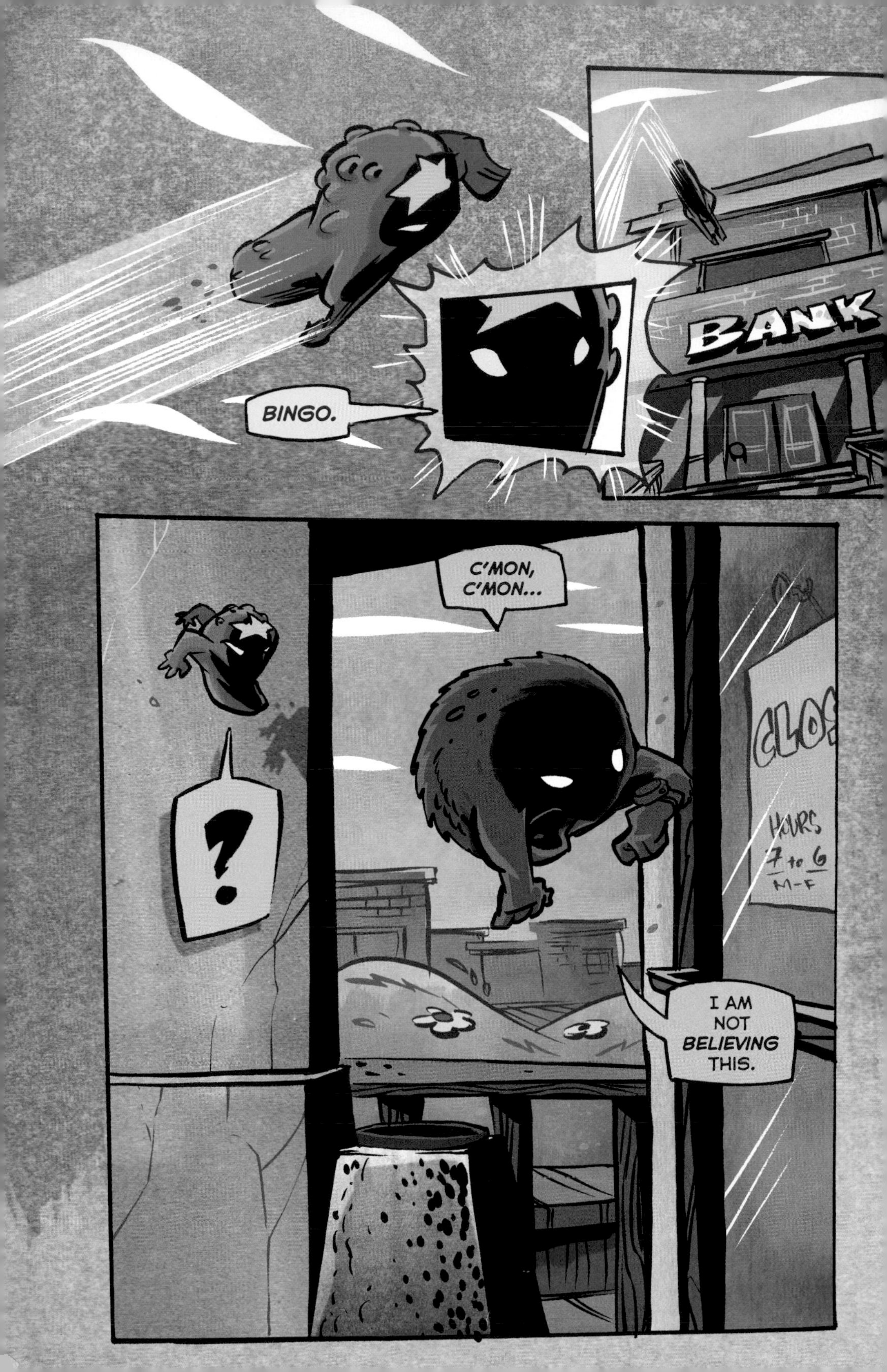
BANK
BINGO.
C'MON, C'MON...
?
CLOS
HOURS 7 to 6 M-F
I AM NOT *BELIEVING* THIS.

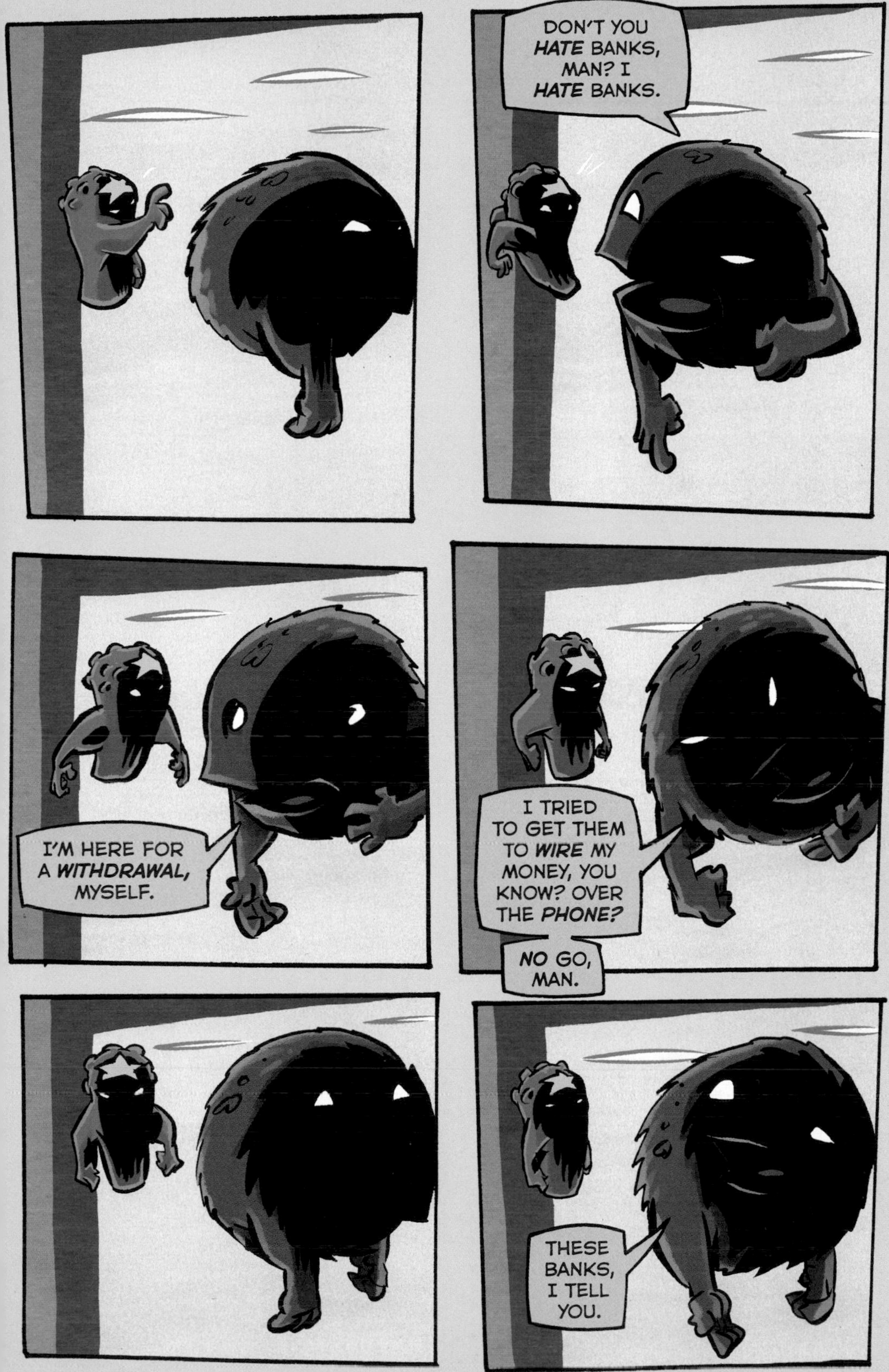

DON'T YOU *HATE* BANKS, MAN? I *HATE* BANKS.
I'M HERE FOR A *WITHDRAWAL,* MYSELF.
I TRIED TO GET THEM TO *WIRE* MY MONEY, YOU KNOW? OVER THE *PHONE?*
NO GO, MAN.
THESE BANKS, I TELL YOU.

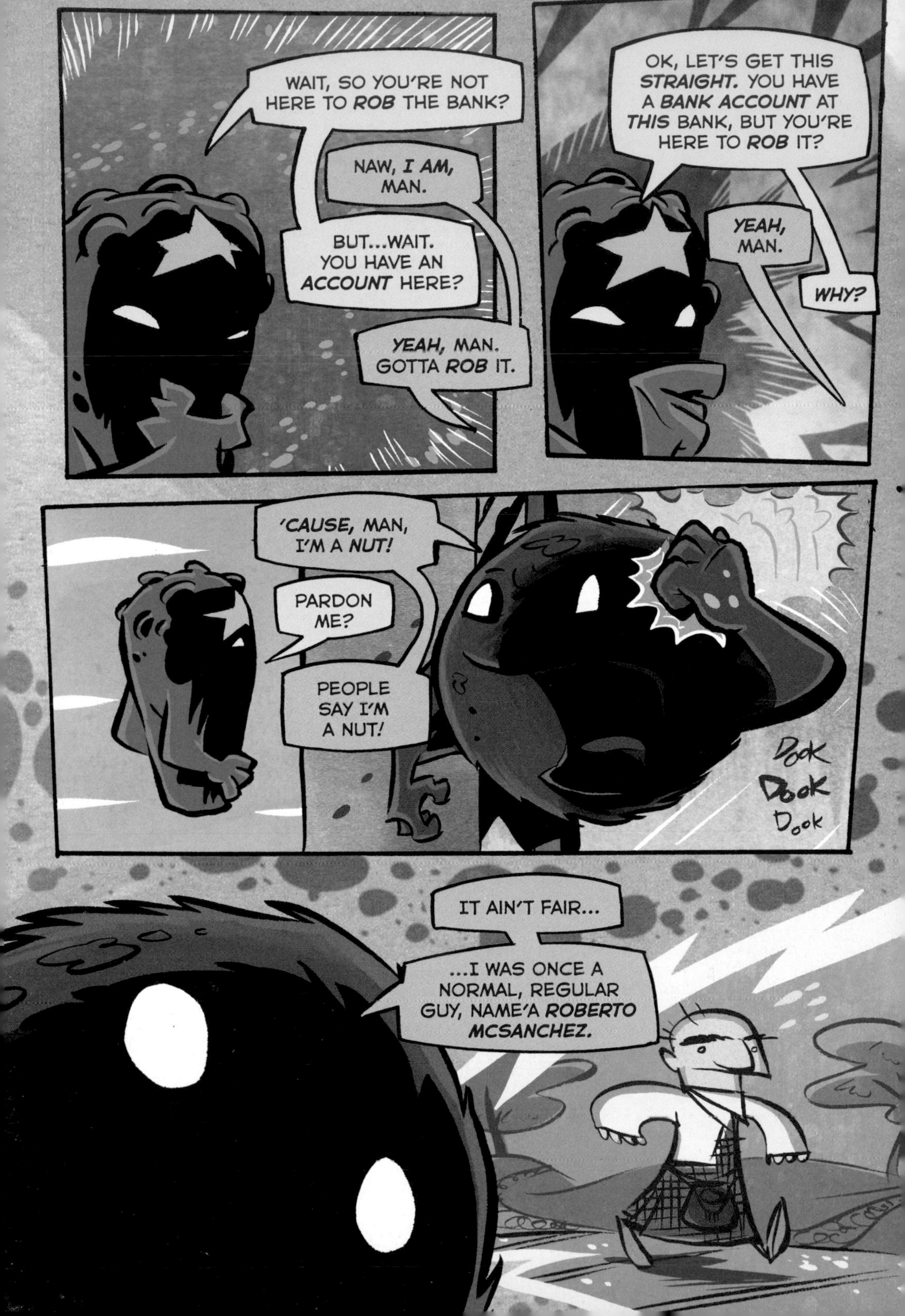
WAIT, SO YOU'RE NOT HERE TO ROB THE BANK?
NAW, I AM, MAN.
BUT...WAIT. YOU HAVE AN ACCOUNT HERE?
YEAH, MAN. GOTTA ROB IT.
OK, LET'S GET THIS STRAIGHT. YOU HAVE A BANK ACCOUNT AT THIS BANK, BUT YOU'RE HERE TO ROB IT?
YEAH, MAN.
WHY?
'CAUSE, MAN, I'M A NUT!
PARDON ME?
PEOPLE SAY I'M A NUT!
DOOK DOOK DOOK
IT AIN'T FAIR...
...I WAS ONCE A NORMAL, REGULAR GUY, NAME'A ROBERTO MCSANCHEZ.

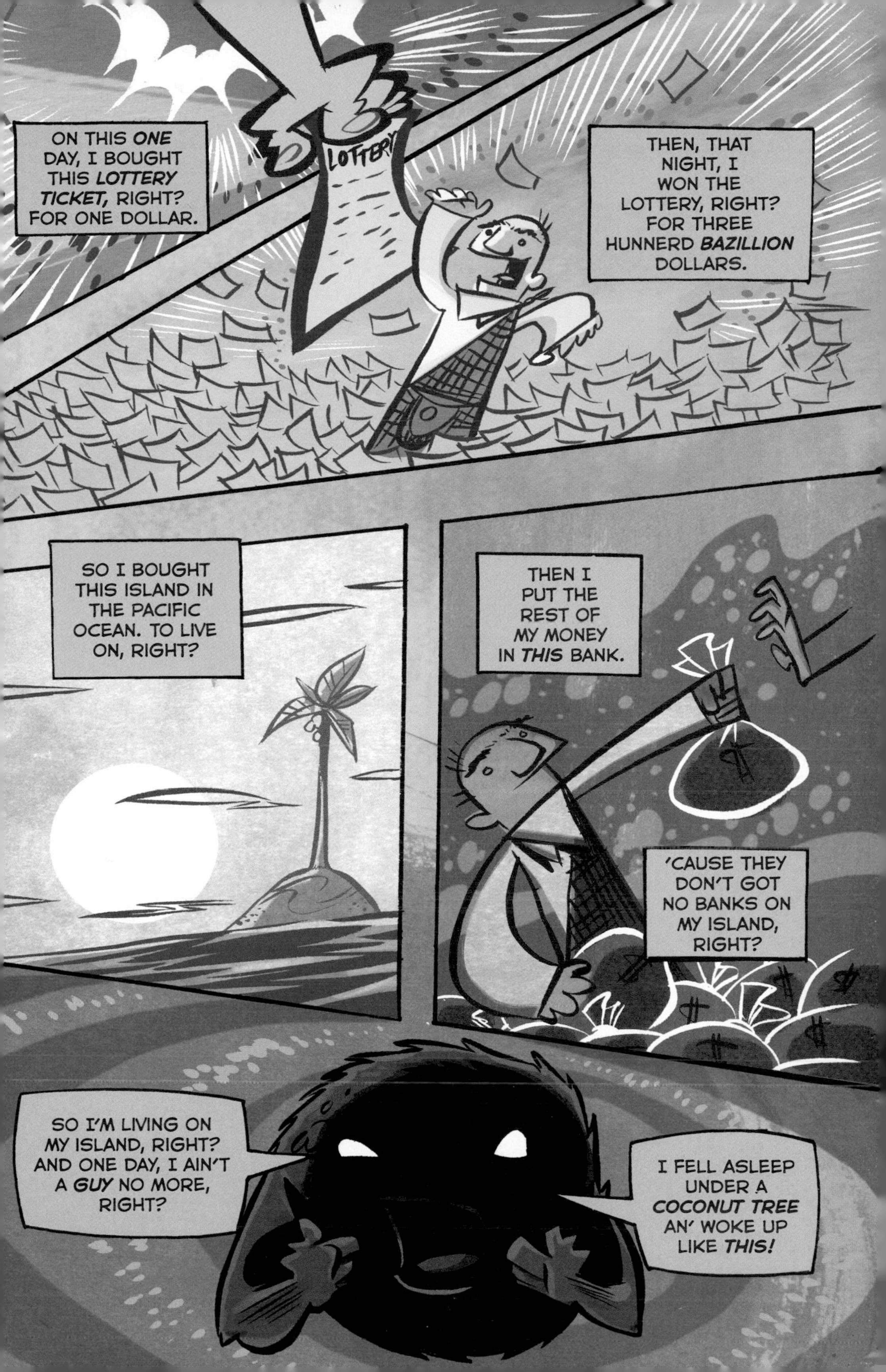
ON THIS ONE DAY, I BOUGHT THIS LOTTERY TICKET, RIGHT? FOR ONE DOLLAR.
LOTTERY
THEN, THAT NIGHT, I WON THE LOTTERY, RIGHT? FOR THREE HUNNERD BAZILLION DOLLARS.
SO I BOUGHT THIS ISLAND IN THE PACIFIC OCEAN. TO LIVE ON, RIGHT?
THEN I PUT THE REST OF MY MONEY IN THIS BANK.
'CAUSE THEY DON'T GOT NO BANKS ON MY ISLAND, RIGHT?
SO I'M LIVING ON MY ISLAND, RIGHT? AND ONE DAY, I AIN'T A GUY NO MORE, RIGHT?
I FELL ASLEEP UNDER A COCONUT TREE AN' WOKE UP LIKE THIS!

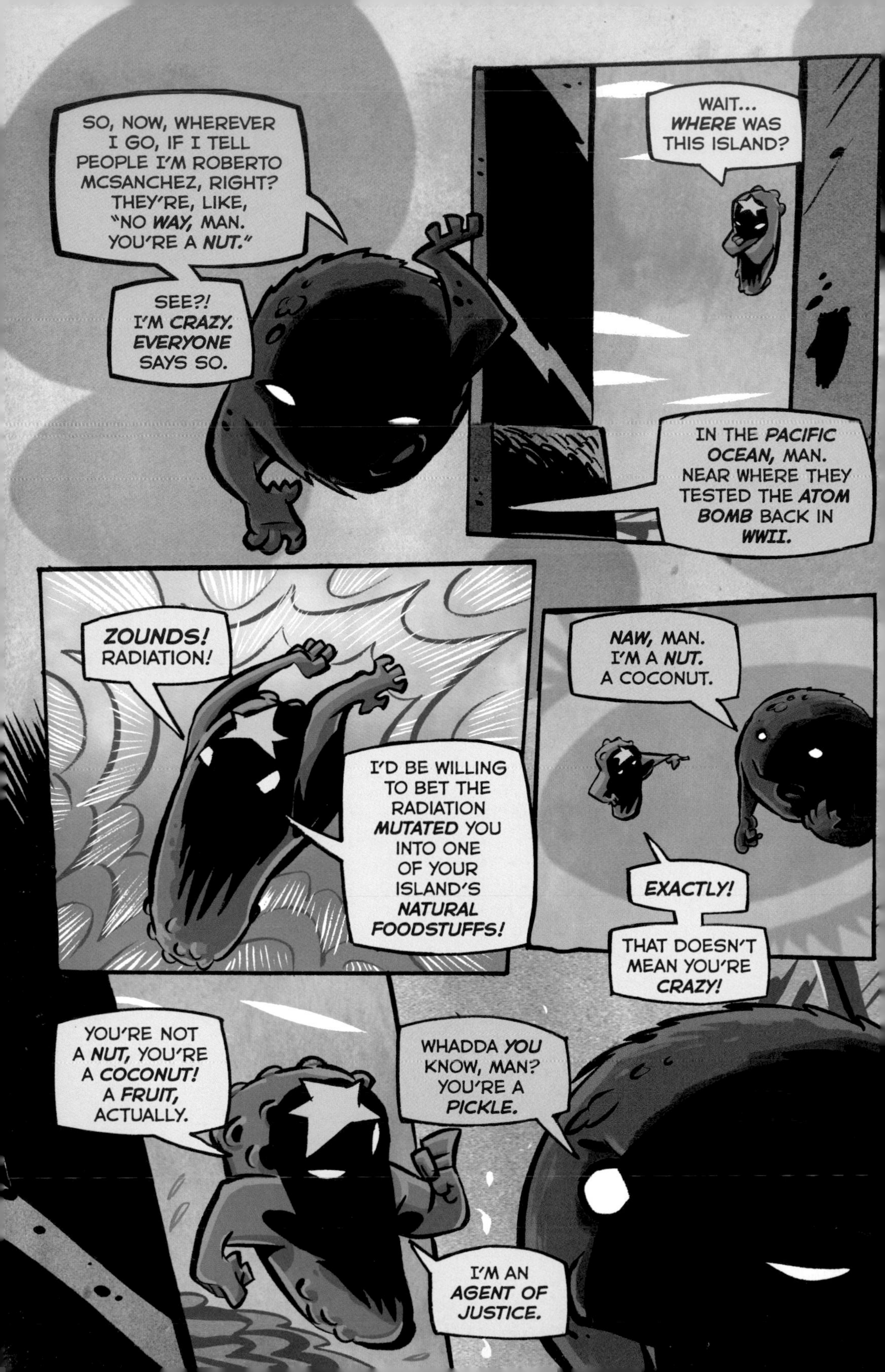

SO, NOW, WHEREVER I GO, IF I TELL PEOPLE I'M ROBERTO MCSANCHEZ, RIGHT? THEY'RE, LIKE, "NO *WAY,* MAN. YOU'RE A *NUT.*"
SEE?! I'M *CRAZY. EVERYONE* SAYS SO.
WAIT... *WHERE* WAS THIS ISLAND?
IN THE *PACIFIC OCEAN,* MAN. NEAR WHERE THEY TESTED THE *ATOM BOMB* BACK IN *WWII.*
ZOUNDS! RADIATION!
I'D BE WILLING TO BET THE RADIATION *MUTATED* YOU INTO ONE OF YOUR ISLAND'S *NATURAL FOODSTUFFS!*
NAW, MAN. I'M A *NUT.* A COCONUT.
EXACTLY!
THAT DOESN'T MEAN YOU'RE *CRAZY!*
YOU'RE NOT A *NUT,* YOU'RE A *COCONUT!* A *FRUIT,* ACTUALLY.
WHADDA *YOU* KNOW, MAN? YOU'RE A *PICKLE.*
I'M AN *AGENT OF JUSTICE.*

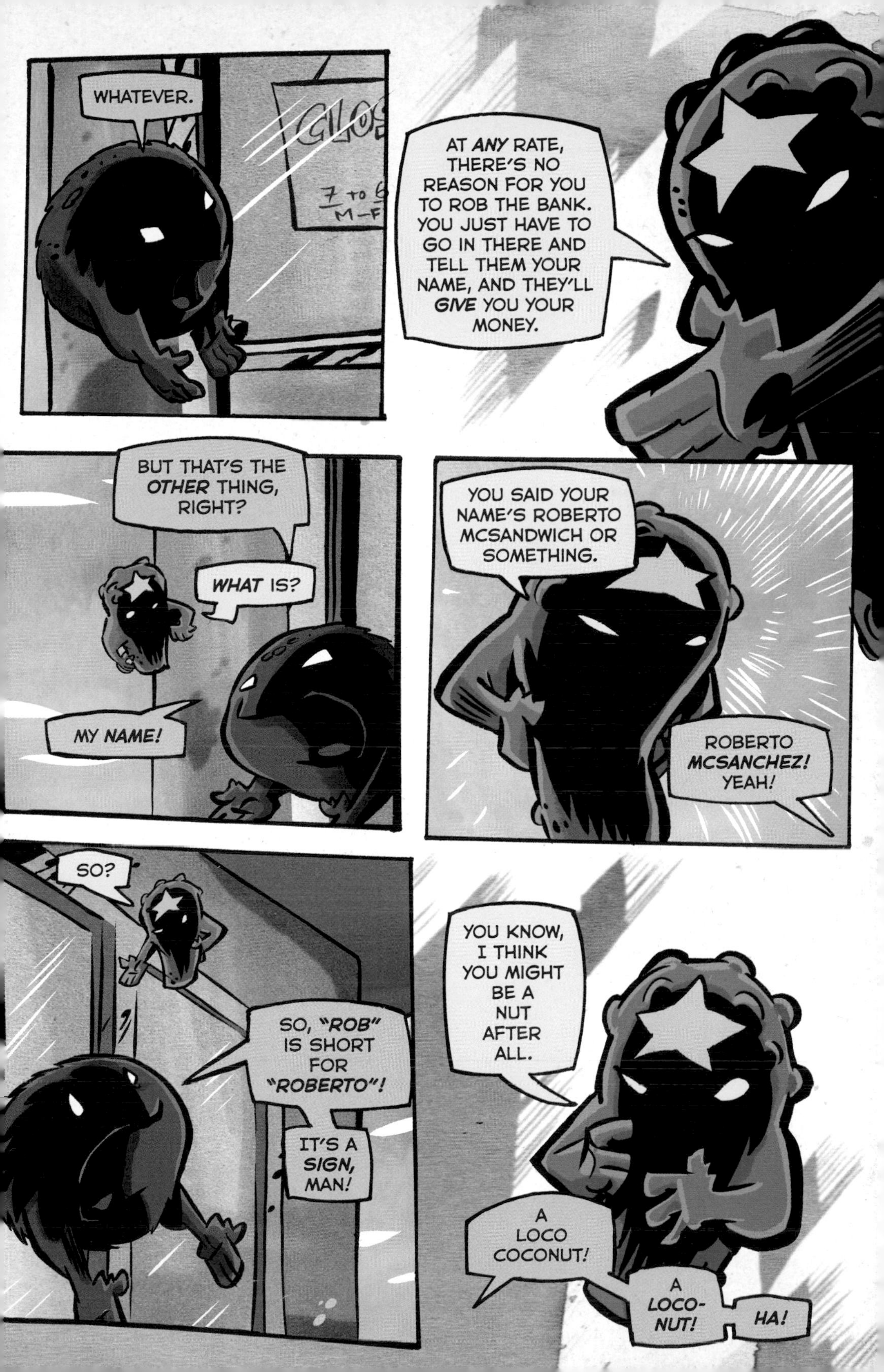
WHATEVER.
AT ANY RATE, THERE'S NO REASON FOR YOU TO ROB THE BANK. YOU JUST HAVE TO GO IN THERE AND TELL THEM YOUR NAME, AND THEY'LL GIVE YOU YOUR MONEY.
BUT THAT'S THE OTHER THING, RIGHT?
WHAT IS?
MY NAME!
YOU SAID YOUR NAME'S ROBERTO MCSANDWICH OR SOMETHING.
ROBERTO MCSANCHEZ! YEAH!
SO?
SO, "ROB" IS SHORT FOR "ROBERTO"!
IT'S A SIGN, MAN!
YOU KNOW, I THINK YOU MIGHT BE A NUT AFTER ALL.
A LOCO COCONUT!
A LOCO-NUT!
HA!

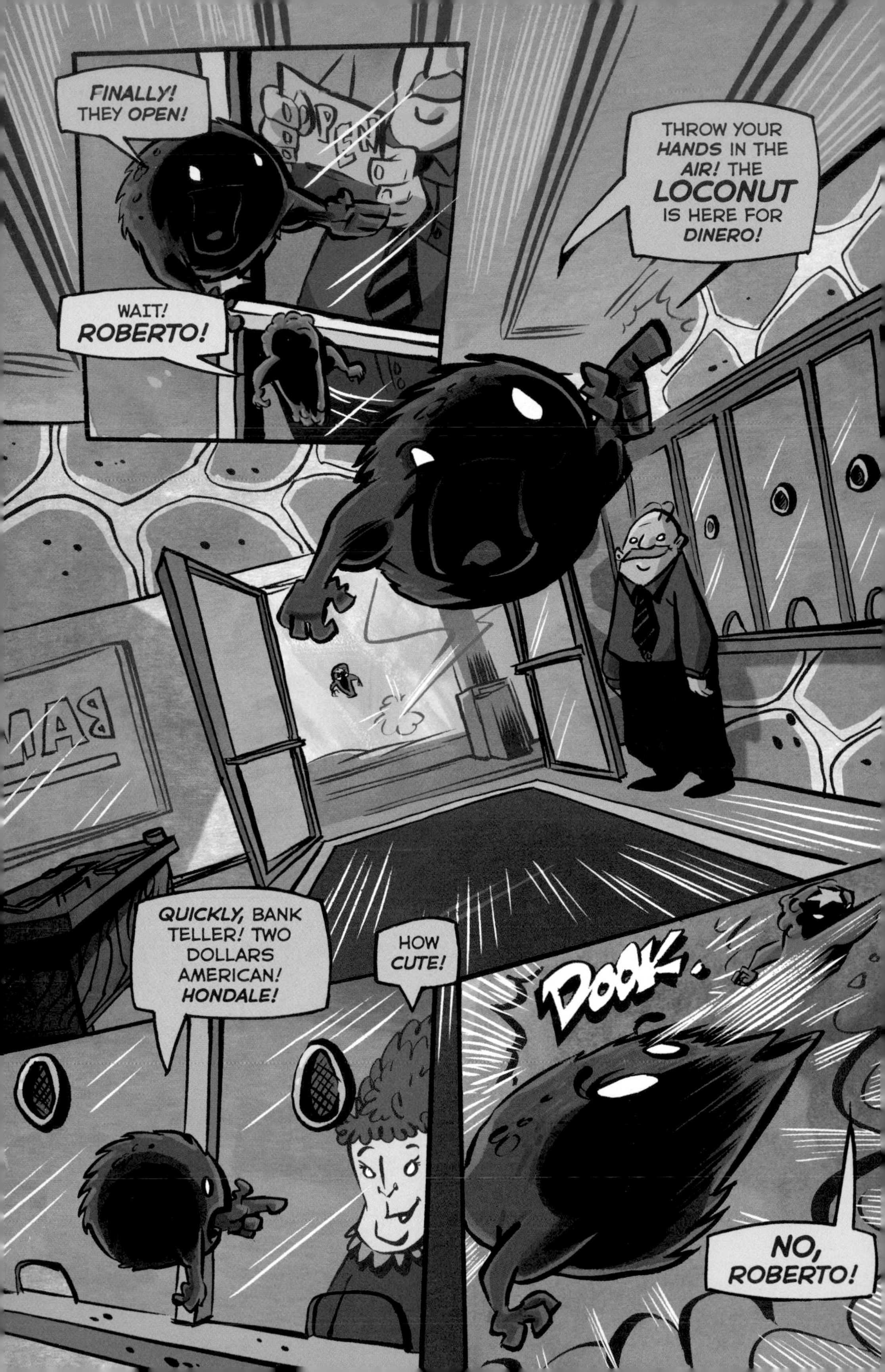

FINALLY! THEY OPEN!
OPEN
WAIT! ROBERTO!
THROW YOUR HANDS IN THE AIR! THE LOCONUT IS HERE FOR DINERO!
QUICKLY, BANK TELLER! TWO DOLLARS AMERICAN! HONDALE!
HOW CUTE!
DOOK.
NO, ROBERTO!

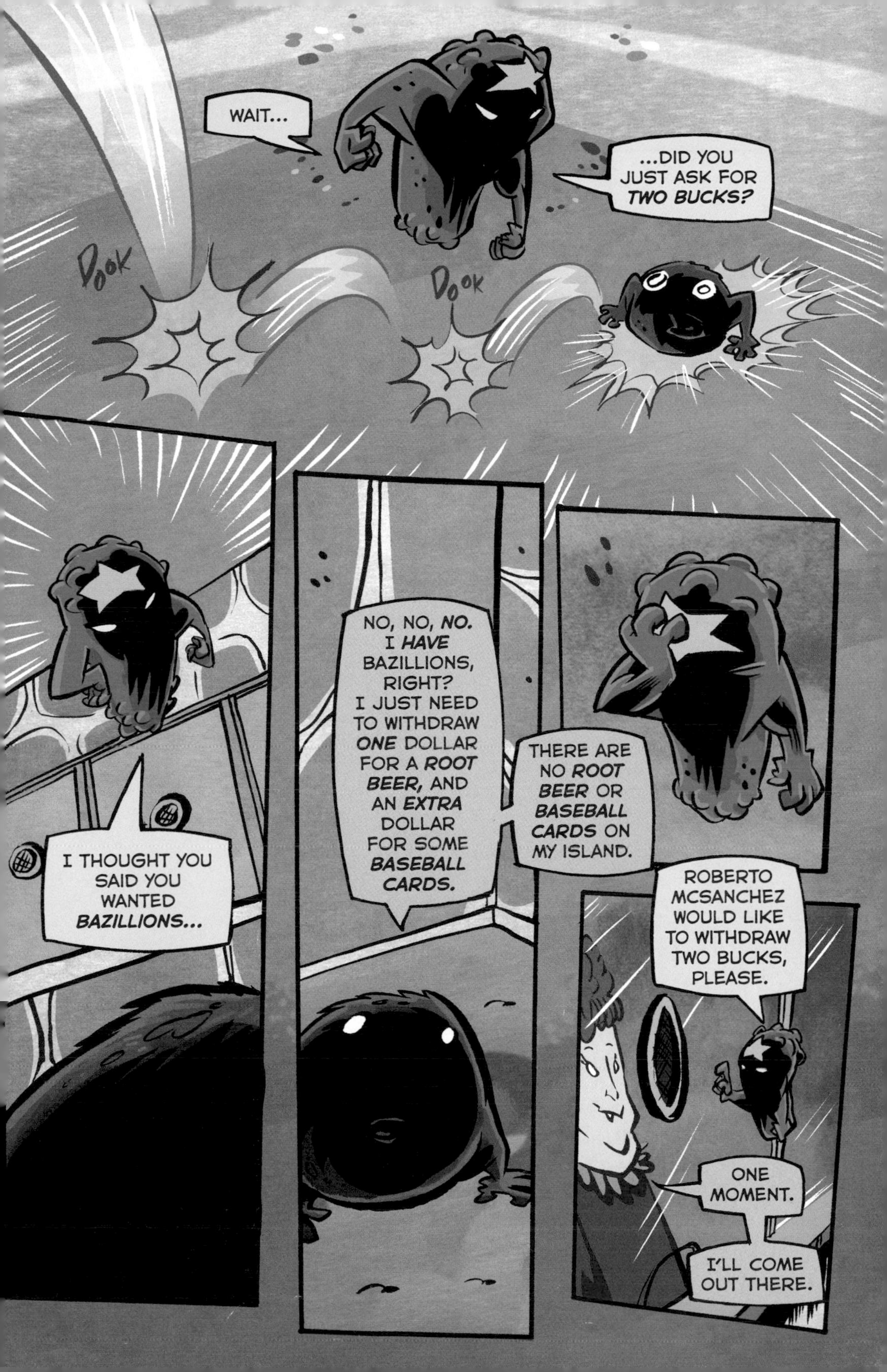
WAIT...
...DID YOU JUST ASK FOR *TWO BUCKS?*
DOOK
DOOK
I THOUGHT YOU SAID YOU WANTED *BAZILLIONS...*
NO, NO, *NO.* I *HAVE* BAZILLIONS, RIGHT? I JUST NEED TO WITHDRAW *ONE* DOLLAR FOR A *ROOT BEER,* AND AN *EXTRA* DOLLAR FOR SOME *BASEBALL CARDS.*
THERE ARE NO *ROOT BEER* OR *BASEBALL CARDS* ON MY ISLAND.
ROBERTO MCSANCHEZ WOULD LIKE TO WITHDRAW TWO BUCKS, PLEASE.
ONE MOMENT.
I'LL COME OUT THERE.

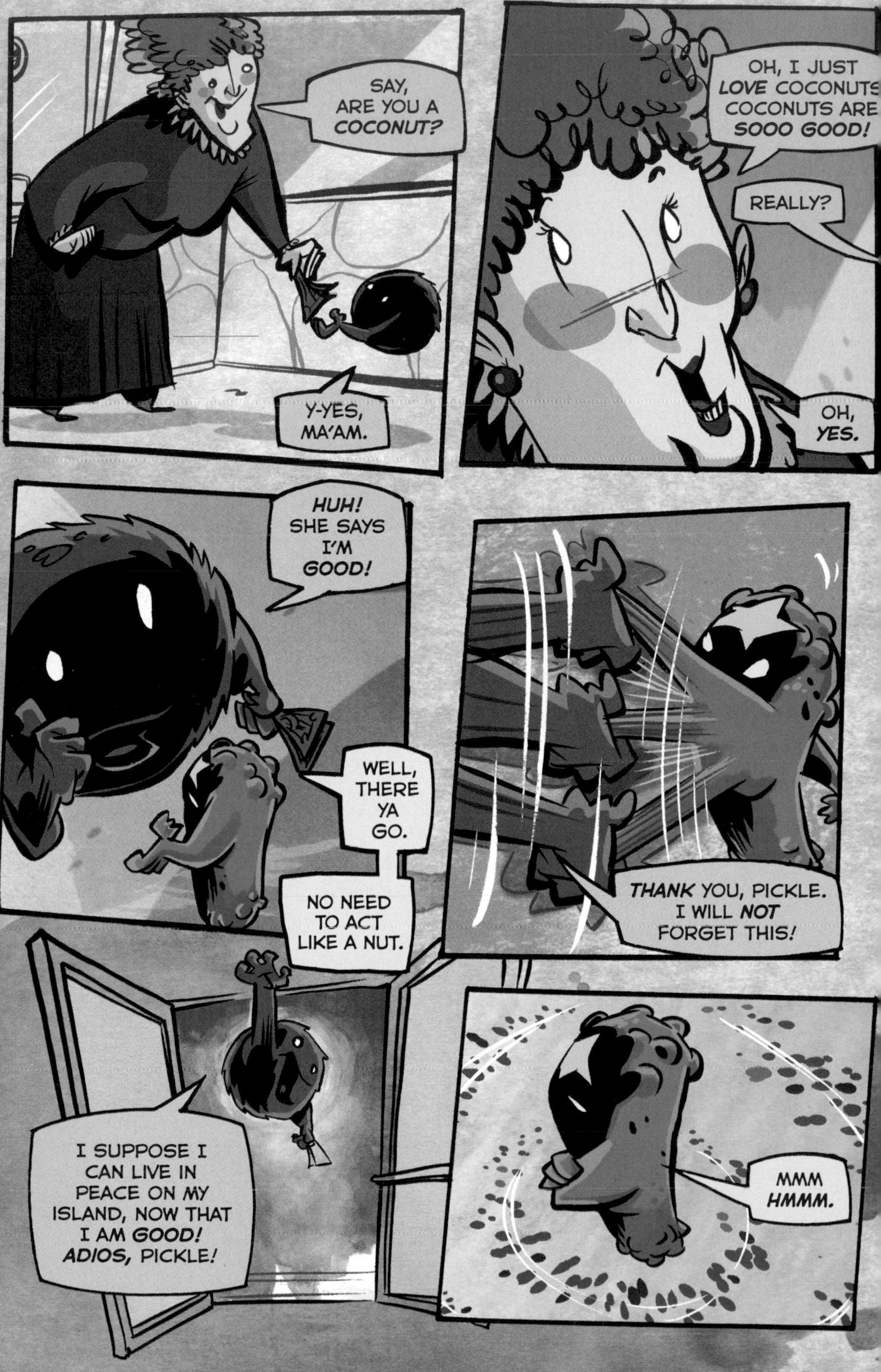
SAY, ARE YOU A *COCONUT?*
Y-YES, MA'AM.
OH, I JUST *LOVE* COCONUTS COCONUTS ARE *SOOO GOOD!*
REALLY?
OH, *YES.*
HUH! SHE SAYS I'M *GOOD!*
WELL, THERE YA GO.
NO NEED TO ACT LIKE A NUT.
THANK YOU, PICKLE. I WILL *NOT* FORGET THIS!
I SUPPOSE I CAN LIVE IN PEACE ON MY ISLAND, NOW THAT I AM *GOOD!* *ADIOS,* PICKLE!
MMM *HMMM.*

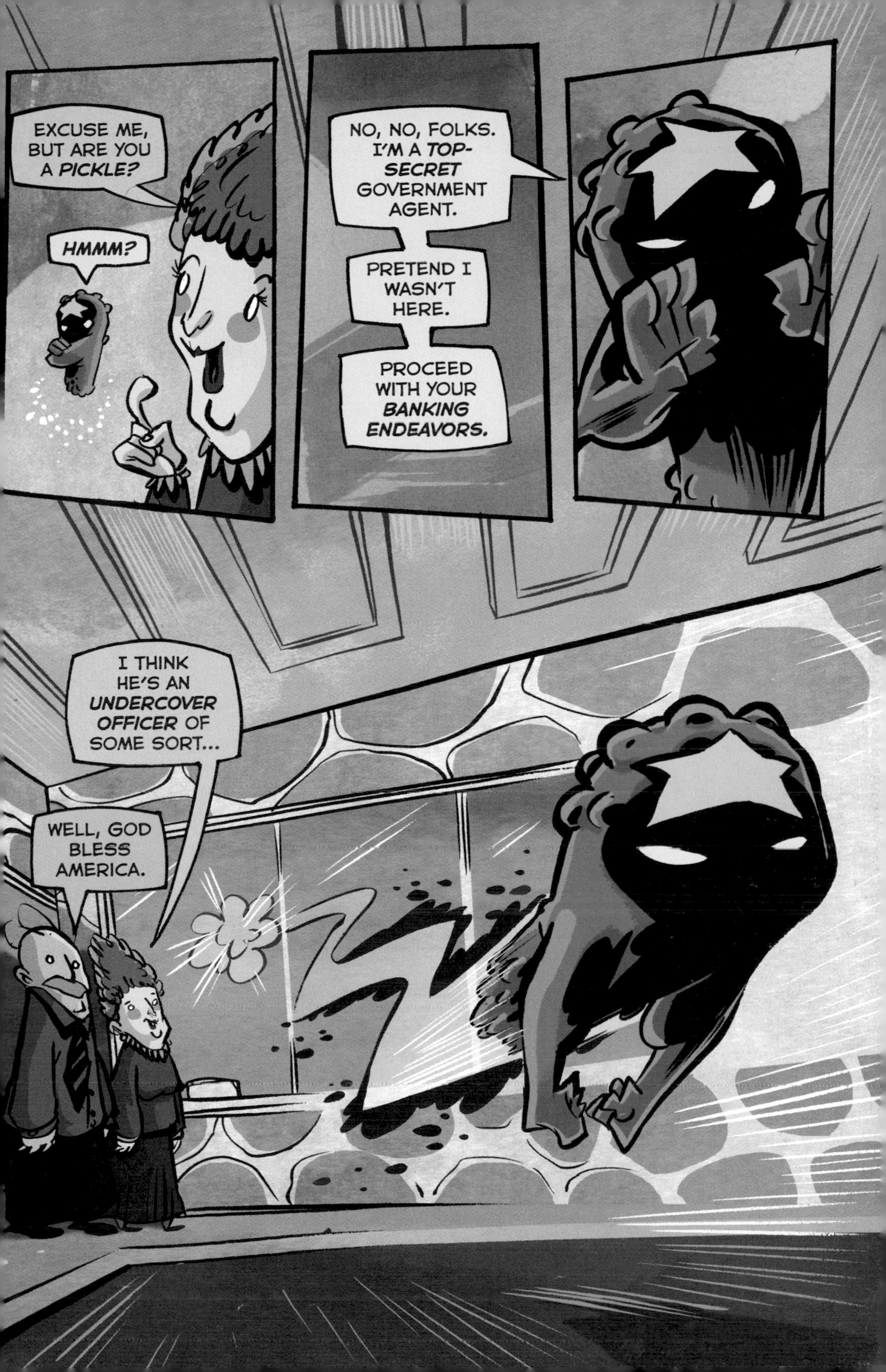
EXCUSE ME, BUT ARE YOU A *PICKLE?*
HMMM?
NO, NO, FOLKS. I'M A *TOP-SECRET* GOVERNMENT AGENT.
PRETEND I WASN'T HERE.
PROCEED WITH YOUR *BANKING ENDEAVORS.*
I THINK HE'S AN *UNDERCOVER OFFICER* OF SOME SORT...
WELL, GOD BLESS AMERICA.

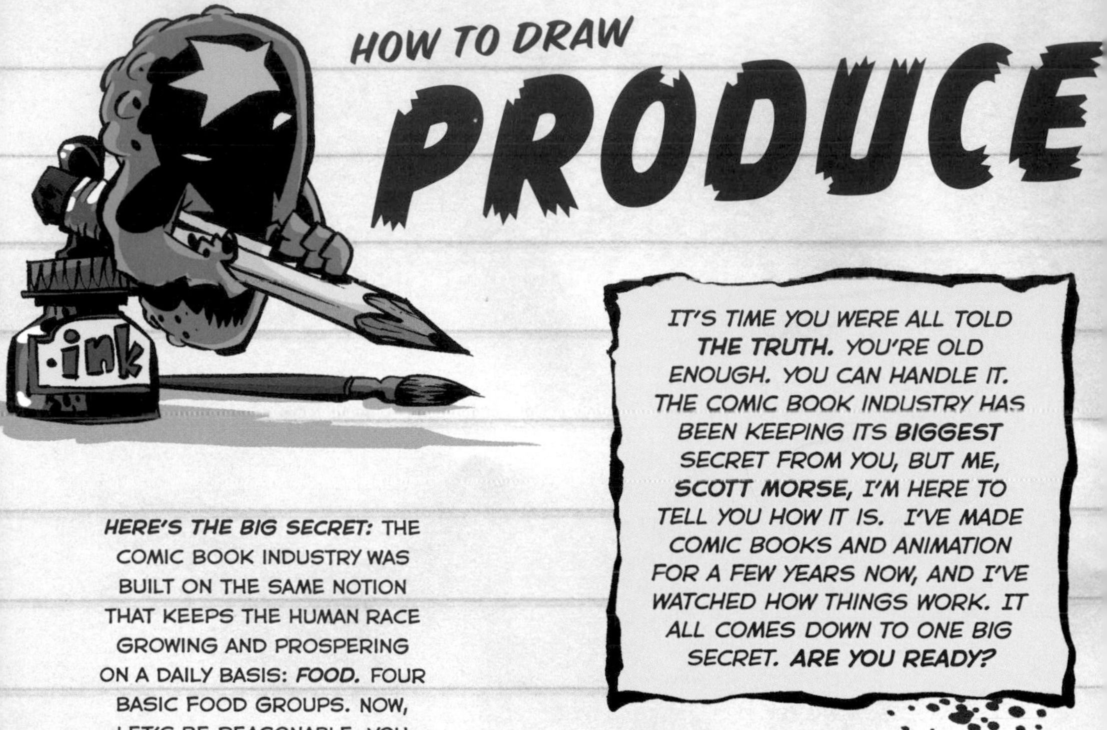
ink

HOW TO DRAW PRODUCE

IT'S TIME YOU WERE ALL TOLD ***THE TRUTH.*** *YOU'RE OLD ENOUGH. YOU CAN HANDLE IT. THE COMIC BOOK INDUSTRY HAS BEEN KEEPING ITS* ***BIGGEST*** *SECRET FROM YOU, BUT ME,* ***SCOTT MORSE,*** *I'M HERE TO TELL YOU HOW IT IS. I'VE MADE COMIC BOOKS AND ANIMATION FOR A FEW YEARS NOW, AND I'VE WATCHED HOW THINGS WORK. IT ALL COMES DOWN TO ONE BIG SECRET.* ***ARE YOU READY?***

HERE'S THE BIG SECRET: THE COMIC BOOK INDUSTRY WAS BUILT ON THE SAME NOTION THAT KEEPS THE HUMAN RACE GROWING AND PROSPERING ON A DAILY BASIS: ***FOOD.*** FOUR BASIC FOOD GROUPS. NOW, LET'S BE REASONABLE. YOU CAN'T ***FEED*** A COMIC BOOK, SILLY, SO STOP THINKING THAT'S WHERE THIS IS GOING. THE SECRET IS ***MUCH*** TASTIER.

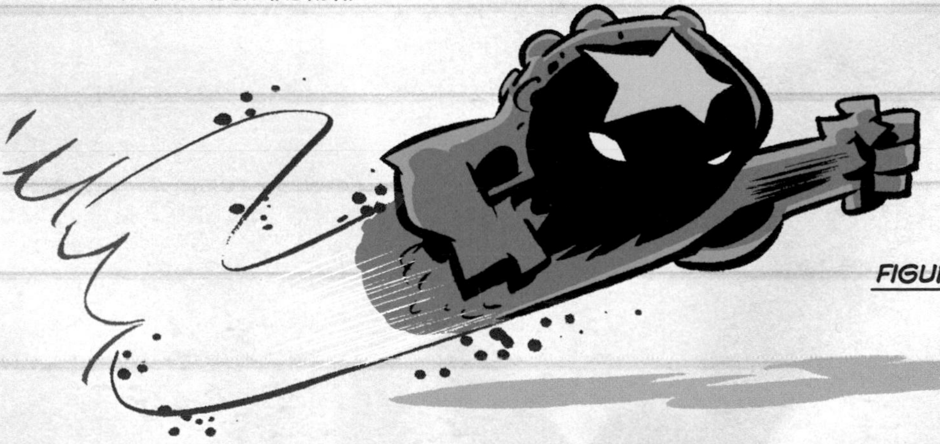

FIGURE A

IF YOU'LL KINDLY REFER TO ***FIGURE A,*** YOU'LL NOTICE WHAT'S BEEN IN FRONT OF YOU SINCE THE BEGINNING, SINCE THE VERY FIRST COMIC BOOK CHARACTER WAS CREATED. ***ALL*** SUPERPOWERED HEROES ARE BASED ON FRUITS AND VEGETABLES. THERE HAVE BEEN FAKES AND IMITATORS, HEROES BASED ON BREADS, OR CEREALS, OR EVEN MEATS, BUT WE ALL KNOW THAT'S JUST ***CRAZY TALK.***

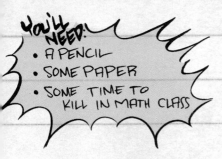

YOU'LL NEED:
- A PENCIL
- SOME PAPER
- SOME TIME TO KILL IN MATH CLASS

FIGURE A
PART 2

HERO

LETTUCE.

ROASTED BELL PEPPER.

WINDSWEPT SIDEKICK

JUST LOOK AT *FIGURE A, PART 2*...A TRUE HERO, *JO JO WIGMAN!* AND RIGHT BELOW HER, *ELLEN CRANSTON!* EVEN SIDEKICKS FOLLOW THE FRUITS AND VEGETABLES FORMULA!

FIGURE B TAKES US ONE STEP CLOSER TO *REALLY* UNDERSTANDING THE SECRET. WHEN CREATING A NEW CHARACTER, YOU'VE GOT TO REALLY THINK ABOUT HOW THAT CHARACTER MIGHT ACT IN YOUR STORY. NOW, TO THE LEFT, OUR VERY OWN ARCHNEMESIS, *LU LU DEEDERLY*, IS VERY MUCH IN CHARACTER... *CORNY!* LOOKING CLOSELY, WE FIND HER VEGETABLE COUNTERPART LYING JUST BENEATH THE SURFACE OF HER DESIGN.

FIGURE B

CORNY VILLAIN

CORN.

REMEMBER: WHEN DESIGNING YOUR CHARACTERS, ALWAYS DRAW FROM LIFE, AS THE PROS SAY. USE A MODEL. THEY'RE REALLY EASY TO FIND! THE BEST REFERENCE IS ALWAYS HANGING AROUND THE FARMER'S MARKET, OR GETTING MISTED IN THE VEGETABLE SECTION OF THE GROCERY STORE. YOU CAN EVEN SPY SOME GOOD IDEAS RIGHT ON THE SUPERMARKET SHELVES (BUT CHECK THOSE EXPIRATION DATES!) STEER CLEAR OF THE FROZEN FOOD AISLE; IT'S JUST NOT AS FRESH AND HEALTHY.

NOW LET'S PRETEND WE'VE BEEN ASKED TO DESIGN A **NEW HERO**, A GOOD GUY, WHO GOT HIS POWERS AFTER ACCIDENTALLY FALLING OUT OF A LUNCH BAG AND INTO A BIG SCIENTIFIC EXPERIMENTAL MACHINE. HE BECOMES A SNAPPY, **FRESH** HERO, PACKING A TASTY **DILL PUNCH**. HMMM. A PICKLE MIGHT DO NICELY FOR REFERENCE: PICKLES ARE SWEET, AND **KOSHER**. THEY START LIFE AS CUCUMBERS, BUT ARE ALTERED SCIENTIFICALLY TO BECOME SOMETHING... MORE. THEY'RE **SNAPPY** WHEN YOU BITE INTO THEM, THEY'RE **FRESH** (IF YOU KEEP THEM IN THE FRIDGE), AND THEY PACK A REAL **PUNCH** TO YOUR TASTE BUDS.

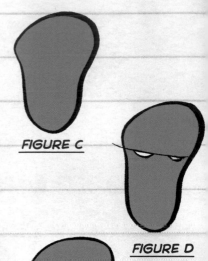

FIGURE C

FIGURE D

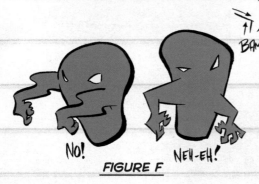

NO!

FIGURE F

NEH-EH!

BAM!

FIGURE E

BOIP

BOIP

BOIP

BOIP

FIGURE G

BOOMP!

FIGURE H

NOW, LET'S START DESIGNING THIS HERO. _FIGURE C_ DEMONSTRATES A GREAT SHAPE TO START WITH...ROUND, AERODYNAMIC, PERFECT FOR A HERO THAT'S PROBABLY GOING TO NEED TO FLY. A SQUASHY OVAL SHAPE IS PERFECT. _FIGURE D_ IS SIMPLE, BUT IT GIVES OUR HERO LIFE: A SIMPLE LINE, WHERE WE CAN HANG HIS EYES. _FIGURE E_ REMINDS US THAT MOST CRIME FIGHTERS NEED WEAPONS, SO A COUPLE OF FISTS (AND ARMS, OF COURSE) ARE NECESSARY. MAKE ANGLES USING STRAIGHT LINES, WITH A CURVED LINE AROUND THE OUTSIDE EDGE TO BALANCE THEM OUT. THE PROS CALL THIS "STRAIGHTS VS. CURVES," AN IMPORTANT DESIGN IDEA, PLUS IT SOUNDS COOL, LIKE A BOXING MATCH OR SOMETHING. _FIGURE F_ SHOWS WHY THIS IS IMPORTANT: TOO MANY "STRAIGHTS" OR TOO MANY "CURVES," AND YOUR HERO BECOMES A SILLY ZERO!

WE'VE STILL GOT TO REMEMBER THAT *"STORY COMES FIRST!"* ALWAYS THINK ABOUT HOW YOUR CHARACTER CAN VISUALLY ADD TO YOUR STORY. MAYBE HE'S HAD SOME ROUGH ADVENTURES AND GOT SOME LUMPS AND BUMPS, LIKE IN *FIGURE G.* COSTUMES ARE IMPORTANT, TOO, AND *FIGURE H* SHOWS US A BASIC YET IMPRESSIVE CLASSIC COSTUME IDEA THAT REPRESENTS GLORY AND FAME. A WELL-PLACED STAR IS *PERFECT!*

FIGURE I

FIGURE I IS A REALLY NEAT TRICK THE PROS USE. IT'S CALLED "DRAMATIC LIGHTING." PRETEND OUR HERO IS SO DARN COOL (AND HE *IS,* YOU DON'T REALLY HAVE TO PRETEND) THAT HE'S CONSTANTLY GOT A BRIGHT LIGHT BEHIND HIM, LIKE HE'S RIDING OUT OF THE SUN ITSELF. THAT MEANS HE'S ALWAYS GOT SHADOWS ON THE FRONT, AND THIS IS *GREAT!* IT HELPS HIDE HIS MOUTH AND HIS NOSE, WHICH MIGHT GIVE AWAY HIS REAL IDENTITY. WE CAN'T HAVE THAT! PLUS IT MAKES HIM LOOK *TOUGH.* I WOULDN'T MESS WITH HIM IF I WERE A TWISTED, EVIL PIECE OF FOOD - WOULD YOU?

GULP.

NOW LET'S SEE WHAT OUR HERO CAN DO! *FIGURE J* SHOWS US SOME NEAT WAYS TO "SEE" HIS POWERS. YOU'VE GOT SQUIGGLY LINES AROUND HIS HEAD SHOWING HOW INTENSE HE IS, PLUS LOTS OF POWER DOTS TO SHOW HIS UNSPEAKABLE MIGHT! AND LOOK AT THAT BRIGHT LIGHT GLOWING BEHIND HIM! *MAN, HE'S COOL.*

FIGURE J

YUCK! PEAS...

FIGURE K

EWWW! CARROTS...

FIGURE L

OUCH! CHILI PEPPERS...

FIGURE M

HOW ABOUT THE REST OF THE CHARACTERS IN OUR STORY? FIGURES K, L, AND M SHOW US HOW TO PICK REFERENCES FOR OUR BAD GUYS: USE FOOD YOU LOVE TO HATE, LIKE PEAS, CARROTS, AND SPICY-HOT CHILI PEPPERS! THEY CAN HURT YOUR TONGUE AND LEAVE A BAD TASTE IN YOUR MOUTH, SO THEY OBVIOUSLY MAKE GREAT VILLAINS. AND FIGURE N HELPS US REMEMBER THAT THERE'S A WORLD FULL OF CHARACTERS THAT NEED SAVING, TOO. THE WEAK AND INNOCENT, LIKE LITTLE MIKEY SPUCHINS, MIGHT REMIND US OF SILLY FOODS, LIKE POTATOES, BUT JUST THINK, IF THERE WAS NO ONE TO KEEP SAFE, WOULD WE EVEN NEED HEROES?

GOOFY NEIGHBOR KID

MOLDY OLD POTATO.

FIGURE N

NOW LOOK AT *FIGURES O AND P!* LET'S SET UP OUR HERO AND A VILLAIN IN A BATTLE SCENE. THOSE "STRAIGHTS VS. CURVES" COME IN HANDY HERE, TOO! LOOK AT HOW NEATLY THINGS CAN LINE UP WHEN YOU PLAY WITH YOUR FOOD CORRECTLY, LIKE THE *PROS!*

FIGURE O

FIGURE P

ALL RIGHT, THE BEANS HAVE *TRULY* BEEN SPILLED! YOU KNOW THE *REAL SECRETS* BEHIND MAKING COMICS! YOU HAVE THE POWER TO STUN THE WORLD WITH THIS KNOWLEDGE, *SO GET TO IT!* IT'S ALL UP TO YOU, KID. DON'T JUST EAT YOUR VEGGIES... DRAW 'EM, AND DRAW 'EM WELL. MAKE ME PROUD, AND YOU'LL BE MY *HERO!*

MORE PICKLE POWER
FROM SCHOLASTIC

CHECK OUT THE GRAPHIX WEB SITE AT WWW.SCHOLASTIC.COM/MAGICPICKLE

BRING ON THE
BRINE BRAWN!

A (graphix) Chapter Book

MAGIC PICKLE AND JO JO TAKE
ON THE RAZIN', A RENEGADE
RAISIN WITH A DASTARDLY PLAN:
TURN EVERYBODY ON EARTH INTO
PLUMP, JUICY, MINDLESS GRAPES,
SO HE CAN RULE THE WORLD.

graphix

DILL JUSTICE
IS AT HAND!

A graphix Chapter Book

THERE'S A ROTTEN EGG IN TOWN
WHO'S OUT TO POACH A WILD KIWI
BUT IN THE PROCESS CREATES
HAVOC AT THE ZOO. MAGIC PICKLE
AND JO JO ARE ON IT!

MEET SCOTT MORSE

IF YOU READ SCHOLASTIC'S *GOOSEBUMPS GRAPHIX: CREEPY CREATURES*, YOU SAW SCOTT MORSE'S SUPERCOOL ART IN *THE ABOMINABLE SNOWMAN OF PASADENA* STORY (AND IF YOU HAVEN'T READ IT, CHECK IT OUT!).

SCOTT IS THE AWARD-WINNING AUTHOR OF MORE THAN TEN GRAPHIC NOVELS FOR CHILDREN AND ADULTS, INCLUDING *SOULWIND*; *THE BAREFOOT SERPENT*; AND *SOUTHPAW*. HE'S ALSO WORKED IN ANIMATION FOR UNIVERSAL, HANNA BARBERA, CARTOON NETWORK, DISNEY, NICKELODEON, AND PIXAR. SCOTT LIVES WITH HIS LOVING FAMILY IN NORTHERN CALIFORNIA.

AND SOMETIMES - IF THERE ARE ANY IN THE FRIDGE - HE EVEN EATS PICKLES.